Destroying Angels

Destroying Angels

Gail Lukasik

Five Star • Waterville, Maine

First Edition
First Printing: March 2006

Published in 2006 in conjunction with Tekno Books
and Ed Gorman.

Set in 11 pt. Plantin by Christina S. Huff.

Printed in the United States on permanent paper.

Library of Congress Cataloging-in-Publication Data

Lukasik, Gail.
   Destroying angels / by Gail Lukasik.—1st ed.
      p. cm.
    ISBN 1-59414-360-9 (hc : alk. paper)
    1. Breast—Cancer—Patients—Fiction. 2. Divorced women—Fiction. 3. Journalists—Fiction. 4. Poisoning—Fiction. 5. Door County (Wis.)—Fiction. I. Title.
PS3612.U385D47 2006
813'.6—dc22   2005029823

For
my husband, Jerry,
my children, Christopher and Lauren,
and my mother, Alvera, who pointed the way

Acknowledgements

The author wishes to acknowledge the invaluable assistance of the following people: breast cancer survivors, Bev Parker and Betsy Evans; bow and arrow hunter, Ron Celesnik; Naturalist, Jean Weeg; Door County Advocate News Editor, Joe Knaapen; and Lake County Coroner, James Wipper.

Halloween, October 31: 20 years earlier

The harvest moon cut thin shadows through the trees, giving just enough light to see by and yet not be seen. She clutched the small bundle close and kept climbing. It was crucial to escape the sound of the water and its repetitious rhythm, which was too much like breathing.

Finally she reached the place: a grouping of caves high above the water on a narrow bluff. She entered the deepest cave, her flashlight leading her farther and farther back into the damp darkness. When she could no longer walk upright, she knelt down and put the bundle beside her. She started to dig with a small shovel that had a slightly bent blade. Within a few minutes, she was satisfied with the hole's depth, and reached for the bundle. As she picked it up, a corner of the towel fell open.

Even in the dim light, she caught sight of a small drop of blood. Just the size of a penny. She thought she'd been careful to press down hard and firmly. Quickly she folded the towel back in place and began to push the dirt into the hole. The blood was a surprise.

1

Wednesday, November 1, Present day

I was driving east on Water's Edge Road and studying the November sky as if my life depended on it. No doubt I should have been studying a map instead. Right now the sky was a translucent blue, like that blue you sometimes see in milk, or the blue glint along a knife's edge. Either way, I was probably late for my first assignment at the newspaper—an obituary—though the time was hard to discern since the truck's clock was busted. And I'd forgotten my watch again.

Earlier, heading north up the Door Peninsula, I'd watched the sky deepen to a navy blue, then suddenly rupture with light and turn a distant stand of birches metallic. And I'd missed this road east.

I'd like to think it was the light that brought me here to Door County. Days like today mostly convinced me of that.

As I crested a hill in my battered red pick-up truck, the restless stretch of green water that is Rowleys Bay rose into view. I stopped the truck abruptly across from the last gravel drive before the bay, and let the engine rattle. The wind was picking up, sending slivers of cold air into the truck. I cranked up the heater and stared at the gravel drive.

I couldn't see a house from the road, and of course there was no address on the tin mailbox. A forbidding tangle of evergreens, the foresty stuff of fairy tales, overhung the gravel drive. This had to be the place, because if I drove any further east on Water's Edge Road, I'd end up in Rowleys Bay—a chilling prospect on this brisk and crystalline afternoon.

What had my new boss, Jake Stevens, editor-in-chief of the *Door County Gazette*, said when giving me directions out here? "You'll know it when you get there."

I had shrugged nonchalantly. "Yeah, I'll find it." I had yet to lose my city veneer.

Ten years of adjunct teaching in English departments at five different Chicago colleges had taught me the value of cultivating a tough exterior. When the purple-haired student high on LSD had threatened me during my lecture on Shakespeare's Macbeth, I had told him to get out or I'd throw him out. When a rowdy group of hockey players wouldn't shut up during a discussion about gothic novels, I had flung an eraser at their heads. I presented myself as unflappable no matter the challenge, because in truth, just about everything frightened me.

"Now listen here, Leigh Girard," I'd tell myself resolutely as I was running from Chicago's Union Station to catch the elevated train to one campus or another, "you don't have time to be afraid."

Little did I know then how much those words foreshadowed my future. After ten years of hopping from college to college and trying to honor a profession that didn't honor me, I had decided to chuck it all—leave my husband of 15 years, leave Chicago for Door County, Wisconsin, and start a new career as a journalist.

Door County seemed an arbitrary choice. We'd vacationed there often in the summer. I knew it, at least as a tourist knows anyplace, and most importantly I could afford it on my meager salary. I'd found a cottage to rent in Egg

Harbor. Situated on the Green Bay side of the peninsula between Carlsville and Fish Creek, Egg Harbor was one of the smaller villages: population 183. If I hadn't landed the *Door County Gazette* job, I have no real idea where I would have gone. I hoped in all this change I'd find what was left of myself.

Because within this change was a part entirely involuntary, that scarred all of my life as it had been before. Cancer will do that—yank you out of your life. Not that I'm dying—at least not presently. I'm just minus one breast—the left one. Instead, I have a six-inch, fuchsia slash of scar tissue that is still angry looking. It cuts across my left side from underarm to sternum. And when I look closely, I can see my heart beating. A faint but steady throb pulsates against this new thin tissue of my skin. I guess I'm a modern version of those Amazon women who supposedly cut off a breast so they could be better markswomen. A friend told me about the Amazons after the mastectomy. "Is this supposed to make me feel better?" I found it hard to believe any woman would do this to herself on purpose, even a mythical woman.

I pulled into the narrow driveway, eventually wondering if there was an end to it, much less a house so far into the trees. When I was about to turn around, I glimpsed a pale green ranch house encased in aluminum siding that looked like a giant breadbox with windows. So much for the Door County charm and my envisioned ambiance of limestone cottages with stained-glass windows and hand-carved doors. Adding insult to injury were four plastic Halloween pumpkins perched on the porch railing. Their ghoulish grins were only likely to scare an interior decorator. Someone had tried to add a touch of native charm by setting a stone fence that encircled the house.

My task was to interview Mrs. Eva Peck about her husband, Carl Peck, who had died yesterday. The *Gazette* had a tradition of writing feature stories on newly deceased residents, instead of standard obits. No matter what Door residents had accomplished in life, in death they gained a sort of celebrity status.

"Obits give you good exposure to the 'Door' ways," Stevens had quipped to me, smiling at his own cleverness. He was a forties-something, hippie-type with a greying ponytail and a six-foot-two body that was surprisingly lean and toned. He was also one of Door County's many poets, though you'd never guess it from hearing him talk.

"Good one," I had responded, more to the irony of an obit as my first assignment. An irony I couldn't or wouldn't share with Stevens or anyone at this point.

Not sure how late I was for this interview, I slammed the door of my truck as a kind of announcement that I had arrived. According to Stevens, Carl Peck had died quite suddenly of liver failure. For about 40 years, he had been the resident artisan/carpenter for the county. He did mostly restorations, including many of the peninsula's older buildings, and in particular, the Cupola in Sturgeon Bay. However, by the looks of this place, his restoration work didn't seem to extend to his own house.

"A real craftsman," Stevens had told me. "You have to see the beamed ceiling he put in my den." Stevens lived in a restored 1875 limestone cottage near the entrance to Newport State Park that he never tired of mentioning.

"Top of my list, after I get my navel pierced," I had thought, not sure if beamed ceilings were the Door County equivalent of etchings.

A woman was waiting expectantly at the front door as I approached the house. This led me to believe I was definitely late.

"Come in, please," she said, before I could even identify myself. "It's getting cold." She held the aluminum storm door open for me.

She was a big-boned and heavy woman with pendulous breasts that even her black, roomy dress couldn't hide. The exposed flesh of her neck and upper arms formed in solid rolls on her body, as if each layer was insufficient to cover her. At one time she might have been called buxom or zaftig, depending on who was doing the leering. But her body had lost even soft definition; now she was merely thick. Her bleached blonde hair showed an inch of dark roots, had been forced into a halo shape, and then lacquered with hair spray. It resembled a steel web, intricate and impenetrable. Under her mud brown eyes hung pockets of skin. I noticed at least one contrast to her dutifully black mourning clothes: a green rhinestone pin affixed to the top of her dress. The stones formed a heart and glistened with a hard, iridescent light.

Ever since I'd entered this modest house, a scent I couldn't quite place was assaulting my keen sense of smell. I hoped it wasn't coming from the abundant Mrs. Peck.

"Mrs. Peck?" I extended my hand. "I'm Leigh Girard from the *Gazette*."

"I know," she said, offering a firm handshake and leading me into the living room. "Don't mind the house, it's a bit of a . . . a mess." She stopped and looked around the room as if she had just realized where she was. Her eyes glossed over with tears. "I'm sorry." She gestured toward the room with a wave of her generous arm.

I looked around the room, not wanting to watch her emotional struggle. White doilies in intricate crocheted patterns covered blonde Formica-topped tables; green and yellow terry towels protected the couch and chairs, all a crushed lime green that matched the shag carpeting. The navy leather re-

13

cliner seemed to shine with polish. If there was a mess here, it was in Mrs. Peck's head.

"Please, sit." She sniffed, and pointed to the chair covered in yellow terry cloth. As I sat down, I noticed a small-framed photo of a little girl on the adjacent table. She had soft brown hair and was wearing a blue dance costume threaded with silver. Her feet were placed in a rigid ballet position—one turned sideways, the other pointing front. The girl looked about five. The scene behind her was this same room where I was now sitting. Except for the terry towels, it hadn't changed much since the photo had been taken.

"I know this is a bad time," I began. "So I won't take long. This must be very difficult for you. But as I explained on the phone, the paper would like to write a feature about your husband." My words sounded trite and rehearsed. I shifted in my chair, cursing Stevens under my breath for giving me this obit assignment. I had come north to write about harvest festivals, high school musicals, and art exhibits. I'd had enough of sickness, death, and grieving.

Mrs. Peck smoothed her dress over her ample thighs with the palms of her hands. She was wearing a thin, gold wedding band. "That's all right. You have your job to do." She blinked her eyes to clear the tears. "It was so sudden, and then . . ." She took a deep breath. "But God is guiding me through." She picked up a black, leather-bound Bible from the table beside her and opened it. I watched her read silently to herself.

As she closed the book, her mouth formed the word, "Amen." She lifted her eyes and looked at me. They seemed a shade darker. "You're new at the paper?"

I had witnessed the erratic early stages of grief before: the ricochet of emotion from staunch denial one minute to full realization the next. I had yet to get used to it.

"Yes. In fact, your husband's obituary is my first feature assignment. For the *Gazette*, that is." I didn't want her to think her husband's remembrance was in the hands of a novice reporter, even though it was.

"And you're from Chicago, I hear?"

Stevens had warned me that everybody in Door County knew everybody else's business. How had he put it? "If you fart, we all know about it." I glanced down at my notebook and answered, "A suburb." Now I wanted to change the direction of our conversation.

Mrs. Peck wasn't quite ready for that, it seemed. "So many people from Chicago end up here. Most don't stay, though. It's too isolated for them. Not enough to do." As she crossed her thick legs at her ankles, her skirt rode up. She tugged on it like a nervous virgin. "I lived there once, in Chicago." She smiled briefly.

"Why didn't you stay?" I was genuinely curious.

"I married Mr. Peck. He wanted to move up here. Say, can I get you anything? A cold drink, perhaps?"

"No, I'm fine, thanks." I cleared my throat. "Now, about Mr. Peck."

"Here's the picture for the paper." From the pocket of her dress, she took out a 5 x 7 black and white photograph and handed it to me. The grainy picture showed a man dressed in an Army uniform, who looked about 20. His eyes stared straight at the camera, as if daring anyone to look away. He resembled a young Harrison Ford.

"Mr. Peck was quite good-looking," I said. "When was he in the service?"

"During the Korean War. He didn't like to talk about it. But he was decorated with the Purple Heart." She smiled so broadly, her fleshy face seemed to swallow her eyes.

"You don't happen to have a clearer picture, do you?

Maybe something more recent? The newspaper needs a sharply-focused photo to get the best reproduction."

"That's his best picture," she said flatly. "I'd like you to use that."

"Okay." I wasn't going to argue with a grieving widow. It was obvious that this was the way she wanted people to remember her husband. I slipped the photo inside my notebook. "Now, where was Mr. Peck born?"

"Chicago." She took a deep breath and looked out the picture window. "I was hoping someone from the paper would come by before I did anything."

The statement puzzled me. "What do you mean, Mrs. Peck?"

She leaned forward, and I could see where she hadn't blended her makeup along her corpulent neck. Her naked skin was the pasty hue of oatmeal.

"I'm going to be filing a lawsuit against the doctor and the hospital." She leaned further forward and whispered, "They killed Carl."

I waited for her to say more but she just sat there, her muddy eyes expectant upon me.

"What makes you think that? I understand that your husband died of liver failure."

"That's what they say. They're claiming that he was an alcoholic. That he drank himself to death. That's not true." Indignation brought a flush to her cheeks. "He was a good man. He hardly ever drank." She set her jaw. "It's a cover-up. He went to the hospital complaining of chest pains. They didn't listen to him. While he was there, he had a heart attack. And it's their fault. He should have been on monitors. They should have done tests."

She stopped and took a deep breath. "I wouldn't leave him, you know. Even after he was gone. I sat there and held his hand and prayed. His eyes stared right at me. And his mouth was open as if he wanted to tell me something. I waited and waited. They tried to get me to leave, those nurses and doctors. But I wouldn't. I couldn't leave him alone with them. Not after what they did."

"Mother, that's enough." In the doorway stood a woman who was a younger, much thinner version of Mrs. Peck, except her hair was so black it made her skin look transparent. She wore bone-hugging jeans that emphasized every crease and crevice of her lower body. Yet the jeans looked more painful than provocative. She came over and stood next to Mrs. Peck. "My mother is upset and doesn't know what she's saying. You need to leave now."

"No, Sarah," Mrs. Peck protested, "you don't understand. You weren't there."

"Mother, I think you should go lie down." The daughter leaned down, and took hold of Mrs. Peck's elbow.

"But I want her to get it right. For the paper!" Mrs. Peck pulled away.

"Didn't I ask you to leave?" The young woman snapped at me.

Mrs. Peck's face went crimson as she hoisted herself out of the chair. "Sarah, I won't tolerate . . ." she began, and then stopped.

Sarah had put her hands on her hips and was glaring at her mother, daring her to finish what she had begun to say. Mrs. Peck's mouth moved back and forth, as if she were chewing on the unsaid words. Then she looked past her daughter and left the room. Before I could say anything, Sarah Peck followed her mother from the room.

So much for Door County hospitality and my first interview.

As I stood up to leave, my empty notebook fell on the

floor. I bent down to retrieve it, and saw what looked like brown clumps of dry mud under the chair. Some of the clumps shone with a gooey substance. Apparently, Mrs. Peck's meticulous housekeeping didn't extend beyond the superficial. As I left the gravel drive and turned west on Water's End Road, the late autumn sun blasted the windshield with light, and a roll of nausea overtook me. I reached for my purse. The familiar migraine symptom was making its slow, sure way across my forehead. Keeping my eyes fixed on the road, I rummaged in the bottom of my purse for the pill box. With one hand, I opened the clasp and took out two red and white capsules. I threw my head back and downed the pills. No water necessary, two pills at the first signs of a headache.

In the distance, field after field opened up before me. Another reason for coming back here, I reminded myself: these clean, uninterrupted vistas where I could see great distances, as if the future was visible before me just down the road.

I gazed up again into the turbulent sky. The clouds were moving fast. It would probably rain again tonight, though who could be sure. I drove toward Highway 42 under a canopy of changing light. It wasn't until I made the left turn on Highway 42 and headed south that the migraine eased, and the realization hit me.

"Stew, some kind of stew." That was the smell in Mrs. Peck's house.

2

The *Door County Gazette* was sandwiched between the Bay Cinema, where movies are always $1.50, and an antique shop in the older section of Sturgeon Bay. The buildings had a feeling of slow decline from better times. Whatever promise this area once had was gone; now it was simply a matter of holding on and not falling apart.

Still, I liked the sturdy gentility of the *Gazette*'s limestone facade, the thick, raised gold lettering and wide windows that I imagined were opened on warm summer afternoons. The lot behind the building overlooked Green Bay; I parked my car and entered through the rear entrance.

Jake Stevens's office was the first door on the left. He had the only office that commanded an unobstructed view of the water. Since his door was open, I tapped it lightly and walked in. One of the first things he told me about his management policy: "No one stands on ceremony around here. If you want to see me, knock once and walk in. If I don't want to see you, my door will be closed." Apparently there was no news around here important enough to bridge his closed door. Back in Chicago, his closed door policy would have had a very different interpretation, especially during lunch hour.

"So what's the story with Mrs. Peck and her daughter?" I said to Stevens's ponytail. With his back to me, he was arched protectively over his computer, like a kid taking a test and fearful someone would copy his answers. For some reason, he still had his coat on—a black leather jacket cracked with wear and reminiscent of James Dean.

"Punch your stuff into Martin's computer. He won't be back till tomorrow," Stevens said, his eyes rapt upon his computer screen.

"There is no stuff." That got his attention. He swiveled around in his chair. The late afternoon sun glinted off his thick lensed, wire-rimmed glasses. I'd yet to catch the color of his eyes.

"What happened? Couldn't find the place?" He was trying not to smirk.

"I found the place just fine. Even though the daughter whisked her mother out of the room before I could interview her in depth. Not, however, before Eva Peck accused the doctor and the hospital of misdiagnosing her husband. According to her, Carl Peck didn't die of liver failure, but a heart attack. She plans to sue."

"Are you serious?"

Finally, I had Jake Stevens's full attention. He took off his glasses and rubbed the bridge of his nose. I noticed that he had those long, fine fingers always associated with artistic types. My fingers look like they could pull potatoes out of the frozen ground in the dead of winter. "That's what she said," I said, and then sat down in the only chair in his office not already full of books, magazines or papers.

"Eva won't do anything. Not her style." Stevens leaned back in his chair and put his hands behind his head. "She's in shock, that's all. From what I heard, Peck's death was pretty ugly. 'He did not go gentle into that good night.' "

I must have had a confused look on my face because he added, "You know, Dylan Thomas." He pronounced Dylan, "die-lynn." Stevens had this annoying habit of quoting poets.

"The folk singer, right?" I asked, trying not to smile.

"Only when he wasn't hacking out words or drinking himself blind at the local pubs." His eyes caught mine. "You should read poetry."

"I should also have my teeth capped. Neither one's worth the effort." I bristled at any advice with "should" in it. I left all those shoulds back in Chicago along with the manicured lawns, the two-story colonials, and the mini-vans.

He smiled and looked away. "It's good for your writing. Makes you cut stuff down to the bone."

"Didn't you say the same thing about writing obits?"

The smile was gone. "Yeah, that too."

"Anyway, I did get a photo of Peck. It's pretty grainy, but this is the one his wife wants us to use." I flipped my notebook open, pulled out the photo and handed it to him.

He glanced at the photo. "Get a year?"

In all the confusion, I hadn't asked about the photo's date. But from here, I could see faint writing on the back. "It's on the back," I said, hoping my hunch was right.

Stevens turned the photo over. "December, 1952." He handed the photo back to me.

If he caught my bluff, he wasn't going to mention it.

"Call Olin Forrest. Used to work for Peck. He'll give you some fill." He put his glasses back on, as if he needed to get a better look at me.

"You sure you don't want me to go 'a callin' at Mr. Forrest's homestead? Introduce myself, bring a cherry pie to show that I'm down home, country folk?" Usually, I wouldn't be so flip on the first day of a new job, but I sensed some weird chemistry between us. Not sexual, more like "Didn't I know you in another life?" I was sure he sensed it too. He'd hired me the day after I walked into his office. Although I'd never worked on a newspaper, small town or otherwise, he told me my ten years teaching experience meant I had good instincts about people. He joked that my Masters degree in English might be a liability. I told him I'd do my best to overcome it.

Now he grinned a slow smile. He was enjoying this chemical mix as much as I was. "Not enough time. We're on deadline. And you didn't get any stuff from Eva Peck."

I was about to defend myself, but thought better of it. Chemistry or no chemistry, I didn't want to push my luck. As pitiful as it was, this was the only income I had at present. I couldn't afford to get on the boss's bad side, no matter how much we both enjoyed this sparring.

He picked up on my mood change. "Look, Girard, this is how it works here. The Door villages are like those medieval hamlets, you know, where every full moon a witch got burned to keep the peasants happy. Maybe because she pissed someone off, or maybe because her nose was long and pointy with a big wart on it, or maybe because her husband croaked suddenly. As a journalist, you walk a thin line. People here know you're after the story, but you have to make them think that's not what you're all about. You have to make them think you want to be their friend. And the thing is, before long, you start to believe it. So if you haven't figured it out yet, nothing ever happens here, bad or otherwise. There's no news, just events. We write about church bazaars, speeding tickets, and the largest trout caught in Kewaunee Harbor. And we do obit features on the local carpenter. Even if he was as dull as dust."

"I take it this paper won't be winning a Pulitzer anytime soon."

"Pulitzer? What's a Pulitzer?"

"Okay, I get your point. I'm not to sully the waters and will try not to be burned as a witch."

"Good. I know a fast learner when I see one." He stared at me as if he were trying to memorize me for a police line up. It took all my will power not to put my right arm over where my left breast should have been. Suddenly, he turned back to his computer, as if whatever he was looking for, he had found.

"And about the . . ." Before I could ask him again about following up on the Peck lawsuit, he interrupted.

"Peck's doctor's name is Porter." He kept his eyes on the computer screen. "Whatever you do, don't say anything about a lawsuit. Just find out what you can about how Carl Peck died. My hunch is Eva Peck's blowing smoke." He paused. "And that obit better be in before five p.m., or you'll be writing the upcoming events section."

"Is that a threat?" I asked, getting up to leave.

"Think about it."

3

I tracked Doctor Charles Porter to the fourth floor of the Bay Hospital. The duty nurse, a pinched-face woman with a missing lower tooth and penciled eyebrows that formed two inverted U's, confirmed that he was making rounds. She refused to page the doctor, and suggested that I wait for him by the nurse's station.

"He should be by in about fifteen minutes." She faked a smile, sat down behind the white partition of the station, and turned her back to me.

"Nurse?" I leaned over the partition. She swiveled slowly around in her chair. "How about pointing him out to me?"

She raised one of her penciled-in eyebrows. "Oh. You don't know the doctor? Well . . ." She paused and took a deep breath. "If I'm here when he comes by, I suppose I can do that."

I left Nurse Ratched to her charts, and sat down in one of those molded plastic chairs meant to survive a nuclear blast. Several tattered magazines, circa 1998, were scattered on the table next to me. To keep myself from thinking about the fact that I was in a hospital, I picked one up. It was a *Women's Circle* with the usual assortment of ten-minute recipes, tummy tightening exercises, and "affordable" family vacations. I was just getting into a photo spread on bathing suits that promised to hide my problem areas when someone addressed me.

"You, there. Miss?"

I looked up.

An elderly man dressed in a white coat stood at the nurse's station. "I'm Doctor Porter. You wanted to see me?"

"Yes." I stood up and walked toward him, as he handed a chart back to the charge nurse.

"Make sure you increase the dosage for Mrs. Gardner as I've indicated," he told her.

"I'm Leigh Girard from the *Gazette*," I said, extending my hand. "I'm writing an article on Carl Peck."

He looked at my hand a second too long before shaking it. His hand felt like damp socks. Doctor Porter appeared to be in his seventies. He was small, with a wiry build and a full head of white hair. There was a vitality about him evident in his clear blue eyes.

"If you have a few minutes, I'd like to ask you some questions about Mr. Peck."

"Young lady," he cautioned me, "if you're inquiring about Carl Peck's medical treatment, I'm afraid I can't tell you anything. I'm sure you know about doctor-patient confidentiality."

I was well aware of doctor-patient confidentiality. That's why I was not only going to mention the lawsuit, but it would be my first question. I wanted to spring it on the doctor and watch his reaction hoping in defending himself he would reveal something about Peck's death. It was worth a try.

"Eva Peck plans on suing you and the hospital," I told him.

"Suing me?" He looked totally at a loss.

"She claims you misdiagnosed her husband. She says he

didn't die of liver failure, but a heart attack. And she was pretty adamant about his not being an alcoholic."

Doctor Porter took a deep breath. "Let me explain something to you about certain kinds of diseases. It's the old story of the elephant in the living room that no one wants to acknowledge."

"So you are saying Carl Peck died of alcoholism?"

"The official cause of death, which you already know, is liver failure."

"So you have no idea why Mrs. Peck would believe her husband died of a heart attack?"

"None whatsoever. Except . . ." he paused. "Generally speaking, sometimes in the case of chronic alcoholics, the cause of death is listed as ventricular fibrillation affecting the nervous conduction system of the heart. Which just means the alcoholism causes the patient to have a heart attack. However, that's not a common occurrence; more often patients exhibit severe and massive liver failure. The body fills with fluid, causing the person to drown in their own fluids. This is a painful death. Having to watch it is extremely hard on the family."

Porter leaned toward me slightly. "Miss, you're new around here, right?" He didn't wait for my answer. "I don't know how much you know about small town living. So let me give you a little advice. We like to spare people's feelings when we can. There's no need to mention in that article of yours how Carl Peck died. That way Eva can hold her head up. For some people, that's extremely important."

A buzzer went off behind the nurse's station. Nurse Ratchet, who had been hanging on our every word as if her next raise depended on it, let the buzzer go two more times before she got up to answer it.

"Was Mr. Peck hospitalized very long before he died?" I thought I'd take another run at the doctor.

Porter crinkled his forehead in annoyance. "The *Gazette* actually announced when he entered the hospital and the day of his death, as I recall, he was in the hospital about a day or so." Then he suggested abruptly, "Well, I've got a house call. So if you don't mind." He held out his hand for a dismissive shake.

I returned his handshake, somewhat perplexed. Why the sudden change? He didn't seem to want to discuss Peck's hospital stay.

"If I have any other questions, would you prefer I call you at your office or at home?" I asked. Doctor Porter wasn't getting off so easily.

"The office. In fact, why don't you come by my office. You look like you could use a B-12 shot."

Not a chance in hell, I thought to myself. I'd had my fill of doctors, thank you. As he departed down the hall, I turned to leave and noticed a patient coming toward me in the opposite direction and awkwardly dragging along her IV bag. My eyes froze on her. She wore a pink satin robe over her hospital gown—the familiar attempt to attach some semblance of normalcy to things beyond your control. As she approached, I focused on her one hand, the one that held the metal IV stand. Across the back was a white tape, which kept the IV needle in place. Around the tape's curling edges flared a yellowish bruise. As she moved past me, I saw that the back of her hair was flat and matted. Automatically, I looked down. There on the hem of her hospital gown was a trail of smudged blood. The old panic rose up from the pit of my stomach. It had a metallic taste.

I had to find a focal point, anything to regain my composure. I didn't think I could make it back to the nest of chairs and magazines. Just then, someone entered the nurse's station behind me. I turned quickly toward the person. A nurse was standing there, reading a chart. I stared at her, trying to bring her into focus. But it was too late. The white hospital walls slipped into sudden blackness.

"How are you feeling now?" A nurse was bending over me, waving smelling salts under my nose.

It took me a few seconds to place myself. The hospital . . . the IV bag . . . the smudged blood. This nurse became my focal point. "I'm fine." Yet I was sprawled across a row of chairs. I tried to sit up, but the dizziness was still there. Somehow I had either fallen back on the chairs, or the nurse had lifted me onto them.

"Maybe you should just sit here a few minutes until you feel better." She had thick chestnut hair in a French braid, and two deep dimples. She smelled like lavender. "I saw you talking to Doc Porter. I hope it wasn't bad news."

"No, I'm just not crazy about hospitals." I sat up. The blood was returning to my brain.

"Most people feel that way. Do you want some water?"

"No thanks, I'm feeling a lot better." My sense of purpose was coming back. "My name's Leigh Girard."

"I'm Lydia Crane. You're new here, right?" She looked down at my suede boots, the ones that had cost me $150 on sale. "My guess is Chicago."

"Is it that obvious?"

We both said it at the same time. "The boots."

"Really, a suburb of Chicago. Ever hear of Libertyville?"

"Hometown of Marlon Brando, or so they claim. I grew up in Lake Forest. Well, welcome to Door. What brings you here?"

"I'm writing a feature, sort of a tribute to Carl Peck."

"No, I mean Door County. Decided to drop out like the rest of us outsiders?"

"Yeah, sort of."

"Well, there's enough of us to keep the place diversified. If there is such a thing as diversification in Door." She smiled, and her dimples deepened, giving her a carefree look.

"Yeah, I've noticed." I sat up straighter in my chair. "As I was saying, I'm writing a feature on Carl Peck. Did you happen to see Mr. Peck while he was here as a patient, before his death?"

"I guess you don't need this anymore." She tossed the smelling salts into a nearby trash bin. "As a matter of fact, I was on duty the morning they brought Mr. Peck in."

"I understand that it was his liver."

She tilted her head sideways. "C'mon. You know I can't say anything about his medical condition."

"I already know about his alcoholism. And that the cause of death was liver failure," I said, reassuringly.

She shrugged. "Sure makes you think about that extra drink." She ran her index finger back and forth across her lower lip. "I guess that wasn't very discreet. Don't quote me on that, okay?"

"No problem." I decided to take another tack. "Have you ever seen someone die of alcoholism?"

"Yeah, back in Chicago. I worked at Cook County Hospital for awhile. Saw a lot of alcoholics die there. And it wasn't pretty."

I must have looked surprised.

"I get it, you're thinking, 'What's a nice girl from Lake Forest doing working at a place like Cook County?' I'm the family's social consciousness. It's a dirty job, but someone has to do it. Couldn't stand the country club life, you know, those debutante balls, junior league luncheons, clothes one-upmanship, etcetera, etcetera."

I was liking Lydia Crane more and more. "So you'd recognize the symptoms. Was there any chance Mr. Peck died of a heart attack and not liver failure?"

"Why?"

"Mrs. Peck is under the impression that her husband died of a heart attack." Stevens wouldn't like this second revelation of the widow's doubts about medical competence, but you can only die once for the same crime.

"Really? I can't imagine where she got that idea." Lydia considered for a moment. "She isn't thinking lawsuit, is she?"

"Maybe thinking, not acting."

"I'm surprised. That would be very out of character for Eva Peck."

"How do you mean?"

"She's one of those martyr types. I can spot them a mile away. Says things like, 'God never gives you more than you can bear,' and 'Suffering builds character.' Which in my opinion is a lot of bull. Anyway, even if she believed her husband had been misdiagnosed, I would have thought she'd find a way to accept it as God's will."

"But you don't think she'd have a case. If she did sue?"

"From my observations and experience, I'd say no."

"Meaning?"

"Meaning, you don't give up easily, do you?"

A buzzer went off again at the nurses' station. "Sorry, but I've got to answer that." She smiled. "If you want to talk sometime about something else or go out for a drink, come by my shop in Fish Creek. It's the Crystal Door. I know, it's too cute. But hey, anything to lure the tourists."

"You run a shop and work here as a nurse?"

"I see you haven't learned about the Door system of

making ends meet. Practically everybody on the peninsula has two jobs, especially if you're a shop owner. My nursing job supports my shop habit." The buzzer repeated. "Why don't you come by Saturday at closing, say around five?"

"Um, okay, I guess I'll see you then."

4

By the time I reached home it was dark, and I had missed the sun making its slow descent into the bay. The ink-black sky was crusted with stars and a three-quarters moon that looked like stage scenery. A few clouds drifted white. I had been wrong about the rain.

As I neared the stone cottage, I rolled down the truck window so I could at least hear the faint lapping of the water. It was the main reason I had leased this cottage—that, and the reasonable rent. The owner was a snowbird widow who summered in Door and spent her winters in Sun City, Arizona. Finding a renter here in late fall and winter is almost impossible, so we'd both lucked out, and my rent was less than what I would pay for a closet in Chicago.

As I drove up, the cottage looked cold and desolate, and I wished I had left a light on. I'd have to remember that in the future. Salinger, my Shetland sheep dog, must be knocking things over in this dark, unfamiliar house. Indeed, I could hear her howling as I walked up the stone path. I always suspected there was some wolf in her lineage. Not only did she howl, but her white-tipped tail was long and bushy, and her whiskered snout was wolf shaped. She had a bad habit of sticking her snout where it didn't belong, such as tail pipes, flowerbeds, and under my covers on cold nights. Her reddish-brown coat also suggested some ancestor had dipped into the fox den. On more than one occasion, she'd been mistaken by suburban joggers for Princess, the Lake County Fox. But then, what can you expect from people who learn about nature from animated Disney movies?

What distinguished Salinger, besides her bold intelligence and hybrid lineage, were uneven splotches of white on both front paws, giving her the appearance of wearing two white socks—one pulled slightly higher than the other. This asymmetry made her look somewhat roguish.

Salinger was the only remnant from my former life that I cherished, besides my clothes, my books, and some art photos. Tom and I had bought her right before I became sick. Where he had overcompensated regarding my cancer, Salinger had instinctually struck the right balance. That first day back home after my surgery, of course, she had wanted to jump up on our bed and snuggle. When Tom yelled at her, she spent the day behind the chair in the corner, not rebuked at all but a silent guardian. Her gesture seemed to say "If I can't touch you, I will sit here quietly sharing your sadness." For Salinger, there was no running away.

So when I left Chicago, I had purged myself of nearly all possessions that would remind me of my former life with Tom. Though he insisted that I take one of the cars, I refused. Instead, I bought my used pick-up from our neighbor's son. A clean break—that's what I had wanted, and that's what I had achieved.

Now as I entered the dusky gloom of the living room, I could see the blinking red eye of the answering machine. It had been a long day, and the only person I could imagine calling me was Tom. I didn't want to hear from him. I had asked him not to write or call me except in an emergency. He was so angered by my departure that he agreed. But I didn't trust his tight-lipped concession.

I had needed to hurt him and make him hate me, so I wouldn't falter. What he wouldn't see, and what I couldn't explain, was that the cancer had taken more than a breast. He still believed if I'd only had reconstructive surgery, then we could have gone on as before. That belief seemed to deny everything I had been through: the shock of discovering the cancerous lump that left me drained and constantly vigilant; the mastectomy that rid me of the cancer but permanently scarred me as undesirable; and the chemo that seemed like a dirge of "this can still come back, maybe in forty years, maybe five years, maybe tomorrow." Tom refused to acknowledge this reality. He just wanted me to get over myself so we could move on. He didn't understand that because my body had betrayed me, I could never count on it again. I would have to stand watch, to wait and see if it would betray me again.

Our last argument had been about the reconstruction.

"I can't ever be that woman again," I told him. "So give it up."

"How about being a woman, period," he snapped, his lower jaw jutting out in angry disapproval.

Later, he tried to apologize. But I wouldn't accept his apology. He no longer tried to touch me. I knew that it was only a matter of time before he left.

A week after the doctors declared that, as far as they could tell, I was free of the cancer, I left Chicago. I needed to be the one doing the leaving.

After much licking and hugging with Salinger, I let her out the back door. I watched her tear through the field of white, weedy flowers toward the water. She was bent on some mission of her own, following some buried scent only she could find. It would be a while before she came scratching at the back door. Not even hunger could deter her insatiable curiosity. Salinger and I had a lot in common.

Determined to ignore the blinking answering machine light, I took my time lighting a fire, leisurely changing into my silky purple robe, and pouring myself a glass of chardonnay. With wine glass in hand, I settled into the moss green velvet chair nearest the massive stone fireplace. The chair's back and seat had been previously worn to a scuffed pattern that now seemed to outline my body. I found this reassuring. When the wine had achieved its warm, relaxing effect, I reached over and pressed the play button on the machine. If it was Tom, I was ready for him.

Instead of Tom's deep baritone, I heard a woman's voice. "Ms. Girard, this is Eva Peck. I just wanted you to know that I'm having an autopsy performed on Carl tomorrow morning." She cleared her throat as if she were about to say something else. Then the machine clicked off.

"What is this woman after?" I wondered aloud. Was she angling for a discreet settlement out of court, enough to keep her comfortable for the rest of her life? She didn't seem like the opportunistic type, though grief can make a person react in strange ways. Regardless of Mrs. Peck's motives, if Doctor Porter and Lydia Crane were correct, she wouldn't be coming into any large sums of money very soon.

Salinger's insistent scratching interrupted my thoughts. When I went to let her in, she was sitting on the back step with her ears back, grinning and panting. Wrapped round her neck like a laurel wreath was a rooted tangle of vines studded with wet leaves. She had found what she had been looking for.

"What do you think Salinger? Greed or grief?" I asked, as I unwound the resistant vine. Salinger gave me one of her pleading looks. "Okay, you're right, dinner is long overdue."

* * * * *

March, 25 years earlier

Now they were driving south past fields the color of chocolate. Deep furrows had already been carved into the earth and stood open, waiting for the seeds. Only occasionally, a farmhouse or small town broke the monotony of the land. And then only briefly, as if each arose from dreams.

As it seeped into the closed car, the heavy scent of manure assaulted her nose. She sat very still, trying not to breathe too deeply.

Soon . . . very soon, they would be past the fields, and the smell would be gone. It would disappear just as quickly as it had come.

There were no other cars on the road, so he was able to keep a steady speed. The rhythm becoming hypnotic as the car hummed softly . . . softly, and as if from a distance, she heard a voice calling her name over and over. Then silence.

Someone was shaking her roughly. "Wake up, wake up. Are you all right?"

When she shook her head yes, it hurt.

"What happened?" he asked.

She thought back. "Something, something I remembered." Then she couldn't tell what it was, because she had fainted again.

5

"Lydia? This is Leigh Girard." I was sitting at Rob Martin's desk, which faced a wall plastered with nature scenes: stags locked in combat, Ephraim Harbor dotted with sailboats, a bull moose feeding in a field of fireweed, coyotes barely visible in the snow, and iridescent orange mushrooms on a dark forest floor. Apparently Martin's taste ran to the bizarre and spectacular. The scenes had been photographed either at sunrise, sunset, or during extremes of weather. They seemed to be at odds with Martin's column, "Nature's Door," which described the area's flora and fauna in respectful and subdued terms. Rob Martin was the resident naturalist/journalist. I'd yet to meet him. He always seemed to be working out in the field.

"Hi, Leigh. Now what makes me think you're calling for something other than my special this week, quartz crystals from Colorado." She laughed. "How are you doing?"

"Okay. And you're right, I didn't call about your special. Though you'll have to enlighten me sometime on the benefits of quartz crystals. What I'm calling about is information on the Peck autopsy."

Uncertain about Lydia's schedule at the hospital, I had called the ICU floor around 11 a.m. and found out that she was on the evening shift. A nurse suggested I try her shop. I

37

wasn't sure if the autopsy results were privileged information, and I wasn't about to ask Jake Stevens and have him spot the gaping hole in my journalistic experience.

"How did you find out about that? Doctor Porter wanted it kept hush hush."

"I got a hot tip." Despite wanting Lydia to reveal what she knew, I was keeping my source confidential.

"Had to be Eva. You don't have to answer that. Just a minute."

I could hear her talking to someone in the shop. But couldn't make out what she was saying.

"Sorry. Where were we?"

I was getting the feeling that she was being purposely cagey. "Look, I don't want you to get in trouble, Lydia. All I really want to do is verify if an autopsy was, in fact, performed."

"Don't worry about me. I don't get in trouble, unless I want to. If Eva told you, probably half the county knows by now that the autopsy was indeed performed. Nothing around here remains secret for long."

"I'm getting that impression. So did Carl Peck die of a heart attack like his wife claims?"

Without my realizing I wasn't alone in the office anymore, a man appeared and stood over the desk, looking annoyed. He had blazing red hair, which also enflamed his mustache and goatee. If it wasn't for the color of his hair, he would have been described as average in build and appearance. I smiled my most charming smile, which caused him to raise a fiery eyebrow.

"Leigh, you know I can't tell you that even if I knew. Besides, it takes at least several days for the written report. If the Medical Examiner sent tissue and blood samples to the State Crime Lab, you're looking at six to twelve weeks for results. Even in Chicago it takes that long, if not longer."

"Well, it was worth a try anyway."

"You might talk to the family, though. That's nineteen-sixty-five." I heard a cash register ring. "One of my friends, who works for the Brown County M.E., where autopsies are performed, told me Carl's daughter, Sarah, argued with the Medical Examiner after the autopsy. She said Sarah seemed pretty upset. The M.E. kept saying, 'If that's what your mother wants, my hands are tied.' Sarah's in the directory under her maiden name. But give it some time."

"Thanks, Lydia." I smiled up at the glaring man, who crossed his arms in annoyance.

"No problem. Us outsiders have to stick together. Don't forget about Saturday."

"Okay." I hung up and turned to the blazing satyr. "Can I help you?"

"My desk." His index finger was a little too close to my face.

I know I should have immediately popped up from the chair and offered some form of apology. But Rob Martin's attitude irked me. He had to know that I was the new reporter. Yet he showed no signs of acknowledgment. So much for professional courtesy. "I'm working on a story, and yours is the only desk with a computer," I explained. In fact, only Rob Martin and the newspaper's production editor/office manager, Marge Lindquist, had computers, and there was only one other desk in the office, which was now mine. This was a newspaper run on a shoe string budget, barely covered with a band-aid, and here I was computerless on the job.

"I'm on deadline. So if you don't mind." He leaned over me and pressed save on the computer.

My face flushed with anger as I unceremoniously pushed back the chair, grabbed my notes, and got up. "Nice to meet you too, Mr. Martin." I held out my hand in defiance. He reluctantly shook it with a little too much pressure. Marge, who I'm sure heard every word, was pretending to shuffle through some papers on her desk.

"I see you two are getting acquainted." In my anger, I hadn't noticed that Stevens had emerged from his inner sanctum. He immediately picked up on the tension.

"Rob Martin, this is Leigh Girard, the new reporter. She'll be covering general stuff. Leigh, as you know, Rob is our celebrated naturalist. His book on Door County flora and fauna was awarded the Aldo Leopold prize for non-fiction last year."

I looked where Stevens was pointing. How had I missed it? Beside the photo of the orange mushrooms sat a gold plaque.

Martin nodded his head in my general direction and sat down in his chair, dismissing both of us. I merely nodded in return, keeping my expression grim. Fine by me if he needed to think he was the big fish in a small pond. Probably also felt we should all kiss his plaque.

"In my office, now." Stevens jabbed one of his long fingers at me.

Like a kid sent to the principal's office, I slunk down the short hallway after his lanky frame.

"What was that about?" Stevens plopped down in his swivel chair and propped his sneaker-clad feet up on the desk.

Words of frustration and anger bubbled up inside of me. Ever since the cancer, I often experienced moments of incredible rage, and I was having one right now. I crossed my legs to steady myself. My right foot was circling round and round like a berserk helicopter blade. "The man attacked me for sitting at his desk." I also tended to exaggerate when I was this angry.

Stevens leaned back in his chair and stared out at the gray water. He seemed to be weighing what he wanted to tell me.

"How's your follow-up on Peck going?" So he decided to tell me nothing.

I filled him in on what I had found out at the hospital yesterday, and Eva Peck's phone message.

"She went ahead with it. The autopsy was performed this morning. And her daughter was upset enough about something to argue with the M.E. I'll find out what and why." My foot circles slowed.

"How are you going to do that?" He kept staring at the water, as if I wasn't physically in the same room with him. He seemed uncharacteristically preoccupied, almost somber.

"I'll call her and . . ." I was going to say interview her on the telephone, then remembered *Gazette* standard procedure. "And make an appointment to see her."

"You can try that. But go easy."

I know he wanted me to ask what else I could try. But I was still angry, and my anger now included all members of his gender. I wasn't going to give him or any man the satisfaction of my asking for their help. "Is there anything else?"

He put his feet down and leaned toward me in his chair. "There's another obit feature I want you to write. Woman named Joyce Oleander. She was a fixture at the Egg Harbor library. Start there. Talk to Ida Reeves. She runs the library." He rummaged through some papers on his desk until he located a pink memo pad. "Here's her number." He tore off the top sheet and handed it to me. There was a tightness in his face that I'd seen before. I suspected it had less to do with a brooding poetic temperament and more to do with some inner demons. Which I guess could amount to the same thing.

I snatched the note from him. "Are these obits some kind of initiation rite? Or have I been permanently slotted as the *Gazette*'s ghoul reporter?"

"For now." He avoided my eyes and looked at the note I held in my hand. "There's some question about this woman's cause of death. Possible suicide."

I started to ask, "Possible? What do you mean?" But remained stubbornly pissed off.

"Talk to Ida Reeves. She found the body last night." He leaned back in his chair and looked out at the water again. "And I made some minor changes in Peck's obit feature. It'll be in tomorrow's paper."

Other than a difference of opinion about a comma or two, I couldn't see what changes needed to be made. I'd even talked to Olin Forrest who had supplied me with enough info about Peck and his restoration work to fill two articles.

"You're the boss," I said, getting up to leave.

"Just remember that." He pulled his eyes away from the monochromatic bay view long enough to give me a chiding look.

I was about to execute my best military salute, but he looked away toward the window again. Rain began pinging the glass and slowly blurring everything.

6

"Joyce was scared to death of the hysterectomy," Ida Reeves explained. "And with good reason, considering her history. She delayed it as long as she could. Kept thinking it would go away. I told her it wouldn't. Classic denial. And in the end, I was right. Anemia from loss of blood." She stared at me through her large round glasses. The thick lenses magnified her sea-green eyes, distilling their color and making them look watery and unfocused. Ida continued. "As it turned out, there were no surgical complications, and she was home within the week. She seemed to be recuperating nicely. A little depressed, but I told her work would cure that."

Obviously, work was Ida Reeves's cure for everything. After all, she'd discovered the body of her co-worker, Joyce Oleander, last night, yet here she was at work the next day. Her fortitude was both amazing and disturbing. We were sitting in the back office of the Egg Harbor Library, which served as a combination office/lunch room. It smelled of moldy books and tuna fish. Ms. Reeves spoke in a voice so low and clipped, I had to lean forward to hear her. Occupational habit, I figured.

"I understand that you found the body." No need to tread gently with this woman. Ida Reeves was as controlled as an IRS agent poised for a sting, and about as warm.

She didn't blink a myopic eye in reaction to my question.

"Ten-thirty-seven p.m. I'd been calling her all day. To make sure she was opening the library today at nine. When she didn't answer, I went over to her condominium in Sunset Shores. I was concerned that she might have had an endocardial infarction." She paused a moment, and added with pride, "that's the medical term for a heart attack. Studying the world of medicine is something of a hobby with me. Anyway, I thought her heart might have given out. The doctors were very concerned about it before the surgery." She shook her head. "It was a logical deduction since both her parents had died in their forties from heart disease. And there's no escaping heredity, you know."

"Really?" I kept thinking how some people fulfill their own stereotypes and destinies while others work against them. Ida Reeves seemed a blend of both. Although she had the requisite librarian's myopia and was dressed conservatively—navy tweed wool skirt, starched white blouse buttoned to the neck, navy cardigan affixed with a gold watch pin and a pearl sweater chain—her gray hair was cut in a stylish shag and her full, thick lips were emphasized with candy red lipstick.

"I'm of the opinion that biology determines your whole life, even your personality." No doubt about the challenge in her statement.

"You don't think there are other factors such as environment or bad luck?" I had to make this query, since no one from either side of my family has had breast cancer. Even the doctors hadn't produced a definitive answer as to why I had developed the disease. None of the common causes—excessive drinking, smoking, fatty diet, too much red meat—applied to me. The conclusion I reached was—sometimes there is no answer. This view left me feeling powerless, angry, and fated.

"No. It's your genes, pure and simple. Did you know that scientists have isolated a gene that causes shyness? I read the study about this that was published in the *New England Journal of Medicine*. Would you like to read it?"

"I seem to remember that study," I said, trying to deflect her helpfulness back to the subject at hand. "So you went over to Joyce Oleander's condo in Sunset Shores," I prompted impatiently. My stomach was making thunderous complaints. I had skipped breakfast, and lunch had consisted of a breath mint I'd dug out of my purse on the drive over to the library.

"Yes. Sunset Shores. Joyce bought a condo there last year. That's where I found the body. Joyce, that is."

She paused for a moment. I noticed how carefully she seemed to be choosing her words, almost with a politician's care. "She was on the floor in the living room, face up. I knew she was dead by looking at her. Her eyes, you understand, were open in a fixed stare. But I checked her pulse to be sure. Then I called the hospital. It wasn't until ten minutes later that I called the police."

"Why the police?"

"Well, after I called the hospital, I found the empty pill bottle. It was on the coffee table. As I told the police, I was very careful. I didn't move the body or touch the bottle. I merely read the prescription label. It was for 20 tablets of Vicodin, and it was dated November 1. And then there was the blood."

"Blood?" I asked, as if I hadn't heard her right.

"Not a great deal. Mostly in her hair, on the left side. About here." She touched the left side of her head near the temple. "I deduced that she lost consciousness after taking the pills, and had hit her head on the coffee table when she fell to the floor. Though probably not with much impact, since

45

there wasn't much blood. And head wounds can be notoriously messy." She pursed her red lips. "She might have been reaching for the phone on the side table."

"What made you deduce that?" I challenged, not liking what she was suggesting. Suicide was bad enough, but to change your mind and fail? "Was the phone off the hook?"

"No, because then I would have gotten a busy signal when I called. But what other logical reason could there be for the body being on the floor in that position?" Ida fingered her sweater chain as if it were a rosary.

"There could be lots of reasons." I knew she was probably right. But I persisted anyway. "Maybe someone before you came to her door."

Ida peered over her glasses at me, as if I had refused to pay my library fines.

I glanced back to my notes. "I'm just trying to get the full picture. So the injury was on the left side of her head, you say?"

"Well, of course, where else would it be? I just told you the blood was on the left side of her head, so logically the injury had to be there." Librarian Reeves didn't like her conclusions questioned. "Joyce took an overdose of Vicodin, tried to get up for some reason, lost consciousness, fell and hit her head. And that's it."

"Was there a suicide note?"

"No, but no one accidentally takes that many pills."

It was unnerving to me how certain this woman was of her opinions, and worse, how detached she seemed from her coworker's death. I wanted to shake her.

"To even consider foul play is . . . well . . . ludicrous," she pronounced, as if I was the village idiot.

Ida had a point, but her self-righteous attitude made me want to challenge everything she said. "What else made it obvious that Ms. Oleander committed suicide? The Vicodin could well have made her woozy enough not to know what dosage she was taking or had already taken. Unless the depression you mentioned before really wasn't attached to her gynecological surgery."

My own deductive reasoning and medical terminology stopped Ida cold.

"That's not what I meant by obvious." She blew out a small breath of air. "Well, that's all I can tell you."

I had pushed her too far. Ida Reeves wasn't going to speculate further about why Joyce Oleander had committed suicide. At least not with me. Still, I persisted. "I just need a few more facts about Joyce for my feature story." I emphasized the word facts. "How old was she at the time of her death?"

Ida folded the plastic wrap from her sandwich over and over again until it formed a tidy, creased square. "She was thirty-six. Her birthday's next month. Would have been next month, on December thirteenth."

I wrote 36 and December 13 in my notebook. "Had she always worked at the library?"

"Yes. She started part-time when she was in high school."

"How would you describe her?"

Ms. Reeves hesitated long enough to make me wonder if she would answer. "Bookish girl. She would sit behind the checkout desk and read."

"Was she ever married?"

"No." Her eyes strayed around the room. I had hit a nerve.

"Boyfriends?"

The librarian, now clearly annoyed with me, took a deep annoyed breath. "She was engaged briefly to Elliott Stillwater right after high school. But they didn't go through with the marriage."

She was supplying the facts, all right, and that was about all. I was willing to bet the only reason she hadn't booted me out of the library was her compulsion, genetic or not, to share information.

"Do you know why they didn't get married?"

"No, I don't."

"She never confided anything to you about Mr. Stillwater?"

Ida put her hand over the collar of her blouse. "She might have said something about things not working out, and that being her fault, or rather, her decision. But you're not to print that."

"Of course not." I decided to try another tack, appealing to Ida as a trusted confidant. I looked down at my notebook as if the next question was already there. "You mentioned that her parents died in their forties from heart disease."

"Yes. The father first, then a year later the mother."

"Was there a connection between the two deaths?"

"I already told you, they both had heart disease. What do these questions have to do with Joyce's obituary?"

She had a right to ask that. What was I after? Maybe some explanation for Joyce's suicide, if that's really what happened. Or maybe I was just trying to force this cold cliché of a woman to show some emotion, even if it was anger.

"I'm just trying to get this right, be accurate. Did Joyce have any friends outside of her work here at the library?"

"No other friends that she mentioned to me. I believe I was her only friend."

This information gave me pause. Then I recovered enough to ask, "How about activities or hobbies?"

"She volunteered at the hospital every Saturday. She worked in the children's ward." Her voiced dropped. "Compensating."

"Compensating?" I knew what she meant, but I wanted to hear it from those lush, red lips.

"For not having any of her own." Ida lowered her voice even more. "Children. Some women have this need to satisfy their unfulfilled maternal instincts."

This obit was going to require a lot of adjectives. Joyce Oleander seemed to have had such a sad and lonely life that it made me depressed just thinking about it. "How about other relatives?"

"She had a grandmother who took care of her after her mother's death. She died about fifteen years ago. I think she once mentioned some distant cousins in Minnesota, but I don't know their names or addresses."

"Who's handling the funeral arrangements?"

"I am. I made arrangements with Father Lewis at St. Patrick's in Egg Harbor. There'll be a funeral mass, even though she was a suicide." There was enough edge in her tone to suggest condemnation. "And she'll be buried in the church cemetery. At nine-thirty, Monday. I expect you'll be there."

An invitation I couldn't refuse. Ida Reeves was like the nuns I'd had as teachers in grammar school. There was an implicit authority in their every demand. After all, they were God's disciples in the classroom. How could they be wrong? How could you ever refuse them?

"Do you have any recent photos of Joyce? I'd like to include a photo with the article."

Ida pushed back her chair and walked over to the green steel desk. "As a matter of fact, I have quite a few." She seemed relieved and suddenly talkative again. "The most recent were taken at a librarians' conference we attended last spring. I had planned to retire in a few years, then Joyce would take over the reins here."

So Joyce's suicide had messed up Ida's neat and tidy life. How could I have missed that? Ida was likely furious at Joyce. That explained her intense control, and her arch coldness.

She came back to the table with a photo album and an envelope. She looked at the watch on her chest. "I still have fifteen minutes." Quickly, she sorted through the envelope, barely glancing at the photos. "Here, how about this one? It's the only one of Joyce alone. She didn't care to have her picture taken."

Joyce Oleander was bone-thin with a protruding belly that made her look three months pregnant. Her skin was sallow, and she wore no makeup to compensate. Her light hair was parted in the middle and pulled back from her gaunt face. A face that, if it hadn't been so stark and haunted, might have been pretty. She had large dark eyes that some poets would no doubt call soulful. They were her best feature, and they were averted away from the camera. She stood huddled beneath one of the stone lions that I instantly recognized as guardians of the front entrance to the Chicago Art Institute.

Ida pushed her glasses up the bridge of her nose and sniffed. "Maybe you can crop it. She looks so sickly."

"What about this one?" A photo had slipped from the envelope. Joyce and Ida were arm-in-arm in front of Chicago's Buckingham Fountain. Neither looked especially happy, but at least they were smiling, or maybe it was just the sun in their eyes.

"No." Ida took the picture from me and placed it back in the envelope. "We want this to be about Joyce. Not me."

"We can crop you out," I suggested.

She patted the photo of Joyce. "I gave you a photo to use."

"Okay. Is there anything else you'd like to tell me about Joyce?"

Ida considered for a moment. "You could count on her."

What a bizarre comment considering Joyce had messed up Ida's retirement plans by dying.

She looked at her pin watch again. "Lunch time is over. So if you don't mind."

I did mind. But there wasn't much I could do about it. Ida had suddenly gone as quiet as the library.

"And I'd like it back," she said, pushing her lunch bag down in the trashcan beside the desk. "That photo. I'd like it back." Ida locked the office door and walked me to the main room of the library. She didn't seem to trust me, or likely anybody else for that matter.

"Was this Joyce's main work area?" I asked, pointing to the front desk.

"When she worked front desk." There was a note of impatience in Ida's voice.

"What if she wasn't working front desk?"

"Then she sat over there." She indicated a wooden desk placed directly under the FICTION SECTION sign. "Now I really do have to open the library."

"Go ahead. I'll just take a look at her desk. If you don't mind."

Ida sniffed again. "I don't know what you expect to find. I've told you everything. Joyce was pretty transparent. There's no mystery here."

"How about why she committed suicide?" I asked, hoping to shake her up.

To my surprise, she answered without hesitation. "If I was to offer up a reason . . ." She paused and clicked her tongue. "I'd say the surgery. It unbalanced her brain chemistry. Quite literally, she wasn't in her right mind. But go ahead, you look through her desk. If you must." She turned away and went to unlock the front door.

I didn't have to explore the desk, but Joyce Oleander's suicide and her repressive life now weighed heavily on my spirit. I needed to find something, anything that might redeem her life and explain her death for me. For whatever reasons, my motives were now purely selfish.

I sat in Joyce's chair, a stiff wooden contraption that was in need of cushioning. Sitting here for longer than fifteen minutes had to constitute thirty days' indulgence from the pangs of purgatory, if those were still available to the Catholic faithful. Alas, the desk proved devoid of any personal items: not a photo, a coffee mug, nor a scraggly plant. I slid open the top drawer. It could have been an ad for an office supply store. Paper, pencils, pens, paper clips, rubber bands, post-it notes: each neatly arranged within an assigned place. The two side drawers were just as business-like. I had difficulty opening the bottom side drawer and was about to give up when it finally jerked open. Buried under a stack of yellow legal pads was a dog-eared copy of *Catcher in the Rye*. One of my favorite books, but hardly the book I expected Joyce Oleander to be savoring. A marker protruded from one end. Curious, I opened the book to the marker. It was a yellowing color photo of Joyce and another girl. They were on the brink of puberty—maybe ten or eleven—that age when they were all arms and legs with the merest suggestion of breasts. I knew it was Joyce because there were those dark, soulful eyes again. Only now they stared directly at the camera. Both girls were dressed in identical bathing suits and had struck rather suggestive poses. Hands on hips, hands behind heads, nubile chests thrust forward. Although they were smiling and showing lots of teeth, their smiles looked forced. The photo made me shiver.

Quickly, I scanned the room for Ida. She was directing a woman toward a back shelf. With my heart doing double time, I slid the photo into my jacket pocket.

After leaving the library I walked down the street looking for a pay phone, cursing myself once again for not recharging my cell phone. I found a phone outside the post office. I flipped to the page in my notebook where I'd written Sarah Peck's home phone number and punched it in. The phone rang five times before a woman answered.

"Is Sarah Peck there?" I asked.

"Speaking. Who is this?" Sarah Peck had a husky voice that I was sure had been enhanced by years of cigarette smoking.

"Leigh Girard from the *Gazette*. We met at your mother's. I want to talk to you about your father's autopsy."

"Not interested."

"Then I guess I'll just have to contact your mother about the autopsy."

"My mother is very upset right now. She doesn't know what she's saying or doing. Why don't you back off?" she snapped.

"Will you talk to me then?"

I heard her take a deep breath. "Fine, all right. I can give you ten minutes. Be at the White Cliffs at four-fifteen. If you're late, tough." Then she hung up on me.

I looked at my watch. It was 2:10; I had about two hours to kill before my meeting with Sarah Peck. Plenty of time to grab a sandwich at the Egg Harbor market and work on the obit. I closed my notebook, shoved it into my purse and walked back to my truck.

The market was at the other end of town. A short jaunt by foot or truck. I decided to drive. I picked up a turkey sandwich and a bottle of water and sat in the market parking lot munching on the sandwich and trying to give Joyce Olean-der's obit some attention.

Joyce Oleander, 36, daughter of the late Frank and Helen Ole-ander, died Wednesday, November 1 after a brief illness. Ms. Ole-ander, a native of Door County, had been a librarian at the Egg Harbor Library for 20 years.

"She will be sorely missed," said Ida Reeves, head librarian. "You could always count on her."

Ms. Oleander's devotion to the library was extraordinary, only matched by her volunteer service and devotion to the children's ward of Bay Hospital.

Ms. Oleander attended Gibraltar High School, and graduated in 1982. She was a member of the GHS French Club.

Funeral services will be held at St. Patrick's Church, Monday November 6 at 9:30 a.m., to be followed by interment at the church cemetery.

I surveyed my paltry effort. Stevens wouldn't be pleased. I needed more "stuff," as he would put it. No one at the high school had been able to offer much of an impression of Joyce, except for what was on record—her B+ average and her French Club membership. I'd have to track down someone from the hospital children's ward who had worked with Joyce. Maybe they could add further dimension to the meager details I'd gathered.

I took out the photo of Joyce and her friend and studied it. Details emerged that I hadn't noticed before. One of the straps on Joyce's suit had slipped down her arm. Her pencil-thin legs were so tightly held together that they almost looked like one leg. The hand on her hip was held in a fist.

I continued to write. As a young girl, Joyce had posed for a suggestive photo with a friend. The unidentified friend said, "No one really knew Joyce."

With a sigh, I realized my need for a story was over stimulating my imagination. The photo could as easily be read as two young girls imitating poses they'd seen on Charlie's Angels or in some magazine like *Seventeen*.

I put my pen down and pulled out Stevens's edited version of my obit on Carl Peck that I'd printed off the computer before leaving the office. It was twice as long as what I had written about Joyce Oleander.

THE DOOR GAZETTE, November 3, PAGE 10

Carl Peck, Egg Harbor, one of Door County's most well-known master carpenters and restorers of Door County buildings, died Tuesday, October 31, at Bay Hospital. He was 67.

Mr. Peck, who came to Door County after the Korean War, was responsible for the restoration of such Door County landmarks as the Cupola, the Stone Gull Inn, and The Meadows. His restoration of the Stone Gull Inn was featured in Wisconsin Yesterday and Today. The magazine praised his attention to historic details and his use of native limestone and other local materials. Olin Forrest, another Egg Harbor resident and a historian, said, "Carl was always a perfectionist when it came to his work."

Mr. Peck served in the 10th Engineer Battalion and was awarded the Purple Heart in 1953. He was born in Chicago, Illinois.

From 1985–1986, he was the president of the Mycology Society. He was a familiar sight roaming the woods in search of rare mushrooms. The current Mycology president, Hank Sullivan, commented to the Gazette, "Carl really knew his mushrooms. Not only did he gather them, he also cultivated them."

"Mr. Peck enjoyed helping other people," said Rebecca Brandt, owner of Rebecca's Antiques. "He must have played Santa Claus for the Egg Harbor Annual Christmas Breakfast at least a dozen times. The kids loved him."

He is survived by his wife, Eva Peck (nee Adams), of the home, and his daughter, Sarah Peck, of Baileys Harbor.

He will be greatly missed by everyone, friends and family alike.

There was no mention of funeral services, because the body had yet to be released by the M.E. I looked at my watch. I still had an hour and a half until I met with Sarah Peck. I got out of the truck and walked toward the pay phone across the street, cursing myself once again for not recharging my cell phone. Someone on the children's ward must have something to say about Joyce Oleander other than, "You could count on her."

After one lost connection, three transfers, and a ten minute hold, I finally reached someone who knew Joyce Oleander and was willing to talk to me: Joe Stillwater, an RN on the children's ward. He ended his shift at three and would meet me at the Land's End Inn in Egg Harbor, where he began his second job as the night clerk. I wondered what his relationship was to Elliott Stillwater, Joyce's ex-fiancé.

"Two jobs? What slacker told you that?" Joe Stillwater had a barrel chest and salt-and-pepper crew cut hair that badly needed pruning. His profile was as sharp as his gaze. "Only rich people on the peninsula have just two jobs."

The Land's End Inn was a twenty-three-unit motel off

Highway 42 at the foot of the hill that led into Egg Harbor. The Inn was built amongst pines and birches. It didn't have a water view, but the surrounding trees were supposed to give lodgers a feeling of "sleeping in the woods under nature's canopy," or so the brochure stuck into each menu proclaimed. From what I could see after I parked and went inside the restaurant, that only applied if your room didn't face the asphalt parking lot. The cozy lobby boasted a floor-to-ceiling fireplace in a sunken seating area. But the briskly burning fire couldn't mask the smell of stale coffee and damp cedar.

I took a sip of the coffee Joe Stillwater offered me. It tasted burnt. I took another sip. I needed the jolt. "What's your third job?"

"On weekends, I run the boat rental in Rowleys Bay. You should come out. I'll teach you canoeing. You don't look like a kayaker."

"I don't, huh?" And I don't look like Dolly Parton either, I thought to myself.

"Kayaking would be too lonely and confining for you." He cocked his head as if to see me better. "You're a people-person."

"Yup, that's me, Ms. Congeniality." He had no idea how wrong he was. Since the cancer, I had trouble connecting with people. Cancer separates you from people, whether you want it to or not.

"You don't think so, but I'm never wrong about people. It's a gift." He patted his chest where his heart was. The gesture suggested such vulnerability that I felt my natural wariness recede.

"What's there to canoeing anyway? You just get in and paddle, right?"

"Ever been in a canoe?"

The very thought terrified me. I had never learned to

swim. "My water sports consist of standing on the shore and watching the sun sink into the bay."

"You come out to the boat rental. I'll show you."

"Sure," I answered, laughing. "When a woman becomes president."

"Okay. I can see you're not biting. So what do you want to know about Joy?"

Joy? That nickname was a surprise. "What can you tell me?"

"For starters, she was almost my sister-in-law. My younger brother, Elliott, was engaged to her for about a millisecond. Then she called the whole thing off. I always thought, his loss."

"Did she give any reason?"

"Some garbage about not being cut out for marriage. At least that's all I could get out of Elliott. It was something else, though. Something had soured her on marriage."

"Why do you say that?"

"Because after their split, she changed, she even looked different. Too thin and sort of dried-out looking."

"So you and she kept in contact?"

"Oh yeah, I'm the one who put her on to the kids' ward at the hospital."

So Ida Reeves wasn't her only friend. I was liking Joe Stillwater more and more.

"That's the thing I couldn't figure about the breakup with Elliott. Joy loved kids. In fact, it was a big reason for their engagement."

"What do you mean?"

"My brother was always complaining that Joy wanted to wait. You know, until marriage. Of course, being the horny bastard that he is, like most guys, he wanted to, you know, before. Jeez, I shouldn't be telling you this stuff. Elliott'll kill me. But hey, he lives in Indiana. You get what I'm talking about."

"I get it."

"But this suicide thing, man, I can't figure it." He ran his hand back and forth through his ragged hair. "I mean, Joy didn't get much out of life, but she loved those kids in the ward, and believe it or not, she loved working at the library. Told me she was going to run it once Dr. Reeves retired. Hey, did you talk to her? I hear she found Joy?"

"I did, but I admit, she wasn't very helpful."

"You sure you just couldn't hear her?" He lowered his voice.

"I heard her too well," I said, smiling.

"Yeah, I know what you mean. Man, that woman, well she's harmless, but you ask her one question and suddenly she's talking genes and glands and hormones. I get enough of that stuff at the hospital." He watched me cross and uncross my legs. "Sorry, what else you need?"

"When was the last time you talked to Joyce?"

"Let me think. D-day." He smiled. "Discharge day. Halloween morning, after her surgery. She was packing up her stuff. I carried her suitcase out to her car."

"How did she seem? Was she depressed?"

"Not depressed, more like, distracted. Like there was something on her mind. Like she was preoccupied."

"Did she say anything?"

"Joy was never much of a talker. I think that's one of the reasons Elliott wanted to marry her. We're a big family of talkers. As I was saying, I noticed she was distracted because I had to remind her to take the bag of meds beside her bed. She was walking out of the room without them when I called after her. 'Joy,' I said, 'you don't want to forget these.' She kinda looked around like she'd forgotten I was there." Joe mimicked a distracted look. " 'Oh,' she says, 'sorry.' I go, 'Hey, you're the one who'll be sorry if you forget these.' Shit." Joe stared into the fire for a few moments. There was nothing for me to say.

Then he got up and poured himself some more of the bad coffee. "I haven't called Elliott yet. Not sure I can even reach him anyway. He's up in Canada on some fishing trip. Won't be back for a couple weeks. I guess the bad news can wait till then. I mean, it's been twenty some years since they were involved. Still, he took it pretty hard when she dumped him. We didn't see him for a long time. He hitchhiked all over the country. We'd get these post cards from places like Intercourse, Pennsylvania. He's got this strange sense of humor. Finally, he settled in Indiana, of all places. Still a bachelor."

"Can you think of any reason why Joyce would kill herself?"

"Like I said, I can't really figure it."

"Anything. A guess."

He looked at me hard, his dark eyes poring into mine. I shifted in my chair. "You're interested in this more than for the story." He wasn't asking me, he was telling me. "But I can't help you with reasons. I can't even guess."

"Okay, then how about before the discharge day, right after the surgery, while she was recovering. How did she seem?"

"I know what you're trying to do, but I gotta tell you, there's nothing to tell. After the surgery, I'd come by the days I was on shift. At first, she was in a lot of pain. But hey, a hysterectomy is big time surgery. Other than that, she seemed fine—her usual quiet self. The only thing, hey . . ." He looked at me and grinned. "You're good at this, huh? The only thing, the day before D-day, when I got there, she wasn't in her room. So I says to the duty nurse, 'Where's Joy?' She says,

'She should be back any minute, she went to visit another patient.' 'Then I must have just missed her,' I says. 'No,' she says, 'she didn't go to the children's ward because I saw her press the up button on the elevator.' I was going to ask Joy about it and then I forgot."

"Any guesses as to who she visited?"

"Nope. Couldn't say. You might want to ask Lorraine Birch, she's the nurse I'm talking about."

"I'll do that."

As I got up to leave, Joe followed me to the door. "One more thing," he said. There was hesitation in his voice. "Don't take this wrong. But I got to tell you cause I like to be up front with people. I said I couldn't figure it, the suicide, but what I didn't say is, I respect it. What she did. It's not my way. But I knew Joy well enough to know she must have had good reasons."

I didn't know why Joe Stillwater felt compelled to tell me this. "You think there are ever reasons good enough for suicide?"

"Like I said, you had to know Joy. I only wish she'd talked to me about it. Maybe I could have done something." Stillwater opened the door for me.

"What could you have done?"

He looked across the parking lot, toward the highway. "If you find out anything about why Joy might have done this, could you let me know? It would mean something to me."

"Joe, this is an obit piece. I'm not doing any kind of investigating."

He put his hand out to me, gave me that, "I can read you like an open book," look and said, "No, you're not doing any investigating. But like I said, Joy must have had good reasons. Just let me know what you come across."

"Okay," I answered, shaking his hand. He'd given me a charge and for some inexplicable reason, I'd accepted it.

As I walked to my truck, I wondered what he would say if I told him that Joyce might have changed her mind. I was struck again by the irony of Joe's calling her Joy. That name had probably fit her when she was in high school and engaged, working at the library, looking forward to a life rich in family and friends. But something had caused her to lose all the joy in life. I took a deep breath. The crisp afternoon air felt clean in my lungs.

7

Sarah Peck had been so adamantly anal about our meeting time, I looked at my watch as I opened the heavy wooden door of the White Cliffs Restaurant: 4:15 p.m. I was on time, give or take a second.

Sarah Peck was waiting in the bar area at one of the round glass tables near the bank of full-length windows. Not surprisingly, she was lighting a cigarette as I approached her.

"You have nine minutes." She took a long drag on her Marlboro Light and blew the smoke in my general direction. I thought about the way some people invite disaster. And that sometimes it comes without invitation.

"Ten, by my watch." I sat down on the black leather swivel chair, trying to control the anger Sarah Peck's open hostility unleashed in me.

"Nine." She flicked her ash with a jerky motion. She was dressed in a chef's uniform, complete with a white kerchief around her neck. Her blue-black hair was knotted near the nape of her slender neck. Divested of her distractingly tight clothes, her face became prominent. She had the fine chiseled bones of a fifties model. Her delicate beauty seemed to be at odds with her mouth, as if she had to defend herself against it.

Since time was a factor, I decided to go for the big question right out of the gate. "Why were you upset at the Med-

63

ical Examiner this morning?"

"I see the grapevine's working overtime, as usual." She took another drag on her cigarette, this time lingering over it. Then she looked me up and down. "You know, my mother's paranoid. That's what living with an alcoholic for close to forty years does to you. Makes you think the world's out to get you."

"So you admit your father was an alcoholic."

She laughed so suddenly that she choked on her smoke. "Alert the media. Anybody who knew him could see he was an alcoholic."

"Some people seem to think he was a nice guy. Not everyone knew about the drinking," I countered.

"Look, I lived with him, they didn't. He was drunk every day of his miserable adult life. Even though he was one of those quiet drinkers, at least in public." She paused and chewed on her lower lip.

I waited. When she didn't continue, I asked, "What do you mean, quiet drinkers?"

"He never was a falling-down drunk. Too much pride. Instead, he drank just enough to keep a constant buzz going. Trouble was, he had to keep drinking more and more to keep that mind-numbing buzz. Toward the end, he had bottles stashed all over the house, in the garage, at work. He even kept a bottle under the seat of his truck. I'd say that makes him an alcoholic."

"But the M.E. ruled your father's cause of death as liver failure. So why would that upset you, since it's totally consistent with alcoholism?"

"You think you're real smart, don't you." She snubbed the cigarette out in the ash tray and pushed back her chair. "Why would I care if he died from liver failure or heart attack? He's dead, that's all that matters."

"Then it wasn't either, was it?"

She moved away from the table. "Your nine minutes are up."

8

As I drove north on Horseshoe Bay Road toward home, I counted to four, inhaling slowly and making sure that my lungs filled with air and my diaphragm expanded. Then I exhaled to the same four count, forcing all the air out. These exercises had gotten me through the worst of the chemo symptoms. I'd hoped never to use them again, or at least not so soon. I kept breathing deeply, slowly, hoping to calm my jittery brain. It had been a frustrating, disturbing day. I'd learned nothing more tangible regarding the circumstances of Carl Peck's death, or Joyce Oleander's, for that matter, but I definitely had learned that Sarah Peck seemed glad her father was dead but wasn't likely to tell me why.

What had she said exactly . . . "He's dead, that's all that matters." I still didn't know what the autopsy report revealed, and her rampant hostility had put a knot at the base of my skull and set my nerves tingling. As for Joyce Oleander's suicide . . . I glanced at my open notebook. Across the top of the page, I'd written in all caps, JOYCE OLEANDER, SUNSET SHORES, followed by the short obit I'd written earlier. I flipped to the next page. It was filled with notes ending in question marks. I read one: "If hit head falling, why body face up?" Without answering any of these questions, I wasn't sure I had enough copy to satisfy Stevens.

If I hurried, I might make it home in time to see the sunset over the bay. The rain had cleared out earlier, and now the sky had all the drama of a purpling, yellowing bruise. Instead, I slowed the truck and turned right on Bluff Pass to follow the winding road up to Sunset Bay. After all, it was on my way home, I reasoned. I had no plans for the evening. There'd be other sunsets.

I pulled into the parking slot in front of Joyce Oleander's town house, and switched off the truck's engine. The sun was starting to set. It would be dark soon. I retrieved the small flashlight I kept in the glove compartment and shoved it into my jacket pocket before exiting the truck. With the setting sun, the wind was picking up. I pulled my jacket hood over my head.

As I walked toward Joyce's building, I wondered what had possessed her to buy this place. Although all three buildings were situated on a high bluff above Green Bay, only Joyce's building was minus a view. It was obscured by a line of dense, towering evergreens. The brown cedar siding was faded, and from the barrenness of the parking lot, it looked like most of the units were occupied only on weekends, if that. Which didn't bode well for my idea of interviewing a neighbor. The place looked about as populated as a mall on Super Bowl Sunday.

I walked up the concrete steps to the unit adjacent to Joyce's, and rang the bell. The whole building felt abandoned. A kid's plastic flip-flop lay in the brown grass, the front door screen had a hole the size of my fist and scraps of paper and debris littered the shrubbery. I rang the bell again. The wind was rushing through the tops of the trees, making me wish I was home soaking in a bubble bath.

Okay, now what? I crossed the slight rise of grass that separated Joyce's front door from her neighbor's. I looked from side to side, then tried the front door knob. It didn't budge.

There was still enough light coming from the west to illumi-
nate the interior of Joyce's town house. I cupped my eyes
against the front door glass and looked in. I could make out a
short narrow hall leading into a sunken living room with a
sliding glass door at the back. I looked around again. No one
in sight. It was worth a try.

Although I was sure her building was deserted, I slunk
around to the back, careful to stay in the shadows, just in case
someone from one of the other buildings saw me. Extending
off the back of each unit was a concrete patio and a six-foot
wooden divider. All the patios were bare except Joyce's. In
defiance of the weather, she had left out a small hibachi, two
lawn chairs, and a small table—forest green and made of that
cheap resin guaranteed to outlive the Sun. Joyce had positioned the chairs so that she could sit with her feet up and
look out toward the non-existent bay view.

I went to the sliding glass door. Again I looked around.
Then I tried the door. It moved easily. I slid it open, stepped
inside and slid it shut.

I was now standing in the living room, the very room
where Joyce Oleander died less than twenty-four hours ago. I
took a deep breath, inhaling a pleasant odor of old pine fires
interlaced with traces of patchouli. The scent seemed a
strange choice for a woman who had supposedly given up on
sex. The rich earthy scents contrasted with the sparse room.
Joyce had favored browns and greens and dark woods. In the
musky light, I saw a mahogany rocker, and an early American
couch with thick wooden arms that was covered in a brown,
green, and yellow print featuring windmills or miniature Rev-
olutionary soldiers. The matching side tables and coffee table
were cumbersome, functional rather than stylish. The furniture was old and sad and probably had been part of her legacy
from her dead parents. I noticed immediately that there was

no TV set. But the built-in bookcases surrounding the ceramic-tiled fireplace were crammed with books. From where I was standing, I couldn't read specific titles, but most were hard cover.

I walked over to the couch and stopped suddenly, as if an electrical current had shot through my body. There on the carpet was a dark splotch. What shocked me was the realization that it was human blood. I'd thought the blood had only been matted in Joyce's hair, not here as such an irrevocable sign of her death just a few hours before. Why hadn't Ida mentioned this?

I stood transfixed in the failing light, watching the stain seem to absorb the falling darkness. Though the sight of it was making me light-headed, I had a strange desire to touch it, as if I half expected it to still be warm and wet.

Instead, I pulled my gaze away and knelt down in the space between the couch and the coffee table, studying the coffee table for signs of blood and tissue. In the fading light, I couldn't see much. I dug out the small flashlight from my jacket pocket and clicked it on, shining it over the table. On the corner nearest the couch and farthest from the patio door was a dark smudge that looked like blood. The table edge wasn't sharp. Age had rounded it. But it was solid. If you got up from the couch, lost your balance and fell forward with all your weight and hit it, it would cause some damage—depending on where your head connected with the edge.

I sat back on my heels, trying to envision how it had happened. Ida Reeves had insisted that she hadn't touched the body except to check for a pulse. And she had said that she found the body face up, and that Joyce had a deep gash on her left temple. Now as I surveyed the room, that information didn't jibe with either the location of the bloodstain or the position of the table and the couch. Either Ida was lying, or confused.

Since the couch was set against a low wall that ran the length of that side of the room and couldn't have moved, and since there was just enough space between the couch and the coffee table for a body to rest, then whatever way the body fell, it would stay that way.

And even if Joyce had somehow landed on her back, because she was bleeding from her left temple, the blood would have been closer to the couch rather than the coffee table. So I came to the conclusion that someone, probably Ida, had turned Joyce over. Then why not admit it? In Ida's case, that would mean admitting that the careful, controlled head librarian had made a mistake. Had been too human.

That knot at the base of my skull spawned by Sarah Peck was now returning, and with it, a headache that squeezed like a band around my skull. My empty stomach felt like it was grinding meat. I stood up, and a wave of dizziness ran through me. I held still until my equilibrium returned. For a change, I thought, my body was speaking loud and clear. Still, I ignored it and moved through the living room and up the carpeted stairs. I wasn't done yet.

When I reached the top of the stairs, I paused to let the pulse that was beating in my head slow down. In the gloomy light, I saw two doorways. I turned right into the larger of the two rooms. This appeared to be Joyce's bedroom, but also a room decorated like a page from *House & Garden*—the perfect décor for the all-American, little girl princess. A queen-sized, four-poster canopied bed dominated the room, the kind you might find in a quaint bed-and-breakfast inn where they charge you an exorbitant fee to stay in their extra bedroom. Arranged against the headboard were different sized pillows trimmed in ribbons and white eyelet, in contrast with a variety of worn teddy bears. The bed was covered with a blue and white diamond pattern quilt that looked handmade.

There was a floor length mirror in a far corner. One wall had a floor-to-ceiling bookcase, again bursting with books. The other walls sported fussy wallpaper with pink tea roses running up and down a green trellis. A white wicker rocker straddled the space between the two windows. There were frilly curtains on the windows that reminded me of a Swiss chalet. I felt like I had wandered into Sleeping Beauty's bedroom before the prince got there and kissed her into womanhood.

I looked out one of the windows. Through a gap in the trees, a sliver of water shimmered in the distance. I turned away from the window and sat in the wicker rocker. I hadn't expected Joyce's bedroom to be so pathologically feminine, so fit for a child. It was as if Joyce could turn back the clock in this room, could be a little girl again, free from the burdens of womanhood. I knew that there were women like that, women who didn't want to leave their girlhoods. They collected Disney movies and elaborate dolls, even made yearly pilgrimages to Disneyland to ride "It's a Small, Small World," and "Pirates of the Caribbean." Getting married and having kids just meant that the dolls they played with were bigger.

As I sat rubbing my temples and trying to ease my headache, something caught my eye on the table beside Joyce's bed. I went over and picked up the slim book: *Ariel* by Sylvia Plath. Great, wasn't that the poet who committed suicide by sticking her head in the oven? Well, if you weren't thinking about suicide, you would be after reading this. I let the book fall open to the book mark. "Lady Lazarus," I vaguely remembered the poem. I'd have to reread it. Maybe it contained a clue to Joyce's suicide.

The other room would have to wait. I could no longer ignore my pounding head and roiling stomach. The sun was completely down, and I was afraid to switch on a light, so I made my way by flashlight down the stairs and into the living room. One more time, I crouched down by the coffee table and thought through the logistics of Joyce's fall and the final position of her body.

Satisfied with my conclusions, I was about to stand up when a flashlight beam bounced around the room. I flicked off my flashlight and ducked down beside the couch, careful to avoid the blood stain. Someone was outside the patio door. Before I could react, the door slid open.

"Don't move there," a deep male voice said. "Or I'll have to shoot. Ya dirt bag, wise guy."

I froze.

"Okay then, get up real slow. Hands where I can see 'em. And no funny business or I'll have to cuff ya. Pretty sneaky comin' in that there truck." The man let out a series of choking sounds. It took me a few seconds to realize that he wasn't choking but laughing.

I stood up slowly with my hands above my head, wondering who this weirdo was and what was so funny. As he panned the room with the flashlight, his silhouetted shadow lengthened, making him appear to be the size of the Incredible Hulk. Finally the light found me. I put my hand up to shield my eyes. He moved the light steadily from my face down to my feet and back to my face again.

"What the blue blazes. You're not Ferry!" He sounded surprised and bewildered.

"Either shoot me or get that light out of my eyes," I bluffed, hoping to take advantage of his momentary surprise.

He switched the flashlight off. For a moment, we stood in

total darkness while he stumbled around trying to locate a light switch. I considered making a run for the patio door, but thought better of it. All the Hulk had to do was make it to the door before me, and there'd be no way around him.

"Okay, then. Should be a switch here somewheres." I heard him pat the wall and scrape something, then a hanging lamp circa 1970s complete with rattan dome cast a diffused glow over the room.

"Who's Ferry, Officer?" I asked the cop standing in front of me. He was big and blonde and solid, like a Viking warrior fully ready to enter Valhalla.

He started to answer, then stopped. "What're you doin' here then, Miss?"

"My name's Leigh Girard. New reporter with the *Gazette*. I'm doing the obit feature on Joyce Oleander." I would have offered my hand, but I wasn't sure I'd get it back in the same condition.

"Jake send ya, then?"

I had two choices, tell the truth or go for the information. "Yeah, he did. And the door was unlocked." I hoped that let me off the hook for breaking and entering. And besides, if the door was unlocked, it was the cops' fault for not securing their crime scene.

"Huh," was all he said, narrowing his eyes. "Ferry's a cop friend of mine. We were meetin' here on official business."

"Do you often threaten to shoot your fellow policemen?"

He pushed his hat back off his forehead and scratched his head. Then he grinned sheepishly. "Kind of a joke with us."

"Aha." I nodded. "Got to keep it interesting, huh?"

"Ya got that right, there," he said, smiling.

"What do you make of this?" I pointed to the blood spot on the carpet.

The smile left as quickly as it came. "Look, Miss Girard. I

can't be talkin' about this here. It's an official case. So ya better skedaddle. No offense."

"Leigh, call me Leigh. I didn't catch your name, Officer?"

"Jorgensen, Deputy Chet Jorgensen. Now let's go, then." He jerked his thumb over his shoulder in the direction of the door.

"Deputy Jorgensen. I already talked to Ida Reeves. I know all about this situation. How Ida found Joyce Oleander lying here dead, on her back with blood in her hair. Considering the bloodstain and the position of the couch and coffee table, it doesn't take Sherlock Holmes to figure out that someone turned the body over. Do you have any suspicion of foul play? I didn't see a crime scene tape, so is that why you're here?"

He scratched his head again. "Now don't ya be jumpin' to no conclusions or puttin' words in my mouth."

He seemed unnerved enough for me to keep at it. "So there was foul play! Could Joyce have been murdered?" I didn't really think that Joyce had been murdered, but I wanted to push the Deputy's buttons and see what came out.

"There ya go. Joyce Oleander died from an overdose of a drug called Vicodin, which ya already know. She washed them pills down with bourbon. And that's what's goin' in the police report. Ain't no murder involved, less someone shoved those pills down her throat along with the booze. And there was no bruising on her throat."

I was doing everything my chief editor had told me not to do, but it was working. "Then why are you here? What's the official business?"

"Just goin' over things one more time. Gotta be careful in cases like this here. You guys handling it like usual?"

I hadn't a clue what "like usual" meant. But I wasn't going to let him know that. "Yeah sure."

That seemed to satisfy him. "Cause we don't want no copycats."

"Right," I said. "We don't want that." He was holding something back, I could sense it. "There's something else, isn't there? Come on, Deputy Jorgensen, off the record. I won't print it, much less tell anyone, even Stevens, Scout's honor." I held up three fingers and hoped they were the right ones.

"What's so important about this to ya? Did ya know Joyce?"

In a way, I felt I did. Except for the fairy tale bedroom, I felt a kinship with this woman, as if I was looking at my own future. But I wasn't about to tell Officer Jorgensen that. "I promised a friend of hers that I'd look into it."

"Who might that be?" he asked.

"Joe Stillwater," I answered.

He sat down in the rocker, and rocked back and forth. He was debating what and how much to tell me. I stood quietly listening to the methodical creaking of the rocker, which probably was in tune with the labored thoughts creaking around that mammoth head of his.

Finally he stopped rocking and leaned forward, putting his palms on his thighs.

"Okay, then. Seein' as you figured it out most ways, so no harm there. But this stays here with us. You can't tell Joe. And I 'spect somethin' in return."

"What?" I wasn't about to complain, but I was a little surprised that this cop was going to share information with me. Stevens was right, I had a lot to learn about the Door ways.

"You find out somethin' about this, you come to me first. Okay, then?"

"Sure. It's a deal."

"Ya ever hear of lividity?"

75

"No, not really. What is it?"

"Lividity is where the blood settles in the body after a person's dead. Has to do with gravity. And in this case here then, we found lividity on the chest and stomach and along the back."

"I don't understand."

"Well, it supports what you were sayin' there about someone turning the body over. Ya see, it takes about six hours for lividity to get a hold completely, which means it's permanent. But it takes only one to two hours for it to start appearing. And according to the doc on the scene, lividity hadn't set in yet. Then the body must have been face down at first for there to be lividity on the chest and stomach. Then someone turned the body over, which caused lividity along the back."

"You mean Ida Reeves? But she said she didn't move the body."

"People say a lot of things, especially when they think they done somethin' they shouldn't."

"So how long did the doctor figure she'd been dead?" I asked.

"Three hours. Close as he can figure."

"How certain is the doctor about time of death?" I was getting an uneasy feeling.

"As certain as he can be," he said. "What you gettin' at?"

"What I'm getting at is this: If the doctor figured she'd been dead about three hours, and there was lividity on both the chest and stomach and along the back, and it takes one to two hours for lividity to appear, then there was at least an hour between Ida's turning the body over and her calling this in. Unless it took you guys an hour to get here. Because how else could there had been lividity on both the front and back of the body? Unless . . ." I thought of another alternative. "Unless someone else was here before Ida. And that person turned the body over but never reported finding Joyce dead."

"It didn't take us no hour to get here." He sounded defensive. "And I'm telling you, Ida turned that body. She just don't want to admit it. As for that hour you're talkin' about, sometimes people go into shock when they find a dead body. They get paralyzed like. That's probably what happened here."

I wasn't convinced. Ida didn't strike me as the kind of person who would get paralyzed by shock. "You check with the neighbors to see if anyone else was here last night?"

He stood up. "Nobody saw nothin.' Just remember our bargain."

Novice journalist that I was, I knew about writing too many details regarding a suicide, for fear of giving disturbed and impressionable people something to copy. My part of this bargain was to keep the details off the record.

Salinger was howling and scratching at the door as I jiggled the key in the back door lock. "Take it easy, girl, I'm hurrying." I inched the door open. She jumped up at me for our obligatory greeting, then tore past me through the field toward the water. I didn't have the energy to even call after her. My headache was still present, albeit faint and persistent, and likely to edge into a full-blown migraine.

I threw my bag down on the kitchen table, kicked off my black suede boots and headed for the bathroom medicine cabinet where I kept the Duradrin.

Standing over the sink, I swallowed two tablets with water and prayed I'd caught it in time. If not, the full-blown pain and flashing light show would soon be upon me, which meant a fun-filled night of light sensitivity followed by vomiting.

Usually about six tablets in four hours did the trick, but that definitely meant no chardonnay and no reading tonight.

I stripped off my ivory-colored silk blouse and black wool trousers and tossed them into the hamper, as if they had a taint on them. Avoiding my reflection in the full-length mirror, I unhooked my bra and slipped out of it, again feeling that jarring sense of disproportion. I pulled on the gray sweatshirt and sweat pants that were hanging on the back of the bathroom door. The tightness in my head was loosening. That was a good sign, but I knew I should eat something too.

On my way to the kitchen, I saw the red eye of the answering machine blinking. "Now what?" I said out loud, irritably pressing the blue play button.

Tom's all-too-familiar voice played back. "I'm just calling to see if everything's all right." Pause. Long pause. "No need to call if it is." Pause. Click.

I punched erase and listened to the tape whirl as I struggled into my jacket and unlaced sneakers. Salinger had the right idea. The night was crisp and black and smelled of dank earth. I sat on the back steps huddled down in my jacket, and rocked back and forth to keep warm. The moon arched over the trees, silvering the field and back lighting the sky. Overhead, two large birds glided and circled. Then suddenly one dove into the field. He rose slowly, his jerking catch held tight in his talons. It looked like rabbit was this evening's entree.

I picked up a rock from the ground and threw it into the field, then another, then another and another.

"Move, damn it," I shouted. "Get out of there or fight!" Things I couldn't see rustled in the tall weeds. It was an absurd useless gesture, but I felt better having made it.

My headache was definitely easing, but now the drug fog was descending. I closed my eyes and leaned back on my elbows, letting the cold air hit my face. Like a series of slides, images flitted across my brain: Ida's watery green eyes, the ruffled edge of Joyce's bathing suit, Sarah's tightly knotted hair, Deputy Jorgensen's black leather gun holster, Joyce Oleander's rust-brown blood. I opened my eyes, trying to shake free of the images.

Why had Joyce Oleander done it? Her suicide made no sense to me. According to Joe Stillwater, she was looking forward to running the library and she loved her work in the children's ward. I didn't buy Ida's explanation that Joyce was the victim of post-hysterectomy chemical imbalance. That sounded like medical mumbo-jumbo covering Ida's refusal to look any deeper. Something had set Joyce upon this course. But what? Joe said that she visited someone in the hospital before her discharge. I had to find out who she visited. It was a long shot, but maybe it tied in somehow with her suicide.

A high screeching sound broke into my musings. I looked up. The other bird had snagged a rabbit. Its screams sounded almost human. I picked up a handful of rocks and started pitching them into the field. The bird flew away into the trees, his prey now quiet.

What kept coming back into my mind was Ida's supposition about Joyce's fall—that she might have been reaching for the phone. That at the last minute, Joyce might have had second thoughts. And then there was the fact that someone, maybe Ida, had turned her over and not immediately called the hospital or the police. My intuition told me that Ida wouldn't have been paralyzed by fear, as Jorgensen suggested. She had done just what she said she had done: first called the hospital, then called the police. Regardless, there'd been no crime committed, except Joyce's crime of taking her own life.

My sockless feet were numb with cold. I stood up, stamped my feet and peered into the dark. "Salinger!" I shouted. The weeds rustled in the distance. I could just make out the tips of her ears as she ran through the field toward me. "Come on, girl. Time to come home."

"No need to call, huh?" I said to myself. "You got that right, Tom."

9

Saturday, November 4, Present day

"Forget church, forget social clubs, there's only one place to meet people here." Lydia Crane cut into her beef Wellington with precision. "Bars."

I raised a skeptical eyebrow. Lydia and I were seated at a corner table in the hearth room of the Stone Gull Inn—aptly named for the blazing red brick hearth that dominated an entire wall. The muted strains of a classical guitar drifted into the room, along with a potpourri of succulent scents. The historic Stone Gull Inn catered to tourists in the vein of a turn-of-the-century hostelry with planked ceilings, white stucco walls, candlelight, strumming guitarist, and serving wenches with cinched waists and prominent bosoms. Both dining rooms had china sideboards whose shelves held delicate dishes painted with pink and white tea roses. The anachronistic atmosphere of the place was just what I needed after yesterday's frenetic revelations. I had spent most of today sequestered in the cottage, rereading Toni Morrison's *Beloved* and trying to ignore the dust bunnies that were haunting my house.

"I know what you're thinking. But it's nothing like Chicago. Walking into a bar is not an automatic invitation to indiscriminate sex." Lydia smiled slyly.

"Does anyone think that anymore, with AIDs and STDs?" I countered.

"People can be pretty careless in the heat of the moment. At least that's been my experience." Her eyes widened. They looked golden in the candlelight, like a cat's.

Lydia just opened the door to another level of intimacy that I didn't want to enter. Singles bars, indiscriminate sex, experiences in the heat of the moment were not on my agenda. "So why do people here in Door County go to bars, if it's not for the sex?"

"Sex can be part of it. After all, it's always there lurking around some corner. But the bars here are where people go to talk. If you don't want to talk, you can listen or 'people watch.' If sex happens, fine. If it doesn't, that's fine, too. There are these unwritten rules."

"Like a medieval hamlet where every once in a while a person has to be burned as a witch to keep everybody happy?"

"What?" She looked at me incredulously.

"Nothing, just something Jake Stevens suggested about Door life."

"How's he to work for?" She smirked knowingly. Sex was certainly lurking around Lydia's every corner.

"Enigmatic."

"Aren't they all?"

"So how do I learn the unwritten rules?" I asked, biting into an artichoke heart. I had ordered the artichoke Romano. The blend of artichokes, asparagus tips, angel hair pasta and Romano cheese was wonderfully rich and satisfying.

"By experience, my dear, how else?" Lydia took a sip of her dark merlot wine. "I propose a field trip after dinner."

"Where?" I was feeling too good for the evening to be over so soon. Thoughts of Joyce Oleander and the way she died could be put on hold for one night.

"I know the perfect place to show you some local color: Bailey's Roadhouse."

"That dive in Egg Harbor with the fifty motorcycles parked outside night and day? Is this part of your rebellion against that Lake Forest upbringing?"

"You do have an ornery streak, Leigh. Yes, that's the place. But don't be fooled by its appearance. It's even worse than it looks." Lydia laughed.

"You're not one of those weekend biker chicks, are you, Lydia?"

"You never know what secrets lie beneath the surface." Her eyebrows went up and down several times. "Come on, don't be so uptight. It'll be good for you."

"Like medicine is good for you? This isn't one of these initiation things?"

"You are a suspicious person, Leigh."

"Goes with the job."

"I have a feeling it has nothing to do with the job. Look, I go there by myself and my virtue's still intact. What's left of it, that is."

"All right, I'll go. But if it's just totally tacky, I'm outta there."

"Speaking of your job, did you talk to Sarah Peck about her father's autopsy?"

"For about nine minutes yesterday. All I found out was that she's a very hostile person." My encounter with Sarah Peck seemed almost insignificant in light of what I'd learned from Deputy Jorgensen about Joyce's time of death, and my supposition that someone besides Ida Reeves may have found her, moved her body, and not called the police.

"That's Sarah. I've concluded that she gets off on her anger. Check out those streetwalker clothes. They're so outrageous, they leave you speechless. You don't know if you should slap her or hug her."

"What's the situation with her family?"

83

"Dysfunctional to the max but hey, whose isn't?" She pushed her dinner plate aside.

"Sarah freely admits that her father was a heavy-duty drunk. Did you ever see him drinking at any of the bars?"

"What do you think I am, a bar fly? Don't answer that. At Bailey's maybe, I saw him a few times on Friday nights."

"Was he drunk?"

"Not so you could tell by looking at him."

"But you could tell?"

"Yes." Lydia was staring over my head, trying to catch the attention of our waitress. I was getting the strong impression that she didn't want to talk about Carl Peck.

"Okay, what did he do so that you could tell?"

She sighed heavily. "Not much, he was just a little too friendly. Kept putting his hand on my arm, leaning in too close, that kind of harmless old man thing. You know, once a stud always a stud."

The waitress returned and discreetly slipped the leather bound bill book on our table.

"So, what's your story, Leigh? I notice you're not wearing a wedding band."

"Separated. And you?"

"Divorced. He was a photographer, of all things. But nobody wanted to buy the pictures he took of the nightlife of junkies and bums—magnificent technique, depressing topic. I admit I used the poor guy to irritate my family. More of that rebel stuff, but of course, I'm past all that now."

I smiled at her comment. "Are you involved with anyone?" Even though Lydia and I hardly knew each other, it was clear we were willing to speak directly to each other. I was curious, but wanted to keep our conversation away from my personal life. The separation, moving here—it was all connected to the cancer. And I didn't want to bring down our evening by talking about cancer.

"It's not easy finding companionship here, male or otherwise." She opened the black leather book and squinted at the bill. "Why don't we just split it?"

She put two twenties on top of the bill. "Oh, what's the difference," she said, pushing back her chair. "It's over now anyway, so why should I care?" She seemed to be justifying her words to herself. "Rob Martin and I went out for awhile. It's no secret. But it didn't work out."

Before I could respond, Lydia left the table and headed in the direction of the Women's Room. Even though I didn't like Martin, I could see the attraction for Lydia. She had a gift for exaggeration. I had a hunch Lydia was one of those people prone to depression who kept the blues at bay by creating dramatic situations. Martin's intensity would keep her from depression's door. I wondered why it hadn't worked out, since it was obvious she still wanted it to.

10

Bailey's Roadhouse was a battered, claustrophobic bar and restaurant in Egg Harbor along Highway 42, just south of County E. Its white paint was grayed, chipped, and peeling away, giving the outside the appearance of an abandoned ship. The back of the bar overlooked the bay, but a tangle of weeds and trees obscured most of the view. It was Egg Harbor's last authentic holdout from pseudo-rural renewal. No one came here for the view.

The interior of Bailey's fared no better than the exterior. The requisite jukebox played Willie Nelson, and I smelled a permeating odor of stale beer. A dark, gleaming bar dominated the room. It was like an oasis in a desert of wooden tables and chairs stained by spilled drinks. The knotty pine ceiling offered the perfect complement to an entire wall festooned with a collection of beer bottles from around the world. As I walked past the bottles, I read a few unpronounceable German names.

The only exception to the usual bar decor was a mural that covered another wall. It depicted an old fishing village. I didn't recognize the place, though I was certain it was one of the local villages. It had a haunting quality, eliciting a way of life that could only be imagined now. In the painting, men in heavy clothing on a trawler near a stone pier struggle with nets brimming with fish. Looking on is a scraggly brown dog. In the distance, another fish-laden trawler heads into shore.

The only female in the scene is a yellow-haired girl in a blue dress. She fishes off the pier. The artist had muted the colors so that the whole scene looked faded.

As we made our way to a table, a few customers called out greetings to Lydia. From the benign, "Where you been lately, honey?" to the more hostile, "Slumming?"

"Don't pay attention to these losers, Leigh. They resent the fact that I work for a living but don't have to. Right, guys?"

"Damn right," one of the more friendly-looking men answered.

Lydia ran her fingers through her auburn hair, which, loose from its braid, gave her a feral quality. I suspected a fierceness to her. She'd be an ardent friend and an awesome enemy. She ordered a pitcher of beer from the waitress who looked old enough to be collecting social security. Probably one of the legions of retirees who lived in Door on meager pensions and worked minimum wage jobs to get by.

"Impressed?" Lydia asked.

"Oppressed is more like it," I answered, waving my hand through the dense smoke.

"Only restaurant on the peninsula that has an all-smoking dining room." Lydia pointed toward a side door.

I started to ask her about the mural when the sound of shattering glass drew everyone's attention toward the bar.

"See what you made me do!" a man shouted. He looked as substantial as a scarecrow. He was middle-aged and wore muddy jeans and a faded-black tee shirt emblazoned with "Jack Daniel's" across his back. It was unclear whether he was talking to the bartender or the woman on his right.

The bartender tried to give him a rag for his hand, which was dripping blood, but he threw it on the floor. "He owes me. He owes me big time."

The bartender leaned close to the man and said something.

"I'm not drunk." He directed his remark toward the woman on his right, who stood up so quickly that her barstool fell over. She had long, straight brown hair that reached halfway down her back. Her thin nose was slightly askew to the right. I wondered how many times it had been broken, and by whom.

"Where d'you think you're going?" he called after her. The woman kept walking as if she hadn't heard him. "I said get back here, bitch." Before he could finish, she was out the door.

The bartender grabbed the man's arm to restrain him from following her. But the man jerked his arm away and slid sideways off the barstool.

"I don't have to take this shit." He looked around the room, swaying with the effort to stay upright. Everyone looked down at their drinks, trying not to make eye contact with the man. I wasn't about to take my eyes off him.

"Sure, look away. But you know that bastard cheated me. I dare one of you to say he didn't."

"Aw, Renn, sit down," a guy playing darts shouted across the bar. "You're ruining my dart game."

"You know where you can stick those darts, Charlie."

"Chris sakes, Renn, they haven't even buried the guy yet. Show some respect," answered Charlie.

"Respect, respect . . ." The drunk's face went dark-red with rage. "What respect did he give me? Dirty, cheating son of a bitch. I'll fight anyone who says he wasn't." He staggered forward, right toward our table, with his fists raised. "C'mon."

I didn't have time to even push back my chair before he was lurching over me. I smelled whiskey, cigarettes, and greasy food emanating from him.

"What's this?" he slurred. He unballed his fists long enough to point at me.

"This is Leigh," I said. I had had just enough wine at dinner to blurt out what I felt and still make sense. "And that," I pointed in the direction of the bar, "is a bar stool. Why don't you go sit on it." I didn't like drunken bullies and I didn't like feeling scared. My usual defense was an aggressive bluff. If this had been a classroom, there'd have been an eraser bouncing off his greasy head. To my disgust, he pulled out the chair next to me and sat down. Everyone went back to what they had been doing, and the low buzz of conversation once again filled the room.

"You know I'm right," he spat across the table at Lydia. He was missing about four of his upper teeth. I doubted if he even knew how he'd lost them.

"Are you talking about Carl Peck?" I asked.

"Who the hell else?" He wiped his bleeding hand across his shirt. "And what do you care?"

"Don't. Just curious. How did he cheat you?"

"Who's idea do you think it was? Huh? Mine! Who did the leg work? Not that bastard Peck. Then he cuts me out of the business. Go on and tell her." He glared at Lydia.

"Whatever you say, Renn." Lydia looked around the room as if for rescue.

He looked down at his bleeding hand, as if he'd just noticed it. "I gotta go. Regina. Gotta find Regina."

"Why don't you have a cup of coffee with us first," I suggested. I wanted to know more about Renn's connection with Peck.

"What? No, I told you." He pushed his chair back, turned and headed for the door.

"Isn't someone going to stop him?" I asked Lydia.

"It's already taken care of." She pointed to the bartender.

He was talking on the phone. "Tony's calling the cops. And Paulie followed Renn outside to stall him until the cops arrive. Impressed?" she asked, raising her glass of beer for a toast.

"Impressed," I answered, clinking my glass with hers. "So, what's the story between Peck and this Renn guy?"

Lydia rolled her eyes as if I was annoying her. "You know that wasn't very smart?"

When I didn't answer, Lydia continued. "Renn Woulff. Name sound familiar?" I shook my head no. "Formerly, of Woulff Orchards."

"Oh." I recalled that Woulff Orchards encompassed the largest producer of cherries on the peninsula.

"Renn sold the orchards to back Peck's restoration business. At the time, no one could figure out why. I don't know exactly what happened, but Renn claims Peck cheated him out of his share of the business. Some kind of legal loophole. Ever since, Renn's turned into a drunken bore. As opposed to being just a bore." Lydia broke off eye contact and was trolling the room like a sailor with one night's shore leave.

"Well, did he?" I asked, not willing to let the subject drop.

"Speak of the devil." Lydia grabbed my arm. "Look who's sitting over there against the wall." I peered through the smoke and gloom of the bar. Across the room with his back to me sat Jake Stevens. He was with Sarah Peck, who leaned toward him, touching his arm. Even from here, I could see the white roundness of her breasts pushing up against her low-cut blouse.

Lydia poured me a beer. "Surprised?" she asked with a mischievous grin.

"To tell you the truth, yes." What really surprised me was their body language. I couldn't see the expression on

Stevens's face, but he slipped his hand over Sarah's in what looked like a very proprietary gesture from my vantage point.

"They're an off again, on again item. It was rumored that Sarah was seeing Jake even before her divorce was final. Which, of course, made things around the newspaper somewhat tense."

"What are you talking about?"

"You don't know?" Lydia smiled, deeply punctuating her dimples. "Rob Martin is Sarah's ex."

My mouth must have hit the table. "Sarah and Rob were once married?"

"For about a minute. They both grew up here. But didn't really 'find' each other until they attended the University of Wisconsin. That's where Rob got his degree in journalism with a minor in environmental studies, while Sarah drifted from major to major. Anyway, Sarah finally found her way back to her first love, painting. That's her work on the wall." I stared in disbelief. I would never have pegged Sarah Peck as a frustrated painter.

"They both had all these plans to make it big. Him writing for the *Chicago Tribune*, her selling her work in the Chicago galleries. Neither dream panned out, and they both came home dragging their tails between their legs." There was an edge to Lydia's voice that confirmed my earlier assessment of her feelings for Martin.

Sarah had moved closer to Stevens and was whispering into his ear. At least it looked like whispering. From this distance, she could have been using her tongue as Q-tip for all I could tell.

"Within six months of being back, Sarah filed for divorce. The rest, as they say, is history. Sarah and Rob went their separate ways, though he remained close to the Pecks. They were the family he never had, I guess. Then about six months ago, he became obsessed with Sarah again. Really strange. It's a shame 'cause he's a real nice guy. Am I talking too much?"

I poured Lydia and myself each another beer.

"Whoa." Lydia held out her hand to stop me. "I'd like to at least see the tree before I smack into it." Finally she relented and let me pour, but only sipped at her beer. I gulped mine. I was starting to feel the accumulation of the evening's alcohol, though it didn't deter me from another generous gulp. I decided a little oblivion would feel good right now. "So, off or on at this point?"

"What, them? I'd say on. But we'd have to check under the table to be sure." Lydia laughed so loud, Sarah looked up. She saw us, said something to Stevens, and he turned around. I gave a cursory wave and instantly regretted it. Stevens ignored it and turned his attention back to Sarah.

"I just never would have figured those two together. I mean from what I've observed in my short time here, Sarah seems a bit obvious for Stevens's taste." Now I was talking too much.

"Not to be catty . . ." Lydia batted her eyes, "but since her divorce, Sarah's been known to take pity on a lot of guys. And Stevens, what can I tell you, he's a man."

I figured she was about to add, "and men are dogs," when the bar door opened and Rob Martin walked in. There was a tenseness in his body, like one sees in a well-tuned hunting dog. He scanned the room, found his prey and headed directly to Sarah's table. All eyes in the bar honed in on the three of them.

Stevens indicated with an arm gesture that Martin should join them. Martin remained standing. Instead, he reached for Sarah's arm. She pulled away from him. Stevens said something that I couldn't hear, but his body language was conciliatory. Martin ignored him and spoke directly to Sarah.

"I said no!" Sarah shouted above the bar chatter.

Suddenly the bar went quiet again. The only sound was Roy Orbison singing that he was all right for a while and could smile for a while. Slowly, Stevens scraped his chair back and stood up. I thought for a moment that he was going to say something macho like, "Let's take this outside," or drag Martin out of the bar by his collar. But he just threw money on the table and walked out. Martin stood silent for a moment. He didn't seem to know what to do. Finally, he picked up Sarah's sweater from the back of her chair and threw it over her shoulders. And as abruptly as Stevens had left, Martin followed. So much for machismo.

Sarah downed the rest of her drink, threw off her sweater, and strolled over to the bar as if nothing had happened. Someone made a place for her, and the chatter rose again.

"How about another pitcher?" I suggested.

"I've had enough." Lydia seemed to have sobered up. "Let's go."

Sunday, November 5, Present day

One in the morning, and I was wide-awake. Salinger was snoring at the foot of my bed. I envied her careless sleep. There would be no careless sleep for me tonight. I knew the drill. Once the middle of the night jolt struck, the only thing that worked short of drugs was to get up and try to figure out what had broken through my subconscious. When I had been in the throes of the cancer, it was no mystery what had broken through. Was I ever going to beat this thing? Could I bear the pain? How long did I have? Would I ever stop feeling singled out for damage?

I sat up and automatically pulled up my left nightgown strap. In the privacy of my bedroom, I refused to disguise my body. I could have worn pajamas or a flannel nightgown. But

I'd always loved the feel of silk next to my skin, especially the possibilities of a spaghetti-strapped gown, even if all those possibilities were now gone. Surely that wasn't what had shaken me awake. I was sure all of that had been worked out months ago in the cancer survivor group.

When Tom and I had resumed our sex life after my mastectomy, my attire had consisted of a cotton nightshirt that buttoned up the front. Not very conducive to erotic ecstasy. In his subtle way, Tom would buy me sexy underwear. "For when you are ready," he'd say, his eyes soft with understanding. The sexy underwear and his understanding look were all a part of his desire for normalcy, for things to be as they were before. I'd lost the energy to convince him that nothing would ever be as it was before. He had only to take one look at my six-inch scar to realize that, its message emblazoned in angry red.

I slipped on my robe and tiptoed into the living room. Salinger reluctantly followed. On the velvet chair was the book Lydia had given me as a welcoming gift. What had she said when she dropped me off earlier? "For the long winter days and nights." I read the title: *Healing through Wild Plants*.

She had driven away before I could properly thank her. Now I figured I'd read a few pages or at least look at the sketches. Then maybe whatever was on my subconscious mind would step forward, or I'd be tired enough to sleep.

I settled back into the chair, pulling the white crocheted afghan over my feet. Without a fire blazing, the room smelled musty and old. Salinger looked up at me, then paced the room a few times. Finally she decided everything was in order and went back to sleep beneath my chair.

I scanned the book's table of contents. It seemed to be a hodge-podge of Native American plant lore, pop psychology, and Door mythology. Must be a local author in town. How was I to take this gift, I mused? I hadn't told her about the mastectomy. Experience had taught me that cancer was a word better left unsaid. Its mere mention seemed to create a contagion. Besides, I had beaten the cancer. I'd been clean for a while. It was behind me now.

So what did Lydia think I had to heal from? As usual, I was being paranoid or worse, narcissistic. What had one of the women in the group said to me, "You think because you have cancer the whole world begins and ends with you." She had had a relapse. At the time, I had chalked her remark up to projection.

Out of curiosity, I paged through the section on white wild flowers. Maybe I could identify those rampant weedy things in the field behind my house. There was a photograph that looked exactly like those daisy-like white flowers with yellow centers. Asters, so that's what they were. There were so many of them that I'd written them off as some kind of weed. What else but weeds could be so prolific? Their fecundity was frightening. Their lack of restraint seemed beyond any necessity, as if something had gone out of control, this field so choked with flowers that it looked like an angry, white flurry.

From a distance, I couldn't distinguish one flower from another. Only when I ventured to the edge of the field, knelt down and looked closely could I see each flower's compact neatness. Each one seemed to be holding itself quiet under the immense pressure of sun and rain, as if this quiet composure could stop their compulsion to reproduce.

I pictured my American Beauty roses back home, their pink petals so frail and faint they almost looked like skin. Years of bone meal, insect repellent and careful pruning had produced niggardly flowers that some years didn't even open. I suppose it didn't help that they were sandwiched between two arbor vitaes and shoved against the stockade fence.

I turned back to the book. It claimed that the Zunis had special uses for this plant. One was a treatment for arrow or bullet wounds, enacted by members of the Priesthood of the Bow. Apparently a tea made from the entire plant would be applied to the wound to cleanse it. By applying this mixture and then pressure, the missile would be extracted and the wound healed. Pretty impressive: healed by flowers. If only it had been that easy and romantic to heal what had ailed me.

Automatically I lifted my left arm slowly and then brought it down even more slowly. This was one of the exercises I did regularly to keep from developing lymphedema, or fluid buildup, in my left arm. This was a constant threat since I was minus twenty lymph nodes. I swallowed hard against the memory of that first day after the breast had been removed along with the twenty nodes. Like a nightmare I couldn't shake, I kept waking up and seeing the drain attached to my left side, siphoning fluid from me like an insatiable monster. The drain had felt hard and round like a tennis ball under my arm. And the needle inserted in my side had been thick and metallic. It looked like something used on horses. No one had prepared me for the drain or the feeling that whatever it was taking away was already gone.

Later that evening, several friends from work had come by with flowers, yellow roses. In the dimly lit room, I had heard one of them gasp, and then a thud. Apparently she had seen the drain and the blood-tinged liquid accumulating in the bottle, and she had passed out. I never saw her again. After that, every time I smelled the cloying scent of roses, I felt sick.

I shook my head as if that could dispel the memory, and looked down at the book. "Mythic elements" was the only section on asters left to read. "Name derived from the Latin and Greek word meaning star. This star shaped flower was sacred to all the gods and goddesses on Mount Olympus. In ancient times, aster flowers were burned to keep away evil spirits. Associated with Venus, the goddess of love, asters were used in talismans of love." Considering these wild flowers were going wild behind my cottage, there was an irony here I didn't want to pursue.

Maybe Martin should consider wearing a sprig of asters to gain Sarah Peck's attention. Or better yet, he should just give up. Obsession was never seductive. Besides, based on what Lydia had told me, Sarah seemed to have other fields to plow. I still couldn't figure out the connection between Stevens and Sarah. He just didn't seem like the kind of guy who was led around by his privates. Needless to say, it was none of my business.

Too many asters, too many drinks tonight. Tomorrow I'd call Eva Peck and persuade her to tell me about her husband's autopsy report. Then I'd track down that children's ward nurse and find out who Joyce Oleander visited in the hospital the day she was discharged. I also wanted to talk to Renn Woulff when he was sober, if that was possible. I took a deep breath. I was doing it again, trying to order things, find answers to questions that didn't concern me. So much easier than fixing yourself.

I closed the book and put it on the floor. Come to think of it, a bouquet of asters would be more appropriate for Lydia.

January, 28 years earlier
It was too cold in the room. The holy water had dried on her pillowcase. And the nightmare was starting again.

It always started the same way, with someone calling her by name in a low voice, barely audible. Then the inevitable shift into dream. This time it had been triggered by a movie. In the movie, the vampire sucked blood from the neck of a young woman and

then she became a vampire. She had no choice. That was the way
it worked. You either died or became one of them.

In the dream, he was outside her bedroom window. She could
see his face, white and drawn and hungry. His eyes were red like
the eyes of animals at night. He smiled deliberately, and his fangs
appeared.

"Like nails," she thought.

She tried to get out of bed, but he was in the room. His face in
the dresser mirror, his body on the sheets, his breath already inside
her. So the scream caught in her throat like the things he was
saying.

"Pretty, you're so pretty and soft."

She pushed one hand against him, but it disappeared into the
folds of his body, which became first a cape, then wings beating,
beating into her flesh.

Like a dog barking, the whooping broke through the dream. It
wasn't until he slapped her face and threw the water at her that she
realized the whoops were coming from her.

After that she avoided mirrors at night.

11

Sunday, November 5, Present day

Eva Peck insisted on meeting at my cottage after her church service, something about it being "more private." She was probably afraid her daughter might show up again and whisk her out of the room before she could tell me whatever was on her mind. I brewed another pot of coffee, having consumed most of the first pot in an attempt to pry myself awake. I still felt fuzzy from last night's nocturnal musings. Somewhere around three, I had made another attempt at sleep and succeeded.

This gray, rainy morning wasn't helping my fatigue either. Masses of storm clouds layered the sky, and the wind rattled the windows to the staccato accompaniment of a steady rain. I had every light on in the living room, but it still seemed like the middle of the night.

Even on a sunny day, my cottage was a dusky place. I had removed the heavy, green brocade curtains in the living room in hopes that a few slivers of light might get through the wall of pine trees that surrounded the place like the briar wall in Sleeping Beauty. I figured the curtains were originally meant to provide protection from the elements, before central heating. Now they invited a damp mustiness that only sunlight could banish.

Although the textured-plaster walls were white, they did

nothing to lighten the tiny rooms, whose ceilings were too low for this century. I had taken down the widow's brooding oil paintings of fourteenth century German hamlets, and hung my scant collection of black and white photographs. Most of mine were desert shots, stark contrasts between sand and sky. They didn't lighten up the place, but at least it didn't look like the Brothers Grimm lived here. This was only temporarily "my" place, so I resisted the urge to paint the kitchen cabinets yellow or to buy the burgundy and emerald Persian rug I'd coveted at a resale shop in Sturgeon Bay. What was mine here included Salinger, my books, my photos, and my clothes—things that could be packed in a hurry and fit in my truck.

A loud rapping on the door interrupted my musings. I opened the door to Eva Peck's back. She turned quickly toward me.

"I wasn't sure you were home. I knocked several times," she said, waiting politely for me to invite her in.

"Sorry, I didn't hear you. Come in." I led her into the house and took her rain poncho. It was soaked, as if she'd walked the whole way.

"Is your dog friendly?" Salinger was giving Eva the once over and circling her feet.

"She's harmless," I said, waiting for Eva to sit down. She chose the sofa, the darkest spot in the dark living room.

"Oh, before I forget, this is for you." From her voluminous black patent-leather purse, she fished out a hand-painted tin. She handed it to me. "I baked them this morning. I hope you like chocolate-chip cookies."

"I like anything with chocolate in it. Thanks." I took the tin from her and put it on the side table. "Before we get started, would you like some coffee? I just made a fresh pot."

"No, no thank you. I had my one cup for the day. Too

much caffeine makes me nervous. Besides, it's not really good for you."

I would never have taken Eva Peck for a health nut. I flipped open my notebook and sat down in the velvet chair. Salinger nestled at my feet.

Mrs. Peck was perched on the edge of the sofa. As before, her hair had been strictly subdued into its round yellow mass, and she was wearing black. She wore a knee-length black skirt and a black turtleneck sweater. Despite her size, her clothes seemed too large and hung on her. She probably thought the largeness disguised her girth. She had on black crepe-soled shoes that were splattered with mud. I longed for the green rhinestone pin to break her stark widow's attire.

"Thanks for seeing me, Mrs. Peck. I know this must be a difficult time for you and your family." I was following the Jake Stevens technique, and I was beginning to sound like a funeral director.

"Well, as I was telling Rob . . . he's Sarah's ex-husband . . . we all handle grief in our own way. 'Judge not lest ye be judged.' "

"That's true." What can you say when someone starts quoting scripture? Amen to that? "What I wanted to discuss with you was your husband's autopsy."

She lowered her eyes and, for a moment, I thought she was going to cry. Instead she opened her purse and took out a sheet of paper, folded in half.

"Is that the report?" I asked, pointing to the folded paper.

"No. The Medical Examiner told me it'll take a few days to write it up. Then he sends a copy to Doctor Porter. Which doesn't seem right to me, since he's the one that made the mistake. I told Rob that. But Rob said the Medical Examiner has to send Doctor Porter a copy, because he treated Carl. But it doesn't seem right to me."

"I'm sure that's standard procedure," I reassured her. "Is he sending you a copy as well?"

"I think so." Her eyes darted around the room. "Oh, I don't know for sure. But I have this paper here. Would you look at it?"

"What is it?" I asked.

"I wrote down some things the Medical Examiner said. He came out and talked to Sarah and me after the autopsy. But he was talking so fast, I couldn't understand what he was saying. I asked him to write it down, but he wouldn't. That's when Sarah started yelling at me. Because I asked him to do that. She didn't even want the autopsy." Mrs. Peck started to cry.

"I'm sure Sarah is as upset about this as you are." Though for very different reasons, I thought, remembering Sarah's hostility toward her father.

Eva took out a tissue from her purse and dabbed at her face. "I don't know. I don't know. She won't even talk to me now. And Rob, he always takes Sarah's side. I can't talk to him about the autopsy. He was so set against it, I don't want to make him angry again." She unfolded the paper and smoothed the crease with the back of her hand.

"I thought maybe you could look at what he said and maybe explain it." She leaned forward and handed me the paper.

Why she wanted me to look at her notes was beyond me. Maybe some affirmation that she'd done the right thing. "Isn't there someone else who can help you with this—another doctor, a lawyer?" I asked, looking over the paper. It was a heavy bond paper with the Peck Restoration letterhead. A few almost indecipherable sentences were scrawled across the middle.

I read the words "Cirrhosis of the liver." Under that, several additional sentences had been written, but the only words I could read were "fat in liver" and "fibrousness."

I looked up. "I can't make much out of this, Mrs. Peck. Did the M.E. say what your husband died from?"

"All the Medical Examiner would say was that he didn't think Carl died of a heart attack. He said that he needed to send some blood and tissue slides to the crime laboratory in Indianapolis, something about it being quicker. He said that he didn't want to make any guesses until he got a pathologist's report. And . . ." she hesitated, "the results of the blood toxic . . . toxicolo . . . toxicology test."

Now that she said toxicology, I deciphered the words "Toxicology—blood, organs." What I knew about medicine related to cancer. However, you didn't have to be a rocket scientist to know that a blood toxicology test indicated suspicion of some kind of toxic substance such as drugs. I wondered if Eva Peck knew that.

"I can't believe it. They think Carl was taking drugs. That he was a drug addict." She had wrapped her purse strap around her thumb so tightly it was stark white.

"Not necessarily, Mrs. Peck. They're just being thorough."

"When I asked for the autopsy, I had no idea." She shook her head. "It just made me suspicious, you know, how fast he went."

"When do you expect the results from Indianapolis?"

"The Medical Examiner said maybe Monday, sometime Monday."

"I'm sure everything will turn out all right."

"You think so? I guess whatever's meant to be is meant to be. It's in the Lord's hands now. What doesn't kill you makes you stronger."

She was a muddle of philosophical adages and religious

quotations. For any problem, apply one, or several. I envied the comfort that they brought her. Especially since I wasn't finished asking about her deceased husband. "Tell me, Mrs. Peck, what do you think caused your husband's death?"

"If it wasn't a heart attack, then it must have been cirrhosis of the liver." She caught my surprised expression. "I know what I said to you. But I didn't want you printing anything about the drinking. We live in a small community. People read things in the paper, and they never let you forget it. Carl drank too much, but not everyone knew. I have our name to protect." She lifted herself off the sagging sofa with the grace of a much slighter woman. In her youth, she was probably as slim as her daughter, Sarah. She moved like a woman who still embodied that lithe, younger self.

After she left, I opened the tin of cookies and sampled one. I know a store-bought cookie when I taste one, and these weren't remotely fresh. Mrs. Peck had all the marks of a woman who lived in a world of her own making.

Hoping to avoid Rob Martin, I came to the newspaper office on Sunday to finish Joyce Oleander's obituary. I'd already stopped by the hospital looking for Lorraine Birch, who was on vacation and wouldn't be back for a week.

"What're you doing here?" Jake Stevens had sneaked up on me again.

"How do you do that?" I asked.

"What?"

"Appear out of nowhere?"

"Practice."

I punched in the last line of text and pressed SAVE on the computer, trying to ignore his looming presence over my shoulder.

"You did hear the part about no overtime?" he asked the back of my neck.

"Just my agreed-upon pay at the end of the month would be fine, boss." I didn't want to discuss seeing him with Sarah Peck last night. "And I might ask you the same thing."

"Just doing some writing of my own." Stevens leaned against the edge of my desk, his long legs crossed at the ankles. Marge had told me that he was a long-distance runner—ranked second in the Midwest in his age category, which explained his lanky yet muscular frame. As usual, his long hair was tied back in a low ponytail, and he was wearing a pair of rather tight jeans with tears in both knees. Today he had on a faded-blue work shirt. I wondered if he even owned a suit.

I tilted my head in disbelief. "All this natural beauty and you come here to write. I thought you poetic types got off on nature."

He crossed his arms over his chest. "Was that the Oleander obit you just punched in?"

"Yup, all done." I wondered what he really was doing here on a Sunday. He never passed up an opportunity to bore me with talk of poetics. Which reminded me . . . "Know anything about Sylvia Plath and her poem, 'Lady Lazarus'?"

He uncrossed his arms and stared at me. "So I finally get you to read some poetry, and you go for Plath? Didn't figure you as the victim type."

"What can I say, she uses images I understand. My first requirement for a poet." I had reread the poem late last night and was pretty sure I knew what it was about. But I wanted to hear a supposed expert's interpretation. "So enlighten me."

"Didn't you read this as an undergrad?" He looked at me skeptically.

"Just wanted your take on it."

"Okay. She's a confessional poet. That means she likes to

write about herself. However, lately the term's been used to refer to autobiographical or personal poetry in general."

"Whoa." I held up my hand. "Too much information, Teach. Give me the Cliff Notes version."

"You're such a difficult student." He patted me quickly on the head, like patting a dog.

I held very still, as if he was performing a delicate procedure.

"Okay, for the underachievers: the poem's about Plath's three suicide attempts, and how she keeps coming back from the dead. You know, like a resurrection, like Lazarus rising from the dead." He moved his one hand upward. "There are lots of holocaust images—Nazi lampshade, gas chamber, that kind of stuff."

"So she keeps offing herself because she feels like such a victim?" So far, he'd confirmed what I figured out last night. And considering Joyce's life, it wasn't hard to see why she identified so strongly with the role of hapless victim.

"Right. And, big surprise, men, or as you feminists like to say, 'the patriarchy,' are the bad guys in her poems."

"If the boot fits," I said, smiling. "What about the ending where she talks about rising from the ashes and eating men like air. What's that about?"

"What'd you think?"

He was taking this teacher thing a bit far, but I played along. "Since my grade depends on it, I'd say in some weird way she gets power from each death and resurrection. And with that power, she can destroy these men." I wondered if somehow Joyce saw her suicide in the same way? As an act of destructive power aimed against males.

"Not bad for a novice." He shifted his weight and moved closer. "So what'd you find out about Joyce Oleander that's got you reading suicidal poems?"

I moved the computer mouse back and forth on the pad, avoiding his intense scrutiny. "Her death was a suicide. Looks like she overdosed on a drug called Vicodin." He wasn't the only one with secrets to keep.

"You didn't put that in the obit?"

"Duh," I said, in my best valley girl voice.

He grinned at me with that sardonic smile. "You know, it's hard to imagine you as a teacher, Girard."

"Speaking of strange things," I said, inching my chair back a little, "I interviewed Mrs. Peck today." I repeated what Eva Peck had told me.

"A toxicology test, huh? Wonder what the M.E. found? Maybe old Eva was right to be suspicious."

"Looks that way. Except she thought he had a heart attack. Now she's saying cirrhosis. We're talking something completely different if the Path report comes back positive for drugs."

"Hard to believe, Carl Peck on drugs, other than alcohol, I mean. That leaves a host of other toxins and poisons. Even harder to believe." He stood up. "If it comes up poison, the pathologist has to notify the sheriff's office. Call the sheriff's office Monday. See what they know. I want you to talk to Chet Jorgensen. Get the details from him. He's a county deputy, and he owes me a favor. Depending on the results, we might want to do a follow-up story." All his playfulness had disappeared, and Jake seemed downright dour.

So Jorgensen was indebted to Stevens for something. Well, that explained his letting me off so easy Friday when I was on the prowl in Joyce Oleander's townhouse.

"And just so you know, Martin sometimes works on Sundays too."

I was about to respond when the phone rang. As I reached

for it, Stevens put his hand over mine. "I'll get it. You go on home."

I slipped my hand away and stood up. It wasn't until I was out of the room that he answered the phone. As I reached the back door, I heard him say, "Yeah, I accept."

12

Monday, November 6, Present day

The rain had blown out to the east overnight, dropping temperatures into the forties and leaving behind a bitter sun. For the third night, I hadn't slept well. So I didn't hear the alarm and was late for Joyce Oleander's memorial service. I had decided to attend, but not because Ida Reeves had insisted. I couldn't free myself of thoughts about Joyce's suicide. It lingered like a heavy taste of garlic on the tongue. Freely chosen or not, the abbreviated life never made sense to me. Maybe because I'd struggled so hard to rid myself of the taint of death. It was a waste no matter how you looked at it. I didn't see what power Joyce could possibly have gained by killing herself. And I also wanted to give Joe Stillwater a reason for the loss of his friend.

I was too late for the funeral mass but not for the burial. As I slogged through the muddy graveyard, past the wet, grassy mounds and rain-stained headstones, I was thinking about the wisdom of wearing my old hiking boots and not about the sparse gathering I was about to join standing in the distance: Ida Reeves, Joe Stillwater, the priest, and Sarah Peck. What was Sarah Peck doing here?

As I neared the graveyard service, Sarah Peck turned her head and glared at me, then looked away. I quietly slipped next to Joe Stillwater, who nodded and made a place for me.

If Ida Reeves noticed my presence, she didn't acknowledge it.

The priest praying over the open grave had to be about six-foot-eight. His liturgical collar was frayed and there was a brown mole the size of a dime over his left eye. After studying the priest, I fixed my attention next on Sarah Peck; she was wearing a black leather jacket with five metal studs on each lapel, black leather mini skirt, also studded, and black tights. There were red streaks running through her black hair that could only have come from a bottle of Mercurochrome. Near her, Ida Reeves wore her usual predictable, nondescript uniform: navy wool coat, sensible shoes, and a matching navy hat. No red lipstick today.

I couldn't see Joe Stillwater without turning my head, so my eyes went back to the priest—anything to keep my mind from imagining Joyce Oleander inside that gray, shiny casket with the angels carved into each corner, her body already beginning its slow dissolution of flesh from bone. The priest ended the formal prayer with the sign of the cross, and cleared his throat. "For those left behind, death is never a happy occasion, especially in circumstances such as these. But none of us can know the mind or soul of another, so we must show compassion and pray for our sister in Christ."

Apparently Fr. Lewis's words were having little impact on Ida Reeves, whose face was pinched with disapproval.

He cleared his throat again. "Would anyone here like to say a few words about Joyce?"

"I would," volunteered Joe Stillwater. He shifted his stance. "Joyce was one of the kindest people I ever knew. She loved children and . . ." His voice broke. "I'm going to miss her." He looked at the priest. "That's all, Father."

"Anyone else?" the priest asked.

"Father Lewis," Ida Reeves whispered. She bowed her

head. "Joyce would have been pleased to be buried here, so near her parents."

For the first time, I noticed that the double headstone adjacent to Joyce's grave bore the names of Frank and Helen Oleander.

The priest waited for Ida to continue. When she didn't, he looked expectantly at Sarah and me. Sarah Peck dug the toe of her stiletto-heeled boot into the mud, and shoved her hands into the pockets of her leather jacket.

"Then I commend the soul of Joyce Oleander to God and His mercy." With those words, the priest turned and walked away from the grave.

Joe shook my hand and said something about "Not able to talk right now," and being late for work. When I turned to look for Ida, she was staring at the open grave with a look of anger.

"Ms. Reeves," I said moving closer to her. "I know how hard this must be for you, but if you have a moment I need to clarify something you told me."

She looked up at me with disdain. "What do you want?"

"Are you absolutely sure Joyce was face up when you found her? It would be understandable if you turned her over. You were probably in shock. Maybe you don't remember doing it." I was giving her the benefit of the doubt.

"I told you what happened. Now if you don't mind . . ." With that she turned and walked away.

For an awkward moment, Sarah Peck and I stared at each other. I decided to break the ice. "Were you and Joyce friends?"

"What the hell are you doing here?" She kept her voice down but the tone was unmistakably hostile.

I started to say that I was writing Joyce Oleander's obituary, but it was written, and Sarah's hostility was so raw that it demanded honesty. "The same as you," I answered.

"You didn't even know her." Her voice was as tight as her stare.

Sunlight moved across the casket, blinding me for a second. "I knew about her," I said lamely.

"Yeah, like what?" She smirked and took a cigarette and lighter from her pocket.

"Okay, I didn't know her." I was on the defensive, and I didn't like it. "Why don't you tell me about her?"

She lit her cigarette and inhaled deeply. "Go away." She blew smoke in my direction.

"I don't understand your hostility toward me."

"Well, understand it." Sunlight washed over her face and seemed to erase her features. "I don't like you. I don't like the way you look or talk or even dress. You make my skin crawl. Now do you get it?"

"I don't know what your problem is, Sarah, but it isn't me."

"You're probably right, but I still don't like you," she said, then turned and walked toward the casket.

She had dismissed me. My face was throbbing with anger. "I know you and Joyce went to high school together." I threw the statement at her back. A wild guess, why didn't I just let it go for now?

She took another drag on her cigarette. I watched the smoke slowly ascend. Then I left.

As I neared the church, I looked back. Sarah Peck was bending toward the casket. There was a red flower in her hand.

13

Deputy Chet Jorgensen grudgingly agreed to meet me Tuesday at 6:30 a.m. near the entrance to Newport State Park. He had some work to do up there that couldn't wait. It was either 6:30 a.m. Tuesday, or I could wait until Thursday when he'd be back at the station. He confirmed over the phone that the toxicology results from Carl Peck's blood and tissue samples had come in Monday afternoon. But he couldn't or wouldn't give me the results over the phone. As a favor to Stevens, he said he'd discuss them with me, but only in person. I didn't want to wait most of the week, so I agreed to his terms and this sunrise meeting. I did appreciate that he never once mentioned our encounter at Joyce Oleander's condo.

I arrived, sleepy and grouchy, at the park entrance. A faint horizon of light pushed at the somber sky. My watch read 6:16, and Deputy Jorgensen was already there. In daylight, he looked even blonder and larger. As I pulled up beside his dark green pickup, Jorgensen was testing the string of a wooden bow. Near his feet lay a container full of arrows.

I slammed the door of my truck, and walked over to him. "That time of year already?" I pointed to the arrows.

He gave me a curt nod and drew back again on the bow string. His camouflage jacket sleeve pulled up, revealing a

113

black leather band that cinched his wrist and looked like some kind of S&M device. I wondered if the band had a practical application singular to bow and arrow hunting, or was merely a male affectation.

"Hunting season, right?" Looking at his thick neck and massive shoulders, and the canny way he handled the bow, I figured he probably always bagged his target.

"Nope, not till November eighteen."

"Oh, just getting in a little pre-season practice?" Hunting was one of my red flags. My best friend's father—a burly, unpleasant man who yelled a lot—had been an avid hunter. His basement rec room looked like a taxidermist's. As a kid I'd been frightened to even go down there. I had a special aversion to the mounted buck head whose eyes had that dead stare and whose tongue was a little too red. I just didn't understand how killing animals could make anybody feel good.

He gave me a cold stare, and for a minute, I thought he was going to cuff me for running off at the mouth. He smiled instead.

"See that, there?" He pointed down the road to a field of neatly planted trees. "Deer are eatin' them new trees. The owner wants me to rid him of his problem."

"Why not use a rifle like everyone else?" I was tempted to amend that sentence with "Like every other blood thirsty idiot hunter," but Jorgensen, the blonde deer slayer, was fairly intimidating up close and personal.

"No sport there." He looked me up and down, as if he was sizing me up for his trophy wall. "Ever shoot a bow and arrow?"

"Never shot anything. And hope I never have to." It was truly beyond me how anyone could hunt for sport or otherwise.

"Ever hear of Darwin?"

"Of course: survival of the fittest, the strongest wins."

"That's why ya gotta hunt. Especially in a situation where ya got too many deer, plain and simple, and no predators. No wolves, no mountain lions. Around here, these deer keep reproducin' like rabbits, eatin' up cherry orchards, flowers, people's gardens, tulips, you name it. Ever see what they do to cars and people?" He didn't wait for me to answer. "Only last week, we had another car crash because of some deer. Damn thing was standin' by the roadside one minute, and in front of this gal's car the next. It was pitch black out, and she didn't see it till it was too late. She tried to avoid the damn thing, and BAM! Smacked right into a tree. Seems the deer just jumped out in front of her. Did ya know they can jump a ten-foot fence? Lucky for her only the car was wrecked."

He ignored my glazed look of flora and fauna boredom. "Ever see a deer starve to death in winter, then?"

"Can't say that I have," I answered, shivering into my down parka. It had started to snow, and just the sight of the wispy flakes swirling through the air was making me cold.

"Well, a clean kill beats slow death by starving, I tell ya that."

Okay, he had my interest, but I wasn't buying his humane white hunter routine. I'd read too many Hemingway novels. Blood lust was always lurking around the page. "And I suppose you eat everything you kill?" I challenged.

"What I don't eat, which ain't much, I give away to friends."

I looked up into Deputy Jorgensen's face for a trace of a smile. There was none. "You're not kidding," I said.

"Now why would I do that?" he asked, grinning broadly.

"Why indeed." It was time to swing the conversation to Carl Peck and his toxicology results. "You said on the phone that the toxicology results came in from Indianapolis."

"Yup, 'round four yesterday. We got 'em first. I told Chief Burnson, run 'em again, make sure. He won't then. Thinks if it comes from Indianapolis, gotta be A-Okay."

"I take it the results were a surprise," I prompted.

"Whadya mean?"

"Well, if the pathologist called the sheriff's office, then Peck didn't die of liver cirrhosis or a heart attack. What was it—some drug?"

He fixed me again with that Norwegian stare. "Nope. There ya go again, jumpin' to conclusions. Ya had to know Carl. Nice old guy. Liked to talk, especially after he'd had a few. Re-did my kitchen, and only charged me for materials."

A flock of Canada geese flew overhead in a honking procession. We both watched in silence. "I hear down where you're from, they don't migrate no more."

"What?"

"The geese. Spend the whole year there cause of them artificial ponds. And so many people feeding 'em. Stupid thing to do."

I remembered an unpleasant al fresco dining experience one summer evening beside an artificial pond in Lake Forest. The geese had boldly approached diners and hissed at them for scraps. "Yeah, I hate those nasty creatures."

He laughed. "Me, too." He paused, lifted the brim of his camouflage cap and scratched his head. "Messy business."

"A real nuisance."

"Nuisance? Nauseating's more like it." He chuckled to himself.

"I take it we're not talking about geese." He gave me yet another stare as if I was being obtuse.

"Only if ya'd shared Peck's last meal, then I'd say your goose was cooked." He laughed. Andy of Mayberry had nothing on Chet Jorgensen.

"Are you saying that Peck died from something he ate?"

He drew one of the arrows out of the container. "According to that pathologist, Peck died from toxic poisoning."

"Did the report name the substance that killed him?"

"Now, that's the interestin' part. He died from mushroom poisoning."

"Mushroom poisoning? Why is that interesting?"

"Didn't ya know? Carl was a mushroom picker." Jorgensen aimed the arrow at a tree.

"I always told 'em, one of these days you're gonna slip up and eat the wrong damn mushroom.' 'Won't happen,' he'd say. 'I know what I'm doin.' " He pulled back on the arrow and let it go. It hit the tree dead center. "Stubborn old bastard. Still, he's been a mushroom picker as long as I can remember. Weird way to spend your time. He even got his son-in-law, well, ex-son-in-law hooked on 'em."

My brain was trying to follow the metaphoric arrow of information that Chet had just let loose, including mention of the son-in-law, who would be my fellow reporter, Rob Martin. "So what kind of lethal mushroom did Carl Peck eat?" I asked.

"The kind that kills ya." Chet thought he was pretty funny. I smiled a weak smile.

"No, really, do you know what kind of mushroom, exactly? For the paper." I indicated my pen.

"Don't know. You'd have to ask the Chief." I wrote down "Call Chief Burnson re: deadly mushroom."

"Are the police going to pursue a criminal investigation?"

Again the stare as if I had two heads. "Ain't no crime to investigate. Who'd want to knock off old Carl?"

Renn Woulff instantly came to mind. "How about Renn Woulff? He claims Peck cheated him."

"Lady, you're way off. Woulff's a dirt bag loser who

couldn't tie his shoes if it weren't for his girl friend, Regina. Ya think he could figure out a poison mushroom and get Peck to eat it? No way, no how. Peck screwed up, plain and simple." He made a motion with his hand, as if he were drinking from a bottle. "Carl had a drinkin' problem, that's for sure. Probably got confused. It's too bad then, but there ain't no crime. I guess he wasn't as smart as he thought he was."

"But aren't the police curious as to why no one else ate the mushrooms? At least they could look into that aspect."

"No need. Everybody knows Carl was the only one who ate them mushrooms he picked. Eva can't stand 'em. Never could. What does she call 'em? 'Slime meat or slime salad,' something like that. And Sarah wasn't exactly on good terms with Carl. So I don't expect she shared any meals with him."

"You seem to know a lot about the Pecks."

He smiled sheepishly. "I've known Sarah since high school. We run into each other, once in awhile."

I could swear he was blushing under his ruddy complexion. "I still think the police should question Eva Peck about the mushrooms." This laissez-faire attitude of the police troubled me.

"Look lady, this ain't Chicago where murders are as common as ticks on a deer. We don't have much crime in Door County. Drunk drivers mostly, some domestic abuse. And if some dirtbag commits a crime and tries to skedaddle, the sheriff radios the drawbridge operators, who are friends of his. And they yank up those bay bridges there. It's like living on a friggin' island." He winked at me.

"What about Joyce Oleander and the person who turned her over?"

"Told ya, that was Ida Reeves. Anyway, it weren't no crime. You find somethin' out?"

"No, did you?"

He shook his head no. "If you're so worried about murderers, maybe you should learn to defend yourself. Here," he pushed his bow toward me. "Why don't ya try it?"

Now I know when someone's having a joke at my expense. But what Deputy Jorgensen didn't know was that when the other girls in my high school gym class opted for softball, I opted for archery. By senior year, I had a letter in the sport. I slipped my pen and notebook into my pocket. "Well, I don't know. It looks awfully heavy." I reached for the bow with both hands.

"It ain't heavy. It's one of them newer bows, made of laminated wood and fiberglass, 'sposed to be lighter and faster. In fact, I've known twelve-year-olds who could shoot it. You're as strong as a twelve-year-old, aren't ya?"

"Well, if you think I can . . ." I batted my eyes innocently up at him. I probably shouldn't use my left arm to hold a bow, no matter how light it was. My doctor had warned me that any overexertion of the left arm could cause the lymphs to swell with lymphatic fluid that would never disperse. The damage would be permanent. He'd told me more than once the story of the patient who had used a Nordic track and permanently damaged her arm. She had ended up with lymphedema. But I also knew that the right arm would do most of the work. Besides, I couldn't resist playing a return joke of my own on Deputy Jorgensen.

"C'mon, try it, then." He walked behind me with the bow and arrow and placed my hands in the proper position. "Now take aim. Pull the string back real tight and just shoot."

"Like this?" I pulled back on the string with my right arm and let the arrow fly. It went left of his arrow, which was centered in the tree. I had been aiming right of it.

"That's damn good," he said.

He seemed to think I had hit my target. I wasn't going to

convince him otherwise. "Just a lucky shot," I grinned. "Have to keep up with those twelve-year-olds."

He cocked his head to one side. "Ya done this before?"

"A long time ago, in another life," I confessed.

He took the bow back. "Ya still got a good eye. Hunting season begins the eighteenth. If you're interested, I've got a spare bow and some arrows."

Before I could say no, he reached into the cab of his truck and brought out another bow and an assortment of arrows.

"Though I should tell ya, shooting is the least part of it."

"What is the most part?" I asked. "Trying not to get shot by your fellow hunters?"

"That only happens to yahoos," he smirked. "Ya know, city people like yourself."

"Okay," I conceded, "I had that coming."

"The most part is knowing your prey, by studying their habits. See, when ya bow and arrow hunt, you're real close to 'em when ya make the kill, so ya gotta know about 'em."

"So, what's there to know about deer? Aren't they relatively docile?"

"What do ya mean? They're moving."

"You know, I mean tame." I wasn't sure anymore which of us was putting the other on most.

"Yeah, okay then. But they're quick too. With deer, ya gotta stand hunt. Look at the land, how it lays, decide what the deer's using the trail for. Once ya know that, ya know when to wait for the deer. See, if the trail's being used for food, then I know to wait for the deer between midday and evening."

"And when the unsuspecting deer arrives, you shoot it clean through the heart. No pun intended," I said.

His forehead wrinkled in confusion. "Pun?"

"You know heart, h-e-a-r-t. Hart, h-a-r-t. Male deer."

"Don't know about that. But shooting through the heart is a macho kill. I don't aim for the heart. I aim for the lungs."

"Why's that?"

"A deer shot through the heart can run two hundred yards before it dies. But if it's shot through the lungs, it can only go about forty-five yards before them lungs collapse and it suffocates. It's better for the deer."

"Either way, it still sounds like a mighty unpleasant way to die." All this talk about clean ways to kill was starting to make me nauseous.

"Most time, deer don't even know it's hit. Ain't no pain, only fear."

"You can't know that," I said. I had often wanted to suggest to my entourage of well-meaning cancer doctors that they try the treatments they were giving me and see how "uncomfortable" it really was.

"I guess you've just gotta see it, to know. Here, give it a try sometime." He handed me the bow and arrows. "Just bring 'em by the station when you're done with 'em."

Reluctantly, I took the bow and arrows. After my truck was out of view, I threw them on the floor behind my seat.

14

"So what's nagging at you?" Lydia locked the front door of the shop and switched off the lights. For a moment, we stood in darkness. I deeply inhaled the potpourri of scents: jasmine, lavender, patchouli and something spicy—maybe cinnamon. Then she lit a candle.

"I'm getting in the mood," she said. As she walked toward the rear of the shop in the direction of the back door, her crimson silk caftan flowed around her like water. I watched her liquid shadow waver across the jewelry display cabinet, a wall of books, then disappear into an archway and emerge again on the back door.

She had called me around noon and asked if I wanted to sit in on her women's group. My spine had instantly stiffened at the idea. I'd had enough of groups and therapy sessions. But Lydia explained that her group was more like a New Age bull session. "We usually start with some type of spiritual ritual, depending on the theme for that week, and then just share what's going on in our lives," she explained. "One of the women recently dropped out. So we could really use another person."

It sounded too intimate for me. "I don't know."

"C'mon. Free drinks," she paused. "And Sarah Peck's a member."

Her father's funeral had been that morning—the day after

Joyce Oleander's. I expressed my doubts about that affecting whether Sarah would show up or not.

"Oh, she'll show up. Our theme tonight is healing."

I mused a moment on Lydia's confidence that Sarah Peck would run anywhere to open up to healing, but decided not to mention it. "Lydia, did you happen to know Joyce Oleander?" The connection between Sarah Peck and Joyce Oleander continued gnawing at me.

"I saw her occasionally around the hospital. What does this have to do with anything?"

"Sarah Peck was at her funeral."

"Really? Wear anything interesting?"

"Her usual attire: back leather and more black leather. Though the mercurochrome treatment to her hair was a nice touch."

Lydia laughed. "You've got to give the girl credit. She does make a statement. So yes or no? Are you coming tonight?"

Of course, I had said yes. Lydia and her wavering candlelight returned from the back of the shop and headed upstairs to her living quarters.

"What's nagging at me are the circumstances of Peck's death. Aren't poisonings from mushrooms pretty rare? And supposedly, Peck was something of an expert. How could he have made such a mistake?" Even after promising not to use the information until after the investigation was concluded, Chief Burnson would only confirm what Jorgensen had already told me: Carl had died from mushroom poisoning. I'd spent the afternoon researching poisonous mushrooms. I'd told Stevens that I needed background for the follow-up story on Peck. He had raised a skeptical eyebrow but didn't stop me.

"All it takes is one," Lydia remarked. "You know, kinda like getting a little pregnant."

"Maybe. But regardless of the circumstances, my guess is that he died from eating one of the amanitas. They cause ninety percent of the deaths from mushroom poisoning. What were his symptoms?"

"You don't really want know," Lydia said, shaking her head. "As I remember, just being in a hospital turns you green."

We reached the top of the stairs, which opened up into a large room. In the candlelight, I could see mammoth pillows scattered around the carpet. All the furniture was pushed against the wall.

"Like it?" Lydia asked. "It makes me feel closer to the earth, more grounded."

The wind rattled the outside shutters. "Did you arrange for this spooky weather?" I asked. "And I do want to know Peck's symptoms. I can handle it."

Lydia laughed. "Okay, I see you're not going to let this go. So here's the deal. You tell me what you know about mushroom poisoning, and I'll tell you if it sounds like Peck's symptoms. But let me get the wine first. I have a feeling you're going to need it."

Lydia left the candle on a low table and lit about a dozen more before she went into the kitchen for the wine. She returned with two glasses and an open bottle of chardonnay. She poured each of us a full glass and handed me one before carefully positioning herself on one of the pillows. I sat down across from her and took a deep sip of wine.

"So Lois Lane, let's hear what you found out?"

"Well," I began, putting my wine glass on the floor. "According to the various books I read, in the case of an amanitas poisoning there are four stages. What makes this poisoning so deadly is that for the first six to twenty-four hours after ingestion, there are no symptoms. And that's when the poison is working on the liver and kidneys. Though it's not until the second stage that the first symptoms appear. The person starts vomiting, has diarrhea, and severe stomach pains. If they don't make the connection between eating the mushroom and the symptoms, a lot of times they think they have the flu or food poisoning. This lasts for about a day. Then there's a latency period that also lasts for about a day. It's sort of like the lull before the storm. If a person's thinks it's the flu or some other stomach problem, they assume they're better. But this is when the second and lethal effect of the poisoning occurs, when the liver and kidneys deteriorate. Then the person dies." I took a deep breath. "And there's no known antidote. So does this fit what you know about Peck's medical condition prior to his death?"

Lydia sipped her wine for a moment, and I thought she wasn't going to answer. "I'm going to spare you the gory details, because I don't want to have to revive you again. And if you tell anyone I told you this, I'll call you a liar. Okay?"

I nodded yes.

"Peck showed up at the hospital the morning before he died with violent vomiting. Plus bloody diarrhea and mega abdominal cramps. And he was thirsty as hell. Kept screaming for water."

I picked up my glass and took another gulp of wine.

"You want me to go on?"

I nodded yes.

"He was a pretty nasty shade of yellow, looked like mustard. Sure sign his liver was shutting down." Lydia had a grin on her face and she looked flushed. She was obviously enjoying painting the agonies of Peck's death. "Then there were the urinary problems. He couldn't, literally. Let's see, what else? Did I say he was blown up like a balloon? When you pressed on his skin, you could feel the fluid. That evening, he went into convulsions. Almost bit his tongue off. We had to keep a rubber clamp in his mouth for a while and tie him to the bed. Both his liver and kidneys failed completely. Then his heart arrested. And as they say, 'that's all she wrote.' So what do you think?"

"Amanita."

"No." She raised her glass. "How's the wine?"

"It's good. Nice and dry." I took another sip and went over the symptoms in my head. "Only two mushrooms fit the whole list of symptoms related to fatal poisoning, along with the relevant geography and season. I'll bet a paycheck Carl Peck ate either an amanita verna or an amanita virosa."

"Amanita what-as?"

"Both mushrooms are deadly. I think verna is commonly known as Fool's Mushroom, and virosa is called 'the Destroying Angel.' They look pretty harmless, though most deaths are caused by amanitas. And they grow in Door County."

"What an apropos name, Destroying Angel, especially when you consider what that mushroom did to him."

"I wonder why he didn't come to the hospital as soon as he had the first symptoms?"

"Maybe he did," Lydia answered. "The mushroom toxins must have hit his already damaged liver like a sledgehammer. His system probably started shutting down right away." She leaned forward and poured me another glass of wine. "How much do you know about Carl Peck?" Lydia asked.

"Just that he had a history of alcohol abuse. Was a skilled artisan, liked to talk. May have cheated Renn Woulff out of their shared business." I cradled my glass and tried to settle onto a pillow on the floor. "Could be too friendly in bars, as you yourself told me."

"Besides his bar habits, let me tell you some other things

about Carl Peck. I'm a fairly unbiased observer, since he never wowed me with any of his restoration wizardry or boozy charm."

I wasn't convinced that Lydia was an unbiased observer, considering how uncomfortable she was the last time we discussed Peck, and how much relish she had just taken in describing his death. Still, I was glad she now wanted to give me the low down.

"Appearance first: he was a jolly looking guy—sort of like Santa Claus, with the flushed face and round belly that shook when he laughed. You get the picture. But when he was younger, supposedly he was strikingly handsome and quite the Don Juan. Of course, I only have the word of one of the nurses who knew Peck way back when. But even though the alcoholism had about destroyed his looks, he remained vain about his appearance. He had a full head of silvery-gray hair that he wore straight back, sort of Rudolf Valentino style. Never wore a hat. I think he wanted to accentuate his strong nose and what was left of his fine features. Pretty obvious where Sarah got her looks.

"Anyway, his clothes were always neatly pressed and clean. He usually wore a matching gray work shirt with gray pants. Even though he didn't do many of the hands-on tasks anymore, I think he was cultivating this blue-collar image. He was always friendly, asked how you were doing. All pretty innocuous, right?"

"Right. So what are you leading up to?" I leaned back against another of the pillows.

"Well, one Saturday I was at the McDonald's in Sturgeon Bay. Occasionally, I've got to have a fast food fix. It was around lunchtime and crowded. Eva Peck was sitting in a booth in the smoking section, since Carl smoked a pipe. Anyway, I was in the non-smoking section, and I don't think she saw me. Whatever they ordered must have been a special order, because Carl stood beside the counter quite awhile waiting for his food. When he finally got it, he brought it to the table and threw one of the sandwiches at Eva. And I mean threw. The sandwich bounced off her chest and fell on the floor." Lydia's hand went over her heart in a dramatic gesture. "I couldn't hear what he said, but it was obvious that he was steamed."

"What did Eva do? Did she throw something back at him?" That would have been my first reaction.

"That's the other interesting part. She left the sandwich on the floor where it had landed, got up from the table and walked quietly out of the restaurant. Carl took his time eating the rest of his food. When he finally left, the one sandwich was still there on the floor." Lydia sighed deeply. She was the storyteller caught up in her own story.

I took what she said with a grain of salt, not certain how much had been embellished by Lydia's need to dramatize. "So, they had a fight. It's not uncommon for couples to have fights."

"Right. But you had to have seen the look Eva gave him when she left."

"What kind of a look?"

"Deadly. Ice cold."

"Are you saying that Eva Peck had something to do with her husband's death?"

"Her? No, of course not. The point of my story was to show you how out of control Carl Peck was because of his drinking. I could easily see him mistaking a poisonous mushroom for a harmless one."

"Because a thrown sandwich is hardly a reason to kill one's husband." I thought for a moment. "Though I suppose people have killed for less."

"Killed whose husband?" Sarah Peck was suddenly standing in the shadows at the top of the stairs. In the dim light, her dark red lipstick shone black. She was wearing the black leather jacket and matching leather mini skirt that had become her uniform. I wondered if that had been her attire for her father's funeral.

"Gossiping as usual." Lydia tried to make light of the situation.

"You were talking about my parents, weren't you? God, Lydia, and with her." She pointed at me.

"Guilty as charged. I'm sorry. You want a glass of wine?" Lydia's diversionary tactic seemed to work. Sarah came into the candlelight and poured herself a glass of wine.

"I'm not staying if she's here." She jerked her thumb at me.

"Sit down, Sarah. She's my guest too."

"Lydia, I told you, she's been hounding my mother since my father's death. Encouraging her delusions."

"She's not here as a reporter. She's here as an invited participant to our group."

"Look, I can leave." Sarah was piercing me with her hostile glare: the one she'd used on me at Joyce's funeral.

"No." Lydia insisted. "Sarah, you're understandably upset because of your father's funeral. Sit down and relax."

Why was Lydia being so insistent that I stay? She seemed to have her own agenda that had nothing to do with me.

"Does she know the rules?" Sarah plopped down so hard on a pillow, I heard air escape. I didn't trust her acquiescence.

"I thought I'd wait until everyone arrived."

Just then a woman huffed into the room. "Sorry I'm late. Had to wait for the sitter. Barb's right behind me."

"Leigh, I think you know Marge."

People at work always seemed to be merging with people I was writing about. A familiar fist closed in my stomach, getting tighter and tighter. The room felt too small already. I was sweating. All I could think about was running away. I took a deep breath. Just give into it, I told myself. What's the worst that could happen?

"Small world," Marge said as she sat down.

"And getting smaller by the minute," I managed to say in return.

"Hi guys," said a tall woman in a blue sweat suit. She surveyed the room. "I know everyone but you." She pointed at me. "So I guess that makes you Leigh. I'm Barb. Lydia's told me all about you."

"Whatever she said, isn't true." I was feeling more uncomfortable by the minute.

"Don't worry, we all know how Lydia likes to exaggerate. Hey, girl, where's the wine?" Barb dangled the empty bottle.

Lydia went into the kitchen and brought back another bottle of wine and passed it around.

"Okay, now that everybody's settled, I'll go over the rules for Leigh and as a reminder for everyone else. Everything said here is confidential. Nothing leaves this room. No one is forced to talk, but you are encouraged. We are here to be supportive, not judgmental, and to work on our spiritual selves. Who wants to start?"

"You get that, don't you?" Sarah addressed me directly. "This is confidential. So you can't use anything we say in the newspaper."

"I got it," I responded, wondering if Sarah had considered that the rules also applied to her. What was she doing in this group? She seemed as far from spiritual as a person could get.

"If I find out you've used anything in any way, I'll get you." Her voice had become menacing.

"Sarah, I know you're upset about your father. But I invited Leigh, and I feel she can be trusted," Lydia pleaded.

"Sometimes I wonder if you can be trusted." Sarah apparently wasn't going to confine her anger just to me.

Lydia bit back whatever it was she was going to say, as Sarah added, "You know damn well I'm not upset about my father. He should have died a long time ago and put everyone out of their misery. At least he died as ugly as he lived."

"You have every right to feel the way you do," Marge encouraged, smiling at Sarah. "It's the same way I feel about my husband when he criticizes me."

Sarah laughed derisively. "You have no friggin' idea, Marge. It's not the same at all, in any way. No one here knows, not any of you can know." She stood up. "Some women's group. You're all a bunch of losers. I don't know why I thought any of this would do any good."

We listened in silence to the click of her heels as she stormed down the stairs.

It was almost ten p.m. when I drove home down the peninsula. The darkness was absolute. Only as I passed through one of the villages did lights appear and quickly disappear. I was feeling shaky and overtired. Every fear I had ever had about groups had manifested itself tonight. Lydia had dismissed Marge, Barb, and me with an "I'll call you tomorrow." Her mantle of control had slipped, and she seemed unable to regain her poise in front of us.

The wind thundered across the peninsula, and every once in a while lightning flashed in the distance, splitting the sky in two. Why had Sarah lashed out at the group? I could understand her fury at me. She saw me as an outsider who kept pestering her mother. Though the accusation wasn't true, I understood it.

131

However, her emotionality about her father was curious. She had said that she was glad he was dead. How had she phrased it, "his death had put everyone out of their misery"? But what really pushed her over the edge was Marge's innocent remark comparing her situation with Sarah's. Marge had only been trying to empathize, but Sarah took it as a lessening of her own pain. I'd been a member of enough therapy groups to recognize when a hidden wound was erupting to the surface and there was no way to stop it. It was like watching your skin split open.

I was no stranger to the ugly side of life, so some obvious and repulsive answers presented themselves to my overworked imagination. Peck had been an alcoholic. Alcoholics were known to lose control, to be abusive. Had he beaten her as a kid or done something worse? But Sarah had said, "put everyone out of their misery." Who did that everyone include? Her mother? Someone else? Yet no one I'd talked to had said anything about Peck being abusive.

I was so wrapped up in my own thoughts from the disturbing evening that I hadn't noticed the headlights behind me. Now the driver turned them up to brights; they looked like truck headlights, and they were moving in too close for comfort. As a good defensive driver, I slowed down, hoping whoever was behind me would pass, but they also slowed down and maintained that uncomfortable closeness to my back bumper. Up ahead, I spotted a side road. It was a gravel road that would take me the long way home, but at least I wouldn't have to contend with this tailgater riding my ass. There were more than a fair share of drunk driving fatalities on the peninsula, and I didn't want to end up one of them.

Without giving a signal, I turned sharply onto the side road. I heard the tires of the vehicle behind me squeal. The truck had also turned and was coming up fast behind me. I realized this was no drunk. This was someone who was after me. My heart started beating so fast I thought it might rip a hole in my chest. I pushed my foot down hard on the accelerator. For a moment the headlights receded in my rearview mirror. I took a deep breath.

It was then that I felt an aggressive thump on my rear bumper, which jerked me forward. The truck was back with a vengeance. I pushed my foot down even harder on the pedal, trying to control my truck as it lurched from side to side on the gravel road. I watched helplessly as the other truck fell back and accelerated again to ram my rear bumper.

Like a mantra I kept repeating to myself, "Faster, faster, don't stop, don't stop." I accelerated. Now my truck was shaking as it spit up gravel and veered all over the road. My arms ached. "Don't stop, don't stop, faster, faster!" My brain was moving as fast as my truck. Maybe I could make it home before this crazed idiot ran me off the road.

I looked again in the rearview mirror and didn't see the headlights. I knew what was coming, and braced myself. The truck had pulled alongside of me. For a split second, I thought of all the pain I had gone through with my cancer to live. Was I going to let some nut job get to me out here in the middle of nowhere, and not even know why? Immediately all the fear drained out of me.

Before the truck could hit me broadside, I slammed the accelerator to the floor and veered toward the truck. The force of the impact surprised the driver who had been heading toward me. We both struggled to keep our vehicles on the road.

The last thing I saw was a field opening up and taking me in.

15

Wednesday, November 8, Present day

I must have forgotten to pull the shades because sunlight was streaming through the windows. My muscles ached, and I was nauseous and dizzy. When did the old familiar symptoms from chemo come back? Automatically I ran my hand over my head. Thankfully, my hair felt thick and lush. Yet there was something sticky on my fingers. I forced my eyes open. I was sitting in my truck in the middle of a field. Last night flooded back.

I quickly looked around. The other truck was nowhere in sight. I was alone except for a flock of crows circling and cawing. I felt the sticky area on my head again and tried to see it in the mirror. There was a small knot of clotted blood near my hairline above my eye. I must have hit my head against the steering wheel.

The key was still in the ignition. I reached forward to turn the key, and a searing pain tore through the left side of my chest. Quickly I opened the door and vomited. Like an internal explosion, the pain had set off a memory. I was standing in front of a mirror staring at the incised left side of my chest. Seeing the flat, nipple-less expanse. Tears ran down my face and fell over the scar. I couldn't feel the tears, only the lingering, burning pain of the surgery.

Out here in the field and the blazing sun, I carefully lifted my blouse away from my body. A large bruise blazed on the left side of my chest in garish greens and purples. I looked under my prosthesis. The skin was pink. No bruise. With great relief, I realized my prosthesis had protected the mastectomy scar.

Gingerly, I turned the ignition key. The truck started on the first try. I backed up and saw what had stopped my truck last night: a stump jutting out of the dirt.

Once I made my way home, the dusky light of the stone cottage cloaked me as I sat huddled with Salinger in the green velvet chair. I had stripped off last night's clothes, showered, and crawled into my nightgown and robe. I know I should have gone directly to the hospital emergency room, but I couldn't stand the thought of anyone poking and probing at my body. They would definitely want a chest X-ray and maybe an MRI. No thanks. I wasn't due for a follow-up exam for five more months. That was soon enough for me. This sanctuary of the stone cottage and Salinger were all I needed. If the nausea and dizziness didn't go away by evening, I'd call Lydia.

I had made strong coffee to keep myself awake in case I had a concussion. For the moment that was all the medication I was willing to deal with. The most important thing was to keep my head clear, if that was possible. Someone had run me off the road last night and left me in a field, not caring if I was injured or dead.

Sarah Peck immediately came to mind. She had threatened me last night at Lydia's group meeting. Maybe running me off the road was her way of punctuating the threat. But there was no way to prove it had been her. I hadn't seen the driver nor really gotten a good look at the truck. Couldn't tell the license plate or if the driver had been a man or a woman.

All I was sure of was that the truck's color was dark: maybe dark blue or black. Other than that, it was like all the countless pickup trucks on the peninsula.

The phone rang and I startled, spilling coffee on myself and Salinger, who jumped off the chair with a yelp. It rang again. I let the machine pick up.

"Girard? Are you there? Pick up or you're dead."

It was Jake Stevens. Damn. I had forgotten that there was a staff meeting at 8:30 a.m., called in my honor. Stevens wanted me to officially meet the rest of the *Gazette* staff. I looked at the mallard-shaped clock on the mantle; it read 10:05.

"You'd better have a good excuse," he continued.

I reached over and picked up the phone. "I'm here," I said. "You don't have to burn me in effigy."

"What's going on? Surely you didn't forget this morning's special meeting to introduce you to the stringers? You know, to build good working relationships, rapport, possibly be able to recognize them on the street." He was on a roll. "I have five reporters with their noses out of joint wondering who the jerk is that I had hired. Do you think you can get your butt down here sometime today?"

"Someone ran me off the road last night," I hesitated, "on purpose."

For a moment, one could hear the proverbial pin drop. I had wanted to sort things out in my mind before telling anyone about the incident. But maybe Stevens could shed some light on it.

"Anything broken?"

"I've got a bump where my head hit the steering wheel. But mostly, I'm just sore as hell from sleeping in the truck all night." No need to go into further detail.

"Have you been to a doctor?"

"I'm fine. I'll come in later this afternoon."

"Listen, I know you think you're pretty tough, but don't fart around with a head injury. Get yourself over to Emergency. Ask for Dr. Waters. He's the best."

Suddenly Salinger ran for the door and stared barking. Someone was outside.

"I gotta go. Someone's at the door. I'll see you later."

"What do you mean, on purpose—?" Before he could finish, I hung up.

In my haste to see who was snooping around outside, I stood up too fast, and a wave of dizziness and nausea overtook me. I grabbed the back of the chair and waited for it to pass. Then I went to the window and squinted around the etched glass. Rob Martin was kneeling beside my truck, running his hand over the dent in the driver's side door. What was he doing here? I noticed that he drove a black Dodge Ram pickup. From the window, I couldn't see if his truck had any tell-tale dents.

I flung open the front door. "What a surprise."

Salinger ran past me to give Martin the once over. He patted Salinger on the head. The gesture seemed uncharacteristic for him. I reminded myself that he was the local naturalist. Flora and fauna were what he loved, not people. Except for Sarah Peck.

"Looks like you had an accident." He stood up.

"You should see the other guy," I said. "Is this a social call?"

"Well, you didn't show up for the meeting, and your place was on my way, so I thought I'd stop by and see if everything was all right." He approached me, with Salinger circling his feet.

I wasn't buying the new improved Rob, but I was curious over his sudden transformation.

137

"Pretty robust field of asters over there." He pointed toward the field.

"They seem to have a will of their own."

"You'd think that, but it's the weather. Tricks them into continuing to bloom. I've seen them around as late as Thanksgiving. Have you seen any purple heads?"

"Not that I've noticed."

He squinted, staring at the field. "Mind if I take a look before I leave?"

"You can look, but don't touch."

I thought he would head toward the field, but instead he asked, "May I come in for a moment?"

I didn't want to invite him into the house, but there didn't seem to be any tactful way out of it and still satisfy my curiosity. "Sure." For a moment my instincts told me to leave the door open, but I didn't want him to know I didn't trust him. Why couldn't his black truck have been the one on my back bumper last night? I shut the door behind him.

As he sat down on the sofa, Salinger jumped up beside him, wagging her tail as if she'd never seen a man before. She and I were going to have a heart to heart when he left.

"Handsome dog. Shelties aren't usually this friendly." He picked up Salinger's ball and threw it across the room. She ran after it as if it were a flying steak. "Most shelties are real loyal to their families, and usually real wary of strangers." Salinger dropped the ball at Rob's feet and gazed up at him.

"What can I say, she has no taste."

To his credit, he managed a smile. He seemed determined not to take offense to anything I said this morning, which set my nerves jangling. He was probably up to something. I took my usual direct approach. "Why did you think everything wasn't all right over here?"

"What? Oh, um . . ." He crossed one leg over the other,

then put both on the floor again. "Well, you don't strike me as the type to blow off a professional meeting. You know, Type A." He smiled, as if he'd scored a goal.

I smiled back. I'd been called worse things.

"From the looks of your truck and your forehead, I was right. Did you have some kind of accident?"

That was the second time he'd asked that question. "You might say that. Someone ran me off the road last night." I didn't add the "on purpose," because I wanted to see his reaction.

He moved his fingers up and down his shockingly red goatee. I had noticed this nervous habit of his before. "Did you get a look at the driver?"

"No, but I did get a good look at the truck." I was bluffing. There was a reason he had come here, and it wasn't to see if everything was all right.

"Then you've filed a police report?"

If he kept at it, he was going to rub that goatee right off his face. "Rob, let's cut the chit chat. Why don't you tell me the real reason you came over here?"

He seemed about to protest, and then thought better of it. "All right, we aren't candidates for best friends. But I bet you don't know why."

"I'm sure you'll tell me."

"See, that's what I mean, that 'in-your-face' attitude. When I lived in Chicago, I ran into it all the time from women like you. Hard-ass career women. I'm not surprised you're living here and working at a fifth-rate newspaper. You're probably burned out, right? Left the husband and kids, came here to drop out. Only problem is, you don't know how to drop out. You have no idea what it means to relax, to let things go."

The tips of his ears were now as red as his hair. I was curious at his chauvinistic tirade. Granted, some of what he said was true—I couldn't let things go. Still, the ferocity of his words seemed based on some personal experience.

"You don't know me well enough to know what kind of woman I am."

"Oh, I know your type real well. Let me give you some advice—back off." He punctuated his advice with a finger pointed forcefully at me.

"Are you talking about Carl Peck?" It was a rhetorical question. "You, of all people, should be at least a little suspicious about his death. After all, I understand the two of you went mushroom picking together, and that he was the one who got you interested in it. Don't you find it strange that he ate an amanita? One of the most deadly of mushrooms."

For a minute, he didn't say anything. Then he took a deep breath, as if gathering himself. "I see I was right, you've been digging around." He grinned sardonically. His sudden self-control unnerved me. One minute he was raging at me about career-driven harpies and the next, he was making bad puns.

"I'm a reporter. I'm suppose to dig around."

"Not here. Maybe back where you're from. But not here."

"What's the matter? Am I digging too close to home?"

He jumped up from the sofa so fast that Salinger barked. "You're going to do what you want to do anyway. Your kind never listens or learns until it's too late and someone gets hurt."

"Learns what?" I didn't like him standing over me, so I stood up. Again I was overwhelmed with nausea and dizziness.

He didn't seem to notice. "To let things go." We were eye to eye, and I didn't like what I saw. His pupils had contracted to pin points. "Just stay out of my way." He moved toward the door, and I inwardly sighed with relief.

"Is that at work or everywhere?" I shouted after him. He slammed the door so hard, it bounced against the frame.

I followed him as fast as my sore body would allow, hoping to catch another glimpse of his vehicle, but ran directly into Jake Stevens, who stormed through my front door like a man on fire. When he turned back to me, he let out a long whistle. "You did say you were fine." He was grinning. My robe had loosened, and he was staring at the top of my chest. I yanked the robe shut, hoping the garish bruise had distracted him from my lopsided appearance.

"Come to see if I'm playing hooky?" I walked back to my chair and sat down, crossing my arms over my chest.

"I thought whoever ran you off the road might have come to pay a visit." Stevens plopped his lanky body across the sofa.

"You don't know how right you might be."

"Martin? You're way off. That's not his style. He's not the violent kind. He's a tree hugger, Mr. Nature, the Ed Abbey of the Midwest. Ever read Abbey? Helluva writer. He could turn a description of a sunset into a reason to live."

"What about last Saturday? At Bailey's? He wasn't hugging any trees that night."

"Did you see him do anything?"

"No, not really," I conceded. "But he looked like he could."

"It's no secret that he's never gotten over the divorce. Sometimes he feels sorry for himself and goes looking for Sarah. No harm there."

"And her lascivious behavior doesn't seem to help his obsession."

Stevens ignored my remark. "Dog suits you." Salinger was curled up on my feet. Stevens didn't interest her. "Besides, what reason would Martin have to run you off the road?"

"I've been asking questions about Carl Peck's death, and

his lady love, Sarah Peck, doesn't like it or me, for that matter."

"Why would Martin care if you investigated Peck's death? You'd better watch out, Girard, you're starting to sound paranoid. I could sooner see Sarah running you off the road than Martin. Say, you have any coffee?"

"In the kitchen." I wasn't going to risk getting up again. It was taking all my strength not to throw up.

"What makes you think Sarah is capable of running me off the road?" I shouted toward the kitchen.

He came back with the coffee and sat down again. "Let's say that she's a woman with a very passionate and erratic nature."

"Is this from first hand experience?"

"You figure it out." He was being coy.

"Gosh, and I thought we were starting to have a meaningful relationship. Sharing secrets and all."

"You tell me yours, and I'll tell you mine."

"You first."

"We'll save that pleasure for a cold winter evening," he said. "Have you learned anything about Peck's death to justify people running you off the road?"

I told him what I knew about amanita mushrooms, and Sarah's angry comments about her father. "I have a hunch that Peck did something to Sarah, some kind of abuse. Maybe physical, maybe even sexual."

I steeled myself for the inevitable denial from Stevens. Men always have trouble with members of their sex acting like scum. But he surprised me.

"That certainly would explain Sarah's anger at him. Or maybe she's mad at him for something he did to her mother?"

"Could be. But it doesn't feel that way. My instinct tells me that Peck did something to her."

"That still doesn't mean she killed him or ran you off the road," Stevens persisted.

"No, but it puts her as my number one suspect."

"You haven't even proved there's been a crime committed. The police don't think there's been a crime. And, do I need to remind you, it's the job of the police to develop suspect lists, not reporters."

"You mean your razor-quick deputy pal, Chet Jorgensen?"

"He may take his own time, but he gets the job done. Don't underestimate him. In fact, you'd better make a report to him about the incident last night."

"There's really nothing I can tell him, except that the truck was a dark color."

"Just do it. That's an order from your boss."

I merely nodded, which could mean yes or no. "You don't happen to know anything more about Sarah's childhood, do you? Something to do with her father that could shed some light on this?"

Stevens put his coffee cup on the side table. "If I did, do you think I would tell you?"

"I think you would."

"You're right, I would. But I don't know anything. Sarah and I don't do a lot of sharing. Of those kind of secrets, that is." He grinned. "Why don't you just ask her?"

"I think I might just do that."

I should have been home snuggled under my down comforter and nursing a cup of tea, instead of standing outside the Egg Harbor market trying to lure Renn Woulff into a conversation. And I would have been, if my headache hadn't reached symphonic proportions just as I ran out of my migraine meds.

"So, you're that new gal on the paper, then," Woulff commented, running his eyes over me with slimy, obvious delight. It was about twenty degrees out, but he wasn't wearing a coat. His hair, which probably was blonde, was so dirty it looked gray. "I swear I've seen you somewheres before. I never forget a pretty face or a great bod." He gave me another spurious scan, as if I were for sale.

"Bailey's," I said, trying not to inhale the whiskey aroma that seemed to encircle him like a fog.

"Okay then, though it's kinda early in the day," he said, starting down the street in the direction of the waterfront.

"No, that' s not what I meant." I walked beside him. "Last Saturday night. We met at Bailey's."

"Nope, can't be it. I seen you in the paper."

"How can you be sure, it was only a head shot?" I tried not to smirk. "You got time for a cup of coffee? I'd like to hear more about you and Carl Peck."

"Liked that first idea better. How about a beer. If you don't say nothing, I won't."

"Secret's safe with me." I reluctantly followed him into Bailey's. It was barely four p.m., and we were the only customers. The bartender raised an eyebrow when Renn ordered a pitcher of beer and two shots.

"Don't you tell Regina, okay?" He winked at me. "She'd be jealous."

I ignored his intimation, and rubbed my temples, trying to ease my headache. "So, what's the story with you and Carl Peck? You seemed pretty upset last Saturday."

"Hey," Renn shouted at me. "What happened there to your head? That's a nasty one." He touched the bruise on my forehead. His shout had cranked up the pulse in my brain, which didn't need to be any higher.

"I head-butted some guy who said something about my great bod."

For a second, he didn't say anything. Just leaned back in his chair so far that I thought he'd fall. Then he let the chair fall forward with a whump! "Okay, I ain't that out of it. Yet. Not used to good-looking babes picking me up."

Tony the bartender set the pitcher of beer and two glasses on the table. "Now I don't want any trouble from you," he warned Renn.

"Just bring them shots, okay? I'm helping this here lady out with her newspaper story. So take a hike."

"And could I have a glass of water?" I asked the beleaguered-looking Tony.

Woulff poured me and then himself a beer. After he'd consumed about half the glass, he said, "Nice and cold. Ain't you drinking?"

"Got a headache."

"More for me then." He grinned and slid my glass protectively toward his side of the table. "You want to know about Carl, huh? Biggest damn bastard on the peninsula. You know what he did? Talked me into selling the orchards and investing that money in that restoration business of his. Then just as that business is making money, he buys me out for a song. My family owned them orchards over a hundred years."

"Why did you sell to him?"

" 'Cause at the time I didn't know the business was making money. He made it look like we was losing money. He doctored the books."

Tony set down two shots and a glass of water.

"Thanks." I tossed two Duradrin in my mouth and gulped down the water. "Didn't you have an accountant or a lawyer check it over?"

"Yeah, I know that now. But I trusted that bastard. We were drinking buddies. He made it seem like he was doing me some favor, saving my ass." He downed the two shots one after another. "Man, that's almost better than sex," he choked out.

"Couldn't you have sued him? Taken him to court?"

"I got no proof. It woulda been his word against mine. It just seemed funny that soon's he buys me out, that business started doing real good."

"So what are you doing now?"

He raised a glass of beer. "Taking the slow train out of here. Trouble is, by morning, it always ends up back in the same damn place."

I moved the water glass in circles and watched the water rings blur.

"Know what I got left?" He lowered his voice. "An old pickup truck, the clothes on my back, and the sign that hung over the entrance to the orchards. Woulff Orchards, it says. Big black letters, real smart like. I got it hung in the cab of my pickup, if you want to see." He downed another glass of beer. "I know what you're thinking."

I didn't say anything.

"No, I do. You're thinking what everyone around here thinks. That I'm a moron and a loser. But the thing is, he took more than that money. We used to be buddies." His eyes looked even more unfocused. "I gotta go." He stood up quickly.

"You'd better have some coffee first."

"No, I gotta go pee." He stumbled away in the direction of the rest rooms.

I sat and stared at Sarah's mural. Although Woulff had motive enough to want Peck dead, he didn't seem capable of doing it. If Carl Peck was murdered, the murderer had to have been clear headed and intelligent—neither of which applied to Woulff. On his way back from the toilet, he stopped at the bar and got another shot.

146

"Here's to lady reporters with great bods!" He lurched over me and downed his third shot. He pulled back his chair to sit down, missed the seat and fell on the floor. "Oops!" He was grinning as he dragged himself up. "Time to go. Want a ride in my pickup? There's plenty room in the cab, if you know what I mean." He leaned over me and put his hands over both my wrists.

"I'm not interested, if you know what I mean." I pulled my wrists out from under his hands.

"So that's the way, huh? Got what you came for, now you're done with old Renn, tossing me away. Like I'm garbage, then."

I stood up and grabbed my coat from the back of my chair. I didn't see Tony, so I threw a twenty down on the table. "Now we're even." I moved toward the door.

"You can't buy me off!" he yelled, following me out into the dark entranceway. "You owe me something."

I tried to open the outside door, but he pushed it shut from behind. He swung me around to face him. We were so close I could count the broken blood vessels in his bulbous nose. He pressed my shoulders against the wall and leaned down toward me. I turned my head away, but his mouth managed to slur across mine. I pushed at him hard, but couldn't budge him. Then as if in slow motion, I watched his right hand grab at my left breast. With all my physical force, I shot my knee into his groin.

He fell back, yelling and holding his crotch. "You meddling bitch!" he shouted at my retreating back.

As I pulled away from the curb, I saw Woulff struggling with the door of his dark blue pickup truck. My bruised chest was throbbing. I wiped my mouth over and over with the back of my hand.

16

Thursday, November 9, Present day

I took Stevens's advice and called Sarah Peck at White Cliffs around six p.m. Wednesday. After my round of slam dancing with Woulff, I was ready for whatever Sarah had to dish out. But she refused to meet with me. Her exact words to my request were: "When you're in hell and it freezes over."

With the tox results concluded, Stevens was clamoring for my follow-up story on Peck. I told him there were a few loose ends I wanted to tie up. He'd given me his blue-eyed stare and a Monday deadline.

After spending most of Thursday spinning my wheels tracking down anyone who'd ever known Carl Peck, I'd come up blank. Everyone expressed their surprise that he had mistakenly eaten a deadly poisonous mushroom. A few mentioned his drinking, "off the record," of course. But most said he was a nice guy who did great restoration work.

By four p.m., I decided to pack it in and head home. I was feeling pent up, frustrated, and in need of some physical release. When I got home, I immediately changed into my navy sweatshirt, sweatpants, and hiking boots. Salinger was practically doing a dance when she saw me lace up the boots. She knew what that meant. A long walk someplace with fragrant scents. And I knew just the place: Peninsula State Park.

It was dusk when I pulled into the Ephraim entrance and

drove down the winding road through the heavily wooded forest. A streak of yellow light hugged the horizon as the trees thickened into blackness and closed in on me. Like a door firmly shut, the last remnants of light extinguished. Since the sun had set, I decided to park by Eagle Tower and take the Sentinel Trail, an easy hike down a meandering path through a pine and hardwood forest.

Even with a half moon perched over the water, the park seemed unusually dark. But I had no difficulty seeing Eagle Tower. It loomed over the trees. In the dark, the leggy structure looked like a tenuous ascent to some ethereal world. It was that time of day when vision plays tricks on you.

I reached over and stroked Salinger's thick fur. A slight pain pulled across my left side, making me catch my breath for a second. Salinger turned her dark eyes toward me with concern. I was glad I'd decided to bring her.

The nausea and dizziness had subsided that morning, but I hadn't slept much. And I still felt shaky every time I thought about that bruise. I'd heard stories in my cancer survivors' group about injuries reactivating cancer. My doctors had dismissed them as old wives' tales. But in my gut, I knew there were many things that the doctors couldn't explain. Like why cancer had singled me out, when I had had none of the risk factors. The tumor had grown silently inside my breast like a black pearl.

I pulled into the parking lot right next to the tower, my headlights illuminating the empty parking area. For a moment I looked at the monolithic giant, which probably afforded a great view of the Green Bay islands. As the dusk deepened, it took on the characteristics of a horror story metaphor in my imagination. Any minute I expected to see it move toward me.

I turned off the engine and started gathering what I

needed for my hike: gloves, hat, pepper spray, flashlight. As I bent over to retrieve my flashlight from the floor, headlights swept over the parking lot.

I sat up, slowly stroking Salinger to keep her quiet. A truck parked on the far end of the lot, near Eagle Trail. To my surprise, Sarah Peck exited the truck, slamming the door hard. Either she didn't see my truck or was in too much of hurry to take note, because she headed straight for the trail entrance without looking around. There was an urgency in her stride, as if she was late for an appointment.

I waited until she disappeared down the trail, then went over to her truck. It was a black Dodge Ram. The passenger side's door was dented, and I was fairly sure Martin had driven this same truck to my cottage yesterday.

As I stood examining the truck, Salinger let loose with a series of howls capable of setting off car alarms in neighboring states. I went back and let her out. Before I could give her my usual lecture about staying by my side, she tore off in the direction of Eagle Trail.

I quickly locked my truck door and ran toward the trail. When I reached the trailhead, I looked down the path searching for Salinger. She was nowhere to be seen. For a moment I hesitated. Eagle Trail was steep and rocky, with sharp ascent and descent points. Tom and I had hiked this trail many times in the summers. Even in full daylight, it was treacherous.

I could just wait until Salinger made her way back to me, I reasoned. But who knows how long that would be? Then there was Sarah Peck and her dented truck. What was she doing all alone, at dusk, walking this trail? I decided to follow her at a distance with the hope I'd also find my adventuresome dog along the way.

The slope downward was as treacherous as I remembered.

As I began descending, an owl's eerie voice ruptured the rhythmic sound of the bay: not a promising sign. In the dappled moonlight, every once in awhile, I caught a glint from the silver studs of Sarah's leather jacket. She was moving fast, thrashing so loudly through the woods, there was no way she could hear me descending behind her.

By the time I had reached the bottom of the slope, I'd lost sight of Sarah. I continued carefully making my way along the darkest part of the trail that skirted the bay. Following the water's edge, the path flattened but grew more narrow. Even in summer, this was a shadowy place to hike. Now the pine trees blocked the frail moonlight. I stopped for a few minutes and let my eyes adjust to the darkness. I didn't want to turn on my flashlight and possibly alert Sarah to my presence. I wished Salinger would finish her meandering and find me. I reassured myself that the path would open up once I began the slow ascent toward the caves. But that thought did little to ease my growing sense of dread.

I quickened my pace and tripped over a jutting rock. As I caught myself, a burning pain shot across my bruised chest. I stood still for a moment to let the pain pass, and concentrated on the sound of the water thumping against the rocks. It moved obsessively across the rocky beach in a mad search for what can't be found. I moved forward carefully.

As the trail turned away from the water, the sharp odor of pine assaulted my nose. When I reached the trail section that ran in front of a group of caves, I saw Sarah. With some small twigs, she had started a small fire just inside one of the caves. The fire smelled like burning Christmas trees. And there was Salinger, sprawled beside the fire meticulously licking her paws.

As I approached, Salinger stopped her grooming, ran at my feet and began circling them.

"Okay, girl," I said, bending over to give Salinger a few pats on her head to settle her down. Sarah didn't seem surprised to see me. She was smoking a cigarette and staring into the fire.

"What is this place?" I asked. I expected her to ream me a new one, but she just continued smoking and staring into the fire as if I wasn't there. I caught the faint scent of alcohol coming from her.

Quickly, I glanced around the cave walls, wondering if the bats had already left for their nocturnal hunt. No sign of bats. But someone had spray painted something on one of the walls. In the dim firelight, I made out the words, "South Heaven."

Sarah followed my glance. "Pretty ironic, huh?"

"Maybe they didn't know how to spell Haven?" I suggested, sitting down on the damp, hard floor near the fire, careful not to jostle my left side. The pain had subsided to a dull throbbing.

"Maybe. But I like to think that's what they meant. South Heaven, as if this was it for them. As if there was a North Heaven as well."

I was seeing a contemplative side of Sarah that I never suspected existed. Her hostility was gone for the moment. She crushed out her cigarette and threw it into the fire. From her coat pocket, she pulled out a quart bottle of whiskey.

"Want some?" She offered the bottle to me.

"No thanks, I'm driving."

"Funny," she said taking a sip. "You'd better watch your dog. No telling what's in those caves."

I turned and saw the white tip of Salinger's tail disappear into the bowels of the cave.

"She can take care of herself," I said, hopeful.

Sarah rested the bottle between her feet and stared out

into the wooded darkness. In the firelight, I could see that the bottle was half empty. I wasn't going to push her. Something was on her mind.

Just then a bird screeched over the trees. We both looked out.

"Probably an owl," she whispered. "They do their best hunting at night." She took another swig from the bottle.

"How can you be sure it's an owl?" I felt I needed to keep her talking.

"I know a lot about predators." She dangled the bottle by its opening and watched the dark amber liquid swish back and forth. "You'd think I'd know better, wouldn't you?"

"Oblivion can be quite persuasive."

She turned toward me, her face flushed in the firelight. "What would you know about oblivion?"

"I recognize pain when I see it."

"Do you also recognize courage?" She put the bottle down.

For a moment, I considered telling her about the women in my cancer survival group, but immediately rejected the idea. Sarah would never appreciate their stories in her present intoxicated state, and I couldn't bear her scorning them.

"What are you doing here anyway?" she asked.

"I wanted to talk to you about Tuesday night. Someone ran me off the road after the meeting at Lydia's."

"And you think it was me?" she snapped. "It had to be me, right? I was the one out of control. I was the one raving. I was the crazy one." A sob caught in her throat. She took a breath. "So it couldn't be anyone else."

I had been right not to confide in her. The alcohol was making her erratic. "You threatened me," I reasoned, trying to calm her down.

"I don't want to talk anymore." She drank the rest of the whiskey. "Why don't you go away?"

"I'm not leaving until you give me an answer. Did you run me off the road?"

"Yes, yes, yes," she hissed. "It was me."

"Why?"

"I didn't intend to run you off the road. I got carried away."

"You left me unconscious in an open field."

She hesitated. "Well, you're okay now. I mean, I checked on you before I left. You were breathing. Your truck was okay to drive." The excuses sounded lame, even to her.

"You didn't answer my question. Why?"

"So you'd leave me and my mother the hell alone." She talked very slowly, as if she was struggling with the words. "It's almost funny. If you'd known the pecker head, you'd stop this. You'd get it."

"Get what, Sarah?"

She picked the bottle up and threw it into the darkness. The sound of glass breaking echoed through the trees.

"Why do you hate your father so much? What did he do to you?"

She stood up and began kicking dirt on the fire to put it out.

"To me, to my mother, to . . ." She stopped herself. "Yeah, he did something. Ruined a lot of lives. I'm glad he's dead. I'll always be glad he's dead."

I watched her recede down the trail into the dark and toward the water. I sat for a moment and stared into the smoldering fire, thinking how its light shut out the trees, the animals, the woods surrounding me. How it erased night falsely, and separated me from the natural world. Carl Peck had ruined Sarah's life. Whatever he had done, he had hurt her to the core. Even in death, his awful light encased her, shutting out everything else.

Suddenly I heard a sound. I held my breath and listened. There it was again, a scratching sound. It was coming from behind me, from the depths of the cave. I turned slowly around and peered into the cave. I couldn't see anything except a deep dark hole. Then I let out a deep breath. "Salinger," I whispered.

I called into the narrowed darkness, "Come on, girl. Time to go home." But there was no sound except the echo of my words. The scratching had stopped.

"Salinger. Come on," I called again, this time in a stern voice. Still no response. Those fine hairs on the back of my neck started doing the lambada.

"Don't make me come in there after you!" The scratching sound started again, only more frantic. Salinger would be covered in dirt from snout to tail if I didn't get her out of there.

Grateful for my flashlight, I moved into the cave. Just in case some of the bats had decided to forego dinner, I pulled the hood of my jacket over my head. Within a few feet, the passage shrunk abruptly and I had to crawl on hands and knees. I slowly inched forward into a darkness that seemed absolute except for the flashlight's narrow beam. Smells arose out of the dark—metallic wet smells, then the sharp scent of ammonia. Suddenly I sensed a presence move toward me.

"Salinger?" I shined the light around the cave, "that better be you!"

I felt something brush against my shoulder and heard a thud. I froze. Then I felt a wet tongue licking my face.

"Salinger, you idiot," I said with relief, reaching toward her. "Let's get out of here." She pulled away from me. I saw her paw at the dirt. Then she ran past me toward the cave's entrance. I crawled quickly after her. By the time I reached the dwindling fire, Salinger was sitting with her paws crossed over something that she was carefully licking. I walked toward her to take a closer look, and she darted back into the cave.

"Salinger, no!" But she was beyond reason.

I crouched down on my heels to examine her treasure. It was small and narrow and shone white where Salinger had licked away the dirt. It looked like some kind of bone. By the time I had decided that it was probably a leg bone, Salinger had brought me another. By the time I had decided that the bones were probably from a dog, Salinger had brought me a skull.

I stared in dumb amazement, not believing what I was looking at—a small skull, the crown caved in but beautifully rounded at the back, and with symmetrical eye sockets, nose hole, and toothless jaw. This was no animal skull. This was human.

It was past two a.m. and my head was aching again, as well as my chest, with a dull throbbing near the base of my spine that I hoped wouldn't make its way up my neck and band my head like the migraine adder. I'd taken four Duradrin, and they'd barely made a dent in my pain, which meant I hadn't caught the migraine soon enough. I rubbed the back of my neck and climbed into bed, burrowing down under the covers. Even Salinger was unusually subdued and curled quietly at the foot of my bed.

I knew sleep would elude me once again. I was still too stunned by the confirmation of Salinger's discovery. I could still see the look of disbelief on the park ranger's face as he asked me for the third time if I was sure that what I'd found was a human skull.

"It looked like a doll's head," I had explained. "Except for the part that's missing."

He had been in the middle of his dinner of meatloaf, mashed potatoes and green beans when I had pounded on his cabin door. I wouldn't have wanted to believe me either.

"Look, I work for the *Gazette*. My name's Leigh Girard. I assure you, I am not making this up."

"I read ya," he said. "But ya sure, this isn't some prank Stevens put you up to?"

"What? No!"

"Okay, then. But let me finish my dinner."

By the time we had reached the cave, the moon had crested the trees. Ranger Johnson had taken one look at the tiny skull and shook his head.

"Guess you're right, there. Looks as human as you or me."

"You're going to report this to the police?"

"What do you think, missy?"

I must have told Deputy Ferry, a short dark man with a mustache shaped like a mascara brush, at least twelve times how Salinger and I had found the bones. Only after I had promised to come by the station at nine in the morning to give an official statement had he been satisfied.

I threw the covers off and shivered over to the far corner of the room, where I had shoved one of my many boxes of books. I dug through the box until I found the one I was looking for, the perfect antidote to the evening's events: Nathaniel Hawthorne's *Tales and Sketches*. Book in hand, I crawled back under the covers. Salinger looked up with an expression of annoyed willingness on her face.

"You've done your work for today," I told her. "You can go back to sleep."

As I read the first few pages of Hawthorne's book, I was

again reminded that he understood how past sins eventually have a way of surfacing. They come back to haunt us, even when they're not our own. In my mind's eye, I saw the small holes in the skull where the eyes had been, felt the lightness and fragility of that extinguished life. Whoever had buried that baby in the recesses of a cave had a secret that had finally surfaced.

17

Friday, November 10, Present day

At seven a.m. I was back at the Bay hospital. Lydia woke me at six, her voice edgy with adrenaline. Sarah Peck had been brought into the Emergency Room around midnight. She had taken an overdose of sleeping pills, which combined with a high alcohol level, had put her in a coma. She was in critical condition and the next twenty-four hours, according to Lydia, would be touch and go.

The nurse on duty directed me to the ICU waiting room. Walking down the green linoleum hall past the patient rooms, I realized my head no longer hurt. As I entered the waiting room, Rob Martin stared up at me.

"What are you doing here?" He looked like he hadn't slept in a week. There were dark circles under his eyes resembling smudges. His clothes were wrinkled and smelled musky.

"I came to see if there was anything I could do." In truth, I was feeling guilty about Sarah. I had pushed her hard, maybe too hard. "You look like you could use some coffee."

"I don't want anything, especially from you." For once, his anger toward me seemed justified.

"What happened?"

"I don't know. I found her passed out in her bed." He caught my look of surprise. "She left a message on my machine asking me to come over, no matter how late. There was something she wanted to tell me. I didn't get home from the conservation meeting until about ten-thirty. By the time I reached her place, she had already taken the pills." In the moment, his need to talk about what happened seemed to outweigh his dislike of me.

"Was there a note?" I asked, wondering if what Sarah needed to tell him had anything to do with those bones Salinger found. In a way, I felt as if Sarah had led me to them.

"No." He glared at me. "What did you say to her last night? You must have said something to make her take enough Valium to kill herself." He stopped. "My God!" He collapsed back against the chair, all the fight suddenly out of him. "I could lose her."

"Sarah told you about our meeting?"

"It was in her message." He looked away.

I let that fact register for a moment. "Did she also tell you she was the one who ran me off the road?"

"Sarah didn't run you off the road." He spoke so quietly that I wasn't sure I had heard him correctly.

"She admitted it to me."

He ran his fingers through his red hair. "She did that for me."

"For you?" I got it, I just couldn't believe what he was admitting.

"You ran me off the road?"

"Sarah was protecting me. She didn't want me taking the blame. She was afraid that you'd go to Stevens, get me fired. She didn't think you'd do anything to her."

"But why would you run me off the road in the first place?"

"I didn't mean to run you off the road. I was only trying to scare you so you'd back off Sarah. I felt I had to protect her from you, even though she didn't want my protection. She said that it was too late for anyone's protection."

He put his face in his hands and shook his head. "I should have done something. If only I'd known. But Sarah never said anything. All those years, she never said anything. It's that old bastard's fault."

"Carl Peck?"

"Who else? After we moved back from Chicago, he was drinking heavily. He'd go into these rages. He didn't even care if I was around. Called Sarah a slut and a loser, right in front of me. I should have done something, at least said something. Maybe if I had, she wouldn't have done this."

"Done what? Taken the pills, you mean?"

He turned his head slowly in my direction and looked at me with such contempt that I felt a flush creep up my neck and spread across my face. "You just never quit, do you? Why don't you just get the hell out of here!"

Eva Peck stood in the waiting room doorway. As before, she was dressed in black. However, this time she was wearing a loose-fitting wool suit, black suede heels and black hose. How had she mustered the presence of mind to dress so impeccably?

Martin stood up. "Has there been any change?"

"No, no change. She's still in a coma." Eva walked over to us. "So nice of you to come, Leigh." She stared at my bruised forehead, which was now a pasty purplish-yellow. "Oh dear, did you have an accident?" Her sense of propriety was unnerving.

"You might say that, but I'm fine." I didn't look at Martin. "Is there anything I can get for you?"

She sat down next to Martin, pulling primly on the hem of her skirt. "A cup of tea would be nice, if it's not too much trouble."

"No trouble at all."

"Would you mind getting it from the cafeteria? I can't stomach that tea from the vending machine. No sugar, but just a little cream."

When I returned to the waiting room with the tea, Eva was holding Martin's hand.

"All we can do now is pray," she said, catching my eye as I entered the room. "It's up to the Lord now. How much was the tea, dear?"

"Don't worry about it," I said, handing her the tea. I looked at my watch. It was 9:10 a.m. I was late for my appointment at the police station. "I'm going to have to go," I told her.

"You haven't seen Sarah. Make sure you see her before you leave."

Martin shook his head. "Eva, they only let relatives see ICU patients."

"Leigh is Sarah's friend, and she took the time to come here." She addressed me. "Tell the nurse you're her good friend. It's the same thing as a relative."

I couldn't understand Eva's insistence that I see Sarah. Especially since she had the mistaken idea that her daughter could stand me. Besides, the last thing I wanted to do was see Sarah Peck attached to mega machines and fighting for her life.

"I really can't right now. I'm late for work."

"Mr. Stevens will understand, won't he, Rob?" She didn't wait for Martin's answer but stood up, took me by the arm and guided me to the hallway. We stopped in front of the nurses' station.

"Julie, this is Leigh Girard, she's Sarah's dear friend from Chicago. Is it all right if she visits Sarah?"

"Sure. Her room is the second unit on the left."

"Oh, I'll go with her. We won't stay long."

There was no graceful way to avoid accompanying Eva into Sarah's room. The only explanation that I could come up with for this bizarre behavior was that the strain of her husband's death and now Sarah's suicide attempt was taking a toll on her. I had seen similar irrational behavior in times of grief. Two women from my cancer group had died, and I had gone through the grieving process with their families.

"There's my little girl," Eva whispered as we stood at the foot of her daughter's bed. The sight of Sarah in a coma clutched at my stomach. Her black hair fanned out starkly against the white pillow. She was hooked up to a heart monitor, oxygen tank, and several IVs. The blipping sound of the monitors bored into my brain.

"Doesn't she look peaceful?" Eva asked me. She moved beside the bed, careful to avoid the multiple wires. "She'll always be a little girl to me." She bent down and kissed Sarah's forehead.

I remained rooted at the foot of the bed. I could endure this if Eva could. "She'll come out of it, Mrs. Peck. She's strong." This was all I could think to say, lame as it sounded.

She stroked Sarah's cheek. "Do you think so? Do you really think so?"

I looked at my watch as I entered the hospital elevator: 9:30. I pushed the button for the third floor. I was already thirty minutes late for my appointment at the police department, so I figured a few more minutes wouldn't make any difference. Lorraine Birch should be back from vacation and on duty, hopefully. I needed to focus on something other than Sarah Peck swaddled to machines.

The third floor station nurse pointed to an elderly woman stacking medicine trays onto a cart.

"I only work part-time now," Lorraine explained to me

when I told her I'd been trying to catch her at work. Her face looked like crumpled linen, and her short hair was bleached a shade of yellow that didn't exist in nature.

"You don't have any other jobs?"

"Oh, goodness, no." She laughed. "I only work here now and then. You know my social security check isn't much. I've been a registered nurse for over forty years. Started out in the emergency room."

"Well, I hope you can help me with a small detail that I bet didn't slip by you. I understand that Joyce Oleander visited someone in the hospital the day before her discharge. Do you happen to know who that was?"

She turned to face me directly, and looked into my eyes for a moment. Then answered, "I'm not even going to ask why you want to know that. But, yes, I do know." She paused, still holding my eyes with her own. "She visited Carl Peck. Joyce and Carl's daughter, Sarah, were friends when they were younger. She was probably paying her respects. Joyce was like that."

"How did she seem after that visit?"

"Seem?" She considered the question. "Let me see. That was the day before she was discharged. Now that I think about it, it was really after her visit with Carl that she became so down. Like all the air had been sucked out of her. In the morning, she was okay. I remember because that morning I told her about Carl being in the hospital, mainly since I recalled that she and Sarah had been friends."

"Did she say anything to you about the visit?"

"No, not really. But . . ." she hesitated.

I waited.

"At the time, I didn't think anything about it. But later, after what she did, I wondered."

"Wondered about what?" I couldn't help feeling exasperated by the convoluted way Nurse Birch was getting to the heart of the matter. But I kept myself in check.

"I wondered if maybe she had been trying to ask for help. You know, one of those warning signs. She said to me, 'Well, I thought I'd feel relief when it finally was over, but I don't.' I guess she was talking about her surgery."

"What else could she have been talking about?" My turn to wonder.

"That's what I'm saying. What else, indeed?"

18

The vision of Sarah Peck lying in a coma haunted me all day. In a fog, I drove to the police station, gave a formal statement about the discovery of the bones, and returned to work. Deputy Ferry assured me that as soon as the medical examiner had completed his examination, he'd call me with the results. He told me he figured the bones had probably been there for hundreds of years. I had been dismissed with the pat attitude of "Don't call us, we'll call you." Chet Jorgensen was off for the day, so I couldn't enlist his help. If Ferry thought he could get rid of me that easily, he was wrong. I wasn't going to be ignored.

For the remainder of the day, I worked on a particularly disturbing story about a Sturgeon Bay man who had hung his Labrador retriever for biting a seventeen-year-old boy. Stevens had finally given me an assignment that didn't involve someone's demise, at least not a human's anyway. I ended the story with a direct quote from the man in an attempt to explain his action to the judge. "I'd told him the next time he bit someone, I'd kill him. So when he bit the neighbor boy, I got angry. I took the dog to a nearby tree and hung him until he died." I was so disgusted I wanted to throttle the guy with my bare hands. The judge let him off with a fine and a warning.

The story left me in a dark mood. When we start hanging

dogs, I thought, we've sunk pretty low on the evolutionary scale. And human or dog, it was still a death story. I was beginning to feel like an albatross. In my short tenure in Door, there'd been one suicide, one attempted suicide, and one suspicious poisoning. If it wasn't bad karma, the only other explanation I could think of was that maybe a lot of death and mayhem had been swept under the carpet over the years. If so, perhaps Stevens hadn't been kidding when he compared the Door villages to medieval hamlets.

I kept expecting Stevens to appear and start asking questions, but either he wasn't in or he was avoiding me. I didn't bother asking Marge where he was because I didn't want to talk to him about Sarah.

Marge took one look at my bruise and, with unexpected tact, did not ask me about it. Neither one of us said anything about the women's group either. She did ask, "Did you hear about Sarah? And would you like to contribute money for flowers?"

I answered yes to both questions, and beat a hasty retreat toward home.

As I drove down Highway 42, an overwhelming urge to call Tom came over me. I needed someone to reassure me, and maybe in the process, also absolve me of what I was feeling about Sarah. Maybe I'd start by saying, "Guess what Salinger found?" Or, "They've got me writing obits. Who'd-a figured?"

I looked at my watch. It was 3:35 p.m. Tom would be at work. I knew how the conversation would go. He'd ask how I was doing. I'd say fine. Then the usual silence would fall between us. We'd both tell each other to take care, and that would be the end of it. There was no point to seeking out this predictable disappointment.

If it was comfort I was seeking, I knew I'd have to find it

elsewhere. I turned left on Clark Lake Road and headed toward White Fish Dunes. The day had turned bright, but windy. I was craving the purity of white sand beach and the openness of possibility. Moving past the open fields, I watched a cluster of dark, iridescent birds. They scattered upward as if they'd been thrown into the sky, and then returned again, arranging themselves on a telephone wire in perfect symmetry. I envied their clarity.

The pavement quickly turned to gravel, and trees crowded the serpentine road. Around the second bend, I slowed my car and peered through an opening among evergreens to see if the gray-scarred fishing boat was still anchored in front of the disheveled cottage with no curtains. No disappointment here: everything still in place as I remembered it from my hikes here with Tom.

When I pulled into the parking lot near the dunes, I saw only one other car—a black convertible with the top down. I got out of my truck, zipped up my coat, pulled on my purple hat and gray wool gloves and headed toward the beach. At the entrance to the beach sat the slate-blue Nature Center. Like a squat lighthouse, the weathered building overlooked Lake Michigan. Although the Center was closed, I could see a telescope perched in the eastern window: ready to spot anyone in distress, or scan a splendid sunrise.

"Doesn't it remind you of Cape Cod?" Tom had asked the last time we were in Door together. Well before my cancer diagnosis.

I quickened my pace and jogged down the wooden slat path toward the beach, careful not to step off the path and walk on the sand dunes. Where the slats ended stood a warning sign: "Casual footsteps take a toll on dunes." Even here, I couldn't escape reminders of the human capacity to destroy.

There was a fierce wind blowing from the east. Whitecaps were breaking close to shore, and for a moment, the brilliant sunlight blinded me. I looked in the distance where the beach curved and saw that the water was silvered with light. This was what I had come for: a vista so beautiful, it frightened. As I trotted toward it, my left chest area began a vague aching.

"Phantom ache," I told myself. Then those garish colors came back to me, the ones I'd seen last night as I stepped out of the bath and looked into the mirror. This area of my chest wasn't healing as quickly as the bruise on my forehead. "But it wouldn't," I reasoned. "It's been traumatized by the chemo and the mastectomy. Makes sense the tissue wouldn't respond as fast."

I turned into the wind. The cold bit into my fingers. I took my gloves off. The cold on my skin was a good clean feeling making the moment sharper, more real.

The waves were high, and the water as green as bottle glass. I looked inland at the rim of trees high on the dunes—the pines gave the landscape a rugged quality that broke through the monotony of maples and oaks. The birch trees drew my eye. They seemed to radiate their own light, even though their white bark was splotched with grays, greens, and blacks where it peeled away. That last time Tom and I had been here, I had asked a naturalist at the Nature Center why the birches peel.

She had answered, "They have to shed their outer bark to accommodate new growth, sort of like a snake sheds its skin, but not all at once. More gradually, over time."

When I reached the wooden lookout shed halfway down the beach, my fingers were numb. As I climbed the steps, I noticed that the sand here ran with fine lines, like cracks in old porcelain. I was somewhat surprised that the water reached this far inland.

I sat on the edge of the lookout platform rubbing my hands together. The view was stunning. The water extended out until it became sky, or maybe it was the other way around. I looked up to see white clouds moving fast across the horizon. This was a sure indication that the peninsula was in for yet another sudden change in weather. Snow, maybe? I watched in fascination as one determined seagull struggled in the stiff wind to right its wings.

Finally, I put my gloves back on and shoved my hands inside my pockets. As the warmth returned, I let myself think about what I had been trying to avoid: Sarah Peck, Rob Martin, and what they might have done together.

Martin had the knowledge, and Sarah had the motive. But if they did poison Carl Peck, how did they do it without Peck knowing? Sarah was a chef. She could have prepared a special meal for him, and Martin could have added the crucial ingredient. If it was loaded with mushrooms, they knew Eva wouldn't eat it.

And if Sarah had helped poison her father, that might explain her attempted suicide. The guilt had overwhelmed her. Or maybe she didn't know that Martin had planned to kill Peck. Maybe he told her the mushrooms would only make her father sick, that it was only right that he should suffer for the years he'd abused her. Martin certainly was obsessed with Sarah, and probably would do anything for her. Was he obsessed enough to commit murder? I wondered just how far he would go to win her back.

No, that didn't make sense. Why kill Sarah's father now? She'd hated him for a long time. Unless something happened recently that made her snap. I shook my head. As I tried to match up the puzzle pieces, something was missing.

Joyce Oleander: how did she fit into this? She had visited Carl Peck the day he died. Lorraine Birch said she'd come back from that exchange seeming depressed. Joe Stillwater said Joyce had been distracted. What had Joyce meant when she had said she thought she'd feel relief when it was over, but she didn't? Was she talking about her surgery or was it something else? And why had she committed suicide? Two friends, both prone to suicide by overdose. What were the odds?

There was something I wasn't seeing. Sarah and Joyce had been friends in high school. Sarah had attended Joyce's funeral. Had Joyce somehow been involved in poisoning Carl Peck? Given him something when she visited him? If she did, what was her motive?

And did any of this have anything to do with those bones? I didn't believe in coincidences. Sarah Peck chose that cave— South Heaven. She'd been there before. Why had she gone there the same night she attempted suicide? Then there was Renn Woulff. He certainly had a motive for killing his former business partner. According to him, Peck had cheated him out of money owed, which ruined him. But he didn't seem to have the wherewithal to commit such a clever crime. Maybe he had moments of lucidity, between binges. Maybe he had had one long enough to poison Peck.

What about Peck's reputation as a skirt chaser? Again, that was the past. Even though he still tried to chase women, what woman in her right mind would find an aging alcoholic attractive?

I gently massaged my forehead. Maybe Deputy Jorgensen was right. No crime had been committed. Carl Peck was a careless drunk who made a critical mistake—one that had been in the making for years, whenever he mixed alcohol with selecting mushrooms that could prove lethal. Why was I so intent on proving that Carl Peck had been murdered? Why couldn't I let this alone?

A shadow suddenly darkened the sand beside me, and I

looked up. There was Jake Stevens, grinning down at me. He was clad in shiny, weather-resistant black pants and a matching parka. He wasn't wearing a hat or gloves. His loose hair reached his shoulders.

"You never come when you say you'll come," he began, quoting a poem. "But on the other hand, you do come."

I interrupted him. "One of yours?"

"Frank O'Hara," he said, sitting down next to me.

" 'Do not go gentle into this good night. Just go'. Leigh Girard." I was grumpy that he had broken into my solitude.

"Has anyone told you you've got a nasty attitude, woman?"

"It's been mentioned."

A silence fell between us as we watched the waves shimmer and roll toward the shore.

"What are you doing here?" he asked.

"It was on my way home."

"No, I mean here in Door. What made you give up the consolations too lovely to leave?"

He was nothing if not persistent. And I wished he'd stop annoying me by quoting poetry.

I could feel his eyes studying my profile. "Let's say I needed a change," I answered, turning toward him. His eyes were cerulean blue, and the irises were rimmed in black.

"For now, that's good enough. But don't expect to get off that easy the next time." He reached down and picked up some sand, let it run through his fingers.

"What about you? What keeps you here?" I asked.

"The winters."

I laughed.

"No, I'm serious. The winters here are unforgiving. The tourists take off before their tails go numb, most of the shops and restaurants close, and the landscape goes stark."

"And these are reasons you stay?" He had piqued my curiosity.

"The change makes me feel alive. No distractions. Just me and this harsh place." He read the doubt in my face. "If you make it through the winter, I guarantee you will discover something about yourself you never suspected. And not necessarily something you want to know." He moved so close to me that I could feel the warmth of his breath on my face.

"What have you found out?" I asked, looking directly into those blue eyes.

"I like living alone." He put his fingers under my chin and pulled my face toward his. "Living alone, not being alone," he added, as if I had asked for clarification.

I knew what was coming, and I didn't pull away. The kiss was part of the wind and the sun, the white beach, the ache in my chest. It was quick and light and held a multitude of questions.

"What a relief to get that over with," I sighed. "I'm never sure when to kiss the boss, or where."

His mouth curled into a slow grin. "You're nothing if not perplexing, Girard." For a moment I thought he was going to kiss me again. Instead, he stared out at the water. "You heard about Sarah Peck?"

I thought I'd probably bruised his vanity. "I saw her this morning at the hospital."

"I don't want her suicide attempt reported in the paper. If she doesn't make it, then we'll print something."

"Okay," I conceded. He was protecting her.

"Your head looks better. Find out who ran you off the road?"

"Sarah told me last night that she did it. But this morning at the hospital, Rob Martin took credit for it. He claimed he

173

was protecting her, said something about his wanting me to leave Sarah alone." I wanted to see his reaction.

"You really have a talent for pissing people off, Leigh."

The kiss seemed to have put us on a first name basis. For now, I let it slide. "Sarah also told me she's glad her father's dead."

He didn't look surprised. "Lots of people hate their parents."

"She said that he should have died years ago and put everyone out of their misery, that he'd ruined a lot of lives."

He let out a deep breath. "Where are you going with this?"

"Don't you think such comments might suggest a motive for murder?"

"Slow down. No one's proved there's been a murder. Besides, even if Carl was murdered, I don't see Sarah as the culprit."

"Maybe you don't want to see her in that light."

He took another deep breath and blew it out. But didn't offer any further defense of Sarah Peck.

"I'm sure you're quite aware how angry and erratic Sarah is. And I'm not sure I believe Martin. Sarah could have run me off the road."

He still didn't answer me. Instead, he stood up and brushed off his sweat pants. The sun was sinking into the water and purpling the horizon.

"It's getting cold. Let's head back."

I followed him down the steps of the shed and onto the beach. He obviously wanted the discussion to be over, but I wasn't quite ready for that.

"You have to admit that if Carl Peck was murdered, his daughter is a strong suspect."

He walked faster, more resolute, back toward the parking lot. I couldn't keep up with him.

"You wouldn't want someone to get away with murder!" I shouted toward his retreating back.

"Depends!" he shouted back.

I stopped trying to gain any ground on him. "On what?"

He kept marching on, right up to his car. "On whether they deserved it," he answered, opening the convertible door and then slamming it shut.

On the drive north down the dark highway, it occurred to me that I had forgotten to tell Stevens about the bones.

19

"Why didn't you tell me someone ran you off the road?" Lydia asked, as she followed me into the cottage. She had been waiting for me when I pulled into the drive at home. She must have come from the shop, because she was wearing a long, black silk dress threaded with silver. A matching ribbon kept her chestnut hair off her face, and her silver snake earrings had crystal tails. There must have been seven rings on her fingers.

I switched on the lights, and let Salinger out the door.

"You're mad because I didn't call you after the meeting?" She took off her suede jacket and flung it across a chair.

"I'm not mad, Lydia." I really wasn't. A little disappointed, perhaps, but I was used to that.

"Good, then that's settled. And I did let you know about Sarah. By the way, she's out of the coma and should be discharged from the hospital Sunday."

"That was a quick recovery. I take it there's no permanent damage?"

"There doesn't appear to be. Got any food in the house?" She went into the kitchen.

I followed her, unsure as to what might be decomposing in the refrigerator. There were three pieces of leftover pizza, half a head of wilted lettuce, low cal Italian dressing, and a bottle of chardonnay. In the freezer, I had a gallon of chocolate chip ice cream that was three-quarters full.

"Does anyone know why she attempted suicide?" I asked her.

"That I don't know." She peered over my shoulder into the refrigerator. "Well, all the basic food groups seem to be here."

"You seem pretty casual about it. Has she ever tried anything like this before?"

She reached over me and pulled out the half-full bottle of wine. "Not that I know about."

"Do you think this had anything to do with her father's death?" I decided not to discuss my suspicions about Sarah. Lydia's talent for exaggeration would only confuse the issue.

"Who knows? I've stopped trying to figure her out." She took the pizza from me and popped it into the microwave.

Lydia's attitude perplexed me. Normally, she'd be squeezing every bit of drama from the situation. Could she also be feeling some guilt about Sarah? "Is something wrong, Lydia?"

The microwave buzzer went off. "Nothing food couldn't fix." She opened the microwave door and pulled out the pizza. "Let's dig in."

After I'd lit a fire and fed Salinger, I settled in front of the fireplace with my cold pizza.

"How did you find out that someone ran me off the road?"

"Marge," Lydia answered, putting her plate on the coffee table. "And what's this I hear about you finding human bones in some cave?" Lydia was waiting to spring this on me. "Don't look so surprised, Chet Jorgensen and I are bridge partners."

She might as well have said that she and Chet had split the

atom. "Whoa. Let me see if I can really connect these dots: Jorgensen mentioned in the same breath with bridge. Don't you have to be able to count for bridge?"

Lydia laughed. "So you were fooled by his 'golly gee, shucks' demeanor. But let's get back to those bones."

"Really not a lot to tell. I was out hiking in Peninsula State Park and Salinger found the bones in one of the caves off Eagle Trail."

Lydia raised an eyebrow. "What were you and that dog of yours doing in those caves at night?"

"I followed Sarah Peck there."

"Oh, this is too good! Back up and start from the beginning. Why were you following Sarah?" Lydia was practically licking her lips with anticipation.

"The night Sarah attempted suicide, I was at the park with Salinger. I was about to go for a hike when Sarah showed up. I had a hunch she might have been the person who ran me off the road. And I wanted to find out if I was right. So when I saw her take off down Eagle Trail, I followed her."

Lydia raised an eyebrow. "You followed her in the dark, down a treacherous, secluded trail? Really Leigh, I'm beginning to think you're one of those people who gets off on danger. Ever hear of a phone?"

"Okay, I know it sounds stupid now. But she refused to talk to me. At the time, catching her off guard seemed the best way to get a straight answer from her."

"And did you?" Lydia refilled her glass with wine.

"Yes and no. She admitted running me off the road. But when I talked to Rob Martin at the hospital, he said Sarah was covering for him, that he had run me off the road."

A few drops of wine spilled on Lydia's dress. "I'll bet it was the other way around. Martin was covering for Sarah.

She was furious at you when she left the women's group."
Lydia dabbed at the wine stain with a paper napkin.
"Frankly, I think she's quite capable of having run you off the
road, and possibly more violence than that."

It was obvious that Lydia's assessment was colored by her
lingering feelings for Martin. "Whatever," I said, not wanting
to pursue it. "Getting back to the bones. Salinger dug up
what looked like the human bones of an infant from one of the
caves. The police think they've probably been there for hundreds of years."

"Wait, let me guess." Lydia put up one of her ring-
spangled hands. "You don't agree with them. You think there
is some ubiquitous killer loose on the peninsula who is mur-
dering babies and old men."

"I didn't say that." I felt defensive. "But you have to
admit, it's odd that those bones were in the very cave Sarah
led me to."

Lydia tucked her legs up and pulled her silvery skirt over
her feet. "What's odd is that you found them."

"What are you saying?" I asked, daring her to finish.

"Nothing. Just stay away from cemeteries, especially when
the moon's full, or the townspeople may get a little suspicious."

"I'll try to remember that." There was a strident sound to
my voice.

"Leigh, it's a joke. Chill already! Has a doctor looked at
that bump on your forehead?" She touched the black stone
pendant around her neck.

"No need. It's fine." I finished my glass of chardonnay.

"At least let me take a look at it." Before I could protest,
she was off the sofa and poking at my head. "From what I can
see, it's healing, but you should have an MRI."

"It's okay, now sit down." She was making me nervous.

She continued to stand over me. "What about your chest?"

I felt my face flush. A person had no privacy on this damn peninsula. "Lydia, please sit down, or I will be mad at you."

She wasn't letting up. "Which side is the bruise on?"

"The left. Now let it go."

I got up and poured myself another glass of wine.

"That's where you had the mastectomy, isn't it?"

I steadied my hand so I could sip my wine without spilling. The acidic dryness stung my nose. "I don't know what you're talking about."

"That day at the hospital when you fainted, your bra shifted up as I lifted you off the floor. I felt under the prosthesis."

I looked skeptical.

"I guess I didn't tell you that I used to work with breast cancer patients until I burned out," she added.

"No, you didn't." Anger flooded my cheeks.

"Leigh, I understand if you don't want to talk about it."

"There's nothing to talk about, Lydia. So drop it." I was shaking with panic. I felt trapped and cornered. It took all my self-control to remain rooted in place.

"I'm only going to say one more thing, and then I will drop it."

I steeled myself for the inevitable lecture on how I should have the area looked at, that I couldn't be too careful, that since I'd had cancer, I was at greater risk with bruises, blah blah blah. I'd listen to her, politely, end the evening, and that would be the last I'd see of Lydia Crane.

She stared into the fire. "I hope you haven't come here to die."

A storm started around midnight, rattling the windows with gusts of wind and snow. Salinger slept fitfully at the end of my bed, punctuated by her jerking legs and deep sighs that

I envied. I had skipped my nightly foraging through Hawthorne's shadowy forest of secret evils, and decided that Hemingway would be a better antidote for insomnia. But after reading all the Nick Adams stories and "Big Two-Hearted River: Part I and Part II," twice, I was still awake.

My mind kept circling back to Sarah Peck. She wasn't going to die. Somehow she had survived her attempt to annihilate herself. I had to talk to her, find out why she had done this drastic thing. I'd go see her on Monday, make her talk to me. With a heavy sigh of my own, I turned off the table lamp and snuggled under the down comforter.

I was in a room with no ceiling. Salinger was standing next to me. It was cold, and the sky was white as snow. Suddenly a car pulled up, and two figures got out. One had fangs like a vampire. I couldn't see the other one's face. But I knew that they had come for me.

I tried to finish the work I had been given: to run blank paper through a printing machine. It was crucial that I read what was printed on the paper. The two figures came ever closer. The one with the fangs had his mouth open, poised to puncture my throat. He was going to drain my blood from me, to suck my life away so that he could live.

I was shivering in a cold sweat. Now they were inside the room. I could see that the other figure was a woman, but I couldn't make out her face because she had turned into a cat. The man lunged toward me, seizing me by the throat. As he sank his fangs into me, I shoved him away with all my strength. I grabbed Salinger. Suddenly Salinger and I floated effortlessly above the scene, and the two figures receded.

I awoke drenched in sweat. The comforter was bunched at my feet, and Salinger was snoring on the pillow next to me. I looked over at the clock: 4:01 a.m. I stared up at the beamed ceiling and let the tears run into my hair.

Lydia's earlier comment came back into my mind. As valiantly as I had fought to survive the cancer, had I come to Door to die? Was I seeking a place to die a clean death free of the messiness of a husband and friends? On some instinctive level, did I believe it was too late? The cancer docs reassured me again and again that I was free of the cancer, as far as they could tell; assured me they had caught it in time. Yet my own G.P. had missed the lump during my annual checkup. I was the one who had found it, by then as big as a golf ball. My body had betrayed me, and I could never count on it again, no matter what they cut out of it or shot into it. This body was a time bomb, and a volcano.

I rolled over toward Salinger and pulled her close. She half-opened her eyes, licked my face and went back to sleep. It was some time before I could erase the picture of Carl Peck biting into my neck, his dark hair slicked back, his gray eyes impenetrable as stone, his callused hands on my skin.

20

Saturday, November 11, Present day

I pulled into Lot 3 of Newport State Park. The snow had stopped, as if it exhausted itself and needed to take a breather. The lake was running hard and fast up the snow-crusted beach. I wrapped a wool scarf across my face and headed toward Europe Bay Trail.

I had awakened at seven with the aftertaste of the vampire dream still strong. A heavy snow had fallen overnight that blocked the doors and rimmed the windows. Though the radio predicted more snow by afternoon, I decided to head up the peninsula. I was going to suffocate if I had to stay in the cottage, where that dream invaded. I needed escape.

Europe Bay Trail partially paralleled Europe Bay, beginning at Lake Michigan and turning back at Europe Lake. Except for the Lynd Point spur, Europe Trail was sheltered by both evergreens and deciduous trees. I knew it well, because Tom and I had hiked it many times during our vacation visits here. It had a picturesque loop called Lynd Point that jutted out toward Lake Michigan. Back home in a box in the bottom of the hall closet were dozens and dozens of pictures I'd taken off Lynd Point. Whenever I'd asked, Tom had patiently posed, giving the stark clean landscape the human element I desired.

The hike was hard going. The snow reached over the tops

of my hiking boots and soon caked the outside of my thermal socks. But the cold felt honest.

I turned right off Europe Bay Trail toward Lake Michigan at the Lynd Point spur. As I reached the beach area, a blast of wind took my breath away. I stood stark still for a moment. Though the sun was blinding, it added no warmth. I shielded my eyes and looked out at the horizon. Sky and water made a single white sheet, distinguished only by movement. Suddenly I sensed that I wasn't alone. I turned around.

Behind me near the rim of evergreens stood a man. From this distance, I couldn't make out his features but it was obvious what he was doing. He was urinating. Either he hadn't seen me, or he didn't care that I saw him. He was standing sideways and taking his sweet time. Finally he zipped up his pants and turned in my direction. For a second, I thought he was going to move toward me. Instead he flipped me off and then abruptly marched down the trail away from the beach.

My heart was beating a little too fast. He had seen me, and he hadn't cared. His hostile gesture confirmed that. I felt I had two choices. I could scurry back to my truck, or I could continue hiking. I had only been walking for about fifteen minutes. I had come here to clear my head, and I was not going to be intimidated by some loser. So I trudged forward down the beach.

By the time Lynd Trail turned inland back to Europe Bay Trail, I was beyond cold. The trees' enclosure offered some relief. I looked back over my shoulder, still wary of the brazen snow whizzer. All I saw was a white canopy of trees bending over the trail. I pushed onward, determined to finish the entire 9.2-mile trek.

When I reached the thickest part of the woods, I heard something moving behind me. I told myself it was probably a squirrel. From the many hikes I'd taken with Tom, I learned that small animal sounds are amplified in the deep woods. Whatever it was, it was coming closer. I quickened my pace. Then I heard a shout and began running. The snow slogged my boots as I headed around a stone mound, and the pursuer was too fast. I felt a yank on the hood of my parka as I was pulled backwards. I lost my balance and fell hard. It took me a full minute before I realized that it was Rob Martin standing over me.

"Why didn't you stop!"

"I'm alone in the woods, and some maniac is chasing me. Would you stop?" I struggled to my feet and brushed the snow off my jeans, trying to regain my dignity. "Besides, the last time I saw you, you were telling me to get the hell out."

"You shouldn't be here by yourself." He shoved his hands under his arms.

I was in no mood for the helpless woman routine. "You made that perfectly clear on the beach."

"On the beach? I haven't been on the beach."

I looked at him quizzically. I hadn't gotten a good look at the urinating man's attire. Though I thought he was wearing a hat. Martin was hatless. I couldn't be sure either way.

"What are you doing here?" I asked, annoyed with myself. "I thought you'd still be at the hospital."

He ignored my ploy to change the subject. "Did something happen on the beach?"

"I ran into some loser taking a piss. He flipped me off."

"And you thought it was me?" He burst out laughing.

"A logical deduction," I answered, "considering you ran me off the road a few nights ago. That is, if it was really you." I didn't think any of this was that funny.

He stopped laughing. "I said it was me."

"By the way, I never did get a chance to ask you. Did you even check to see if I was breathing before you left me there?"

185

His face went blank. "I told you I never meant to run you off the road. I panicked. It was a stupid thing to do. I'm sorry."

Martin's hostility and anger, I could deal with. His contriteness threw me off guard.

"You've got every right to alert the police," he continued. "But I hope you won't. Sarah needs me right now."

So that was his motive. Everything for Martin circled back to Sarah Peck. "I'll think about it." I pointed to his reporter's notebook, which was sticking out of his pocket. "Doing research for your column?"

He looked down. "Always. Aren't you? That is, always pursuing some angle?" He left me with the rhetorical question, and started walking down trail.

"I hear Sarah's out of the coma." I followed after him. "Has she said anything to you about why she attempted suicide?"

He stopped and turned so abruptly that I almost ran into him. "Sarah's been through enough. She needs to be left alone." There was a clear threat in his last comment.

"Look, I'm only trying to help."

He grabbed my arm. Through the layers of down filler, I could feel the strength of his grip. I was grateful he had clenched my right arm and not the left, where I was still so sore. "Let go of me," I growled in a low voice.

His face was close enough for me to see gold glints in the red stubble on his cheeks. "What did you think I was going to do to you?" His tone was neutral, as if he was asking me what I had had for breakfast.

"What do you mean?" I could feel his fingers loosening on my arm.

"Before, when you were running."

"I had no idea, since I didn't know it was you chasing me."

186

"But now you know it was me. Think about that."

I waited until he disappeared into the woods before I headed back to the parking lot. Maybe it had been him on the beach.

Nearing my truck, I spotted a dark blue, rusted-out pickup parked at the other end of Lot 3. My stomach clutched at the Woulff Orchards sign hanging in the back of the cab. I looked around quickly, but didn't see Renn Woulff. Hurriedly, I jerked open my truck door and jumped in. I jammed the key in the starter, revved the engine, and put the truck in reverse. A thump sounded. I looked to my right. There he was, grinning at me through the passenger side window. Before I could react, he pressed his open mouth on the window and ran his tongue up and down the glass, smearing it with his saliva.

"Get the hell away from my truck, you drunken pervert, or I'll run you over!"

He pulled away slowly. "You know you want it, baby! Don't fight it!" he yelled. His hand went for the door handle.

I pushed my foot down hard on the gas and tore out of the lot, slipping and sliding on the snow-slick surface. When I looked in the rear view mirror, Woulff was standing perfectly still, still wearing that shit-faced grin and giving me the finger, for the second time that morning.

21

Monday, November 13, Present day

"Miss Girard?"

"Yes," I answered groggily into the phone. I looked over at the clock. It was eight a.m. I had slept through my alarm.

"This is Deputy Chet Jorgensen. Officer Ferry asked me to call you, about them bones ya found. Only got the preliminary report here, from the pathologist. He sent 'em on to a forensic anthropologist for further analysis."

I waited for him to continue. I heard a rustling of papers. Then he cleared his throat. "The bones are probably those of a human newborn. Okay, then. Looks like ya were right there. About 'em being human and all."

"What about the age?"

"Newborn," he repeated.

"No, how old were the bones?"

Again I waited, and Deputy Chet took his time to answer. "Like I said, gotta wait till we hear further from that forensic anthropologist. Could take one, maybe two months."

"But you're going to investigate this, right?"

"Ahead of you on that. Already run it through missing persons. Didn't turn up nothin'."

"Is that it?" I was so frustrated that I actually pulled the phone away from my ear and looked at it cross-eyed.

"Till we hear from that forensic anthropologist, nothin' else we can do."

"This child was buried in a cave. Was there any sign of trauma?" I was now fully awake and wishing Jorgensen was here so I could shake some sense into his thick Viking brain.

He didn't say anything. I could hear voices in the background. "Hold on, there. Let a man finish."

I sighed deeply.

He lowered his voice. "The pathologist who first looked at the bones said something about the top of the head bein' caved in. But he wasn't goin' to speculate. So until we hear . . ."

I finished his sentence for him. "From the forensic anthropologist, there's nothing else you can do. There must be something else." I was beginning to think that if I ever wanted to commit a crime, Door County was the perfect place. The fact that the police felt crime didn't happen here seemed to make it so in their minds.

"Look, you do your job and let me do mine, okay then?" His tone was even, but I knew that he was annoyed.

"That's what I'm trying to do." I wasn't about to let him have the last word.

"We'll handle it."

"We'll see." I wasn't sure if he had heard me because the line went dead. I hung up the phone and called the paper. "Marge, it's Leigh. Is Stevens in?"

"Well, good morning, early bird." I didn't know if she was being sarcastic or not. "No, he's not in yet. What can I do you for?"

"Give him a message."

"Just a second, hon. Okay, shoot."

"Tell him I'll be a little late this morning. And that I've got the preliminary results on the post mortem examination." I hesitated, not sure how much to say about the post mortem.

"Now what post mortem examination would that be?" Marge asked. This time I knew she was being sarcastic.

"What one do you think?" She knew exactly what I was talking about.

"I'm only making sure you weren't working on something else, hon," she replied. "That's something, isn't it? You finding those bones. Makes you wonder how many bodies are buried in the woods around here."

Monday morning: I decided not to call Sarah Peck, but just drive over to her house. Freshly released from the hospital, I expected to find her home, and I wanted the element of surprise. Besides, I was pretty certain she would refuse to see me.

Eleven inches of snow had fallen over the weekend. This morning, a hard sun bleached the snow crystalline white. The blueness of the sky was blinding. In Chicago, the streets would already be aslosh in salt and dirty snow. I savored the open expanses of pure white.

Sarah lived just north of Bailey's Harbor, the more secluded side of the peninsula. The nature conservancy preserve, the Ridges Sanctuary, and various other pieces of protected land saved the Lake Michigan side from the quaint over-development of bayside villages like Egg Harbor and Fish Creek.

Unlike her parents' mailbox, Sarah's was stenciled with her name and address and edged with tiny, hand painted lady slipper orchids. Sarah's handiwork, no doubt. I pulled into her driveway and followed the winding, deeply wooded gravel road. Patterns of light splattered my windshield here and there, lifting the gloom created by the dense evergreens.

As my truck emerged into a clearing, it was struck by full sunlight. Immediately the feeling of claustrophobia lifted. I felt as if I'd stumbled into an alternative world. Ahead of me high on a bluff stood Sarah's house: one of those silver Airstream mobile homes from the fifties that slightly resembles an alien space ship. I climbed out of my truck and heard the familiar lapping of water. Sarah had wisely situated her glittering house so that it afforded a spectacular view of Lake Michigan.

As I ascended the gentle bluff toward the mobile home, I noticed a small cedar outbuilding several yards to the right of the trailer. It too, overlooked the water. I knocked several times at the front door of the Streamliner, but no one answered. Sarah had to be home, and in that small a trailer, she had to have heard me knocking. For whatever reason, she wasn't answering the door. I was about to leave when I caught the sound of music coming from the cedar house. As I walked toward it, I recognized Billie Holiday's smoky voice singing, "God Bless the Child."

The outbuilding was a structure of brown cedar shingles and glass windows. The wall of windows faced the lake in an expansive view of the water. Its whole purpose was to capture light. This was indeed a perfect studio for an artist. The vista was so dazzling, I had to shield my eyes as I looked out over the water. The lake flashed and rolled in azures and aquamarines of such changing translucence, I figured a person could spend a lifetime trying to capture it and never succeed. Everyday the canvas and the palate would be obstacles that had to be overcome, because the scene could only be interrupted, not translated.

Again no one answered my knock. I knew Sarah was inside. Against all propriety, I turned the front door knob. Though I was still uncomfortable with the idea of unlocked houses and keys left in car ignitions, I took advantage of the situation and walked in.

Sarah was standing before a wall-sized canvas that was bathed in light. Fiery yellows, raging reds, blasts of blue, garnet greens swirled over and off the edges of the canvas. Where there was no color, the white shone with an intensity that almost hurt my eyes. She didn't hear me come in, and I was so taken by the painting that I didn't announce myself. I looked from the canvas to the wall of windows. Then it struck me. She was painting the view from these windows, but the colors were all wrong. The serenity of the realistic scene had been blasted open to what Sarah must be seeing underneath.

The music tape clicked off, and I jumped. Sarah turned around to switch the tape and saw me. If she was surprised, she hid it well.

"I'm working," she said, grabbing another tape and slipping it into the recorder. Bob Seger's raspy voice scratched and rolled out around us.

"That's pretty powerful," I said.

She wiped her brush across a paint-smeared rag. It looked like blood.

She squeezed another color from a tube and swirled it on the palate with a knife. She wouldn't even look at me.

"It's definitely not your usual Door scene," I continued.

"Don't try and con me," she said, purpling the horizon with slashing strokes.

"Okay, I won't," I conceded. "Did your mother tell you I visited you in the hospital?"

"My mother says a lot of things, most of which make little sense." She had thickened the horizon in her painting until it looked like a barrier that kept the water quiet. Sarah wasn't going to let me ease into asking what I needed to know.

"What happened Friday night after you left me at the caves?"

She turned toward me with a hard stare. For the first time, I saw her in full light. Her face was drained of color, and her eyes had dark circles under them.

"Not interested in talking now. You know where the door is."

"I'm not going away, Sarah, until you tell me why you tried to kill yourself." My persistence matched the beat from Seger's drummer.

"I said, I'm not interested in talking." She turned back to the canvas.

I looked around the room. There were canvases everywhere, multiple paintings of this view from these widows in a variety of styles, from the realistic to the imaginary. It was as if she couldn't decide who she was or what she wanted to say.

There had to be a way to reach her, to get her to talk. "Rob feels responsible."

She put her brush down and stared out at the sunlit water. "He has nothing to feel responsible for."

"He thinks he should have done something." I hesitated, "About your father."

In the glare from the windows, her eyes were as flat as glass. "I repeat, what should he feel responsible for?"

"Your suicide attempt, he feels responsible for that."

"There was no suicide attempt."

"Then how do you explain the pills they pumped out of you?"

"I can't."

For some reason, I believed her. "Then tell me what you remember, what happened?"

"My memory's not too reliable, you know."

It sounded like she was talking about more than that night. "Why don't you let me decide that?"

She shrugged her shoulders. "I came home. Left a message on Rob's machine. Drank a bottle of wine. Couldn't fall asleep. So I took a few Valium. That's the last thing I remember. Satisfied?"

"How do you account for the rest of the pills?"

"How do I account for feeling nothing but anger since my father's death? How do I account for my mother's enormous grief for a man who belittled her and betrayed her every day of her life? I can't."

She picked up on my sense of shock at her frankness. "Can't you see I don't care? Doctor Porter thinks I had traumatic amnesia. He thinks I'm an alcoholic like my father. That I took the pills during a blackout. Maybe he's right."

She tossed the palate down on the worn wooden floor. Some of the paint spattered across the floor. I watched in fascination as she very slowly and purposely stroked the canvas with her right hand molding the colors, thinning them in some places, thickening them in others.

"Did you know that Van Gogh painted with his fingers?" she said. "Sometimes the paint on his canvas dripped on the floor. As if the painting was bleeding. Can you see it?"

"I can understand it."

"No, I asked if you can see it?"

"I think I can."

"You think." She smirked at me. "Then you can't see it."

"Maybe I need you to show me."

Her fingers swirled and streaked the paint as she talked. "It starts with a child and her nightmares. They're so frightening that sometimes they have to slap her to wake her. And she never knows when they'll come. And the nightmares never go away, even after she's an adult. Until finally she sees them in the daylight. And the funny thing is that after she sees them in the daylight, the nightmares stop. I mean the ones at night."

I waited for her to continue. "So maybe I did take those pills." The paint was running down her arm. She wiped her arm against her shirt, which now looked like another canvas. "He also ate it—the paint—Van Gogh."

"That's probably what made him crazy," I said.

She shook her head. "Yeah, you would think so." She licked a drop of blue paint from her index finger and smiled.

"Sarah, tell me the rest." For once, I held back. I would ask her about the bones later, when she didn't look as if she were made of air, more spirit than body.

She walked past me toward the door. "I'm tired," she said, and left.

I switched off her tape. I had let her go, hadn't called after her. How many others had done the same, I wondered. Just let her walk away carrying that immense pain, so they didn't have to know, didn't have to feel it too.

I turned to leave and knocked over several paintings resting against the wall. The first painting fell forward revealing the painting underneath. The painting was of an enclosed space—all done in muted shades, as if the room was in an attic or a basement. What riveted me to the painting was a doll, painted near a corner as if it had been thrown there. It didn't look like any doll I had ever played with. Although it had a thick child's body, it also had small pointy breasts. The doll wore a gingham dress, black Mary Jane shoes and lace anklets. Its dress was crumpled and pushed up. Under the dress, the doll had on black lacy panties, the skimpy seductive kind you see on Victoria Secret models. Its shiny dark hair was braided. The glass green eyes were open but dull, the dullness of death. The image was both repulsive and fascinating.

As I picked up the painting that had fallen, I noticed the words "Lynd Point Trail" painted on the back. I put the painting over the doll picture. It was a nature scene done in a realistic style. Sarah could evoke the Door scenes quite well. The painting was of the deep woods. Conifers, birches, and oaks crowded each other on the canvas. A filtered shaft of light pierced through an opening between two trees. I followed the light to where it fell on the forest floor and created a dim halo. I looked closer. It wasn't a halo of light, but a group of white mushrooms clustered at the foot of an oak. I was no expert but those mushrooms looked a lot like amanitas. Sarah had titled the piece, "Destroying Angels."

As I drove down Highway 57 toward Sturgeon Bay, the images in those two paintings kept flashing behind my eyes. It was becoming clear to me that the evidence in the death of Carl Peck, although circumstantial, was pointing to his daughter. If Sarah did poison her father, how had she done it? How did she get him to eat poisonous mushrooms? Her painting proved that she knew about amanitas and where to find them.

Then there was the suicide attempt. Had she become overwrought with guilt? Yet she claimed that she didn't remember taking the pills. I turned right abruptly on County E toward Egg Harbor. Lydia would know about traumatic amnesia. I'd call her from home, where I could be assured that neither Rob Martin nor Jake Stevens would be listening in the background.

"Calling to make an appointment for an MRI?" Lydia asked in her professional voice.

I had half expected the question, but it still rankled me. "I thought we had an agreement?"

"Okay, I give up, for now. What's going on?" I could hear her shuffling papers.

"Can you talk?"

"For a few minutes. You're up to something. I can hear it in your voice."

"I just saw Sarah."

"I have to say one thing for you, Leigh, you've got guts. Well, I know you weren't there to discuss the weather. So why did she try to kill herself? No one around here seems to have a clue."

"She claims that she doesn't remember taking the overdose. And that Dr. Porter attributes it to traumatic amnesia. Is that possible?"

"Considering the amount of alcohol in her system, it's very possible. What it amounts to is that she had a blackout. Quite common with alcoholics. That's why they never seem to remember dancing on the table or screwing their best friend's wife. Convenient, isn't it?"

"So, she could have tried to kill herself?"

"What else? Some other person overdosed her?" She took a deep breath. "Leigh, you're not still thinking Carl Peck was poisoned?"

"Why wouldn't I? There's Sarah's strange behavior the night of our meeting in the woods. And then the incident of someone running me off the road. And now her suicide attempt. If that is what it was . . ." I was holding back on the two paintings I discovered at her studio.

"Nothing you've said implicates Sarah. You're way off. You haven't even proven Peck was murdered, let alone that Sarah did it."

"Not yet."

197

"Maybe you should let this go, Leigh. For your own good. Just stop a minute and think. Maybe something else is going on here that has nothing to do with Sarah or her family."

"Like what?"

"Like you obsessing about the Pecks so you don't have to deal with your own problems."

A cold rage shot up through me. "Was it before or after you burned out in the cancer ward that you moved on to the psyche ward?"

"I'm going to pretend that I deserved that."

For a second, neither of us said anything. Then Lydia broke the silence.

"There's something I was going to ask you, but now I'm not certain this is the right time."

I should have apologized, but I couldn't. For some reason, her being angry at me felt good. "You brought it up so you might as well ask."

"I'm having a small dinner party at my place Friday. You're invited."

"Who's going to be there?" I was stalling, trying to figure out how to get out of it gracefully.

"The usual suspects: Sarah, Rob, Chet Jorgensen, and Jake Stevens. I'd think Jake's being there would be enough incentive for you."

"I'll think about it and let you know."

I was about to hang up, when she added, "Leigh, you'll see that as winter closes in up here, people get strange. They start to imagine all kinds of things. That's why it's important not to spend too much time alone."

"I said I'd think about it."

22

"So you finally dug up a murder, literally," Stevens confirmed, as he leaned back in his chair and stared out at the bay. His feet were propped up on the radiator. He wasn't wearing any shoes, and his one sock had a hole in the heel.

"My dog did," I responded, flopping down on the chair with the smallest pile of papers. That familiar soreness radiated across my chest and under my left arm. Although the pain had lessened, it was still with me.

My editor swirled around, folded his arms across his chest, and tilted his head sideways, as if he was trying to get another view of me. "Like I said, that dog suits you."

He wasn't mentioning our last exchange. So it was like that—whatever happened between us on the beach had been a mistake. We weren't going there again. "I've got the preliminary results on those bones," I announced, all business, and flipped open my notebook to the page where I'd written down what Deputy Jorgensen had told me.

Stevens rocked back and forth in his chair as he recited: "Human, newborn. Possible trauma to the crown of the head. Bones sent to forensic anthropologist." He stopped rocking, picked up a pencil and stuck it into the back of his ponytail.

I closed my notebook. No need fighting over the effectiveness of the Door County grapevine. "Did Jorgensen also tell you who led me to that cave?"

"Sarah Peck. On the very night she tried to kill herself." He took the pencil back out of his hair and began moving it back and forth between his fingers.

"C'mon, Stevens. You're not going to tell me that's just a coincidence."

He raised one eyebrow and gave me that sideways look again. "Girard, do you do it on purpose or does it just happen to you?"

"What?" I asked, knowing he was going to tell me anyway.

"This talent you have for trouble. You're like the eye of an endless swirling storm. Debris is flying all around you, but somehow you stay in the center, serenely watching things get blown to bits."

He put the pencil down and leaned toward me, making me wish I was invisible. "I'm curious. What's it like in there? What do you see on that private inner screen, Leigh Girard?"

"This isn't just grist for another one of your poems, is it?"

He smiled. "Only if you want it to be."

We were now clearly alluding to that kiss on the beach. "You didn't answer my question about the coincidence of Sarah's going to the very cave where the bones were buried."

"What about it?" His teasing tone was gone. "Lots of people hike around those caves. It doesn't mean anything."

"You know anything about Sarah having a baby when she was a teenager?"

He shook his head. His expression reminded me of a disappointed parent dealing with an unruly offspring. "What is this thing you have about Sarah Peck?"

"I could ask you the same thing," I spat back.

He bent down and reached for his shoes. "Look, first of all we don't even know how old those bones are. Even if they're fairly recent, it could be anybody's baby. Think about it.

Some young girl gets knocked up, gets scared, kills the kid. It happens. It's not pretty, but it happens. So drop it."

I was beginning to see that when it came to Sarah Peck, Jake Stevens was as blind as Rob Martin. "Anything else, boss?"

"Keep it clean."

"What?" I felt a flush creep up my neck remembering our kiss on the beach.

"The story. When you write it, keep it clean. No editorializing. No five dollar adjectives. No speculating."

"Got it."

"One more thing."

"Yeah?" I got up casually, trying to ignore that slight ache under my left arm.

"Get that dog of yours a leash."

23

It was 3:40 p.m., and the sun was already dancing danger-ously close to the water's edge. I sat in Sturgeon Bay at the Bayside Café, nursing a lukewarm cup of tea and watching a large freighter maneuver its bulk into the harbor. Plain and simple, I was stalling the inevitable moment when I would go home and open the door on the empty space inside the cottage. Lately even Salinger's presence didn't dispel the length-ening nights and what they implied.

I had written the story about the discovery of the bones just the way Stevens had wanted: clean, no speculation, no editorializing. And I didn't like it. Just like I hadn't liked Joyce Oleander's suicide. Someone had robbed a child of its life. There had been no catcher in the rye, I reflected. Whether the bones had been there ten years or twenty years, a child had been buried under mysterious circumstances.

My jacket was hanging next to the booth. I reached over and pulled out the crumpled photo I'd retrieved from Joyce's desk at the library. I laid the photo on the table and smoothed it with my hand. In the intense glare of the November sunset, the photo's subtleties sharpened. I bent toward it and studied it closely. Then I noticed something I hadn't seen before, as I was focusing on the other girl in the picture. How had I been so blind? There was the woman in the making, she of the translucent white skin, black hair, and a fierceness already in place even as she smiled for the camera. The girl standing next to Joyce Oleander was Sarah Peck.

At once I had an explanation for Sarah's presence at Joyce's funeral. After all, they'd been friends since childhood, according to Lorraine Birch. I took in a deep breath. Two friends, a single proclivity for suicide. I was more sure than ever that their connection had something to do with Carl Peck's death. I was reminded of Joyce's comment to Lorraine Birch that she thought she'd "feel relief when it was over." Despite the suppositions of others as to what she meant, I was sure she had not been referring to her hysterectomy.

I looked at my watch, knowing the confidence in my conclusions would either reveal long hidden crimes, or bring disaster upon my own head. Still, I made the decision to hurry so I could make it to Joyce's town home while it was still light.

That sense of abandonment came over me again as I pulled into the parking space in front of Joyce's town home. The lowering sun and the cloud-dappled sky created a backdrop of gray and slate washes that only added to this place's desolation.

I turned off the engine, and took the flashlight and a screwdriver from the glove compartment. I couldn't count on the back door being unlocked this time. I shoved them into the pocket of my down jacket and got out of the truck, careful not to slam the door in case someone was around.

But the building seemed as bereft of people as before. I rang the neighbor's bell anyway. The plastic flip-flop had moved and become entangled under the shrubs with the other assorted debris, and the front screen door still held a fist-sized hole. No one answered. I rang the bell two more times, then headed toward the back of the building.

As I expected, the glass door was locked. But there was

enough give between the door and the lock for me to maneuver the screwdriver in and push back the lock. A trick I'd learned in college on those nights when I'd not made curfew. Not bothering to look around, I went inside. Again my nose was assaulted with the scent of pine fires and patchouli. I breathed in the loamy smells and let my eyes wander around the room. Everything was as I remembered it—the cumbersome worn furniture, the tiled fireplace, the bookcases overflowing with books.

"Books," I thought to myself. "Her antidote for loneliness."

I walked over to the couch and forced myself to look at the bloodstain. Its redness had faded and turned brown. It was as if the green carpet was absorbing Joyce's blood along with all trace of her existence.

I swallowed hard. "You don't get away that easy, Joyce."

This time, I did a much more careful search of the living room. There was a set of coasters on the coffee table, with different designs of nautical flags. I'd missed the magazine rack the first time. Her taste was eclectic—*Harper's*, *Audubon*, *Nature Conservancy*, *Elle*—the last one was a surprise. I flipped through each magazine. Nothing between the pages but those ubiquitous inserts.

I walked over to the bookcases. Joyce had arranged the books in alphabetical order by author, and also by genre. She had fiction, poetry, art and nonfiction sections. I scanned some of the books that were not shelved. They included the usual fiction classics as well as a slew of mysteries. Her poetry section was small but rich—Elliott, Whitman, Dickinson, William Carlos Williams. Even an Audre Lorde collection.

Her nonfiction section consisted mostly of nature books, and books about Native American mythology. She had all the Audubon field books—from North American Birds to Mushrooms of the World. I pulled out the mushroom field book. The cover was creased and dirty, yet the spine wasn't broken. It had the appearance of much use but good care. I opened it to the table of contents. On the opposite page was a short dedication, and under the dedication Joyce had written: "Joyce Oleander, 5387 Spruce Lane, Ellison Bay, Wisconsin." I took down the other field books. None of them had her name in them.

I could think of only two reasons why she would have written her name and address in the mushroom field guide and not the other field guides. Either she used the book frequently or she'd loaned it to someone. Had she too been a member of the mycology society? Had she, like Rob Martin, been a student of Peck's?

Connections were getting more convoluted by the minute. I sighed heavily, trying to sort things out. Maybe Joyce just had an interest in mushrooms. Maybe she didn't even buy the field book. She might have received it as a gift. I sat on the raised hearth with the guides piled in my lap.

Maybe Lydia was right, and I was obsessing about the Pecks and now Joyce because I didn't want to deal with my own problems. My stomach was grumbling, and my left side ached. I should go home, have a glass of wine, make dinner and forget about all this. I had come to Door County to find some peace.

So far, batting a thousand on that score.

I re-shelved the field guides, stood up and started for the door. A shaft of low sunlight shot through the clouds and momentarily blinded me. I turned from the door. The light illuminated a dark ladder-back chair revealing the subtle grains of its highly varnished wood. Draped sideways across the chair's back was a deep purple sweater, one sleeve dangling down toward the carpet as if reaching for something. The other sleeve touched the chair's seat. Both were ragged with wear. One of the sweater's gold buttons was missing. My brain nearly went haywire with questions: when was the last time Joyce had worn this sweater? The night of her suicide? Before she went to the hospital? Had she thrown it there before taking the pills? I could see her gaunt face and swollen stomach in that photo Ida had given me, of the two of them in front of the Art Institute. I remembered that Joyce had been wearing this sweater.

"I was her only friend," Ida Reeves had claimed. Yet I knew for a fact that Joe Stillwater counted Joyce as a friend, and so did Sarah Peck, at least for a time in her life. For some inexplicable reason, I felt I'd become a friend to Joyce Oleander too, even though our acquaintance was post mortem. I could see there had been a depth to Joyce that was visible in her choice of books and her quiet existence. I sensed she had suffered deep losses. Yet she had built a life in spite of them. Something had come along and shattered it.

The room dimmed as the clouds closed over the shaft of fading sunlight. I walked through the living room, up the green-carpeted stairs and directly into the smaller bedroom. After Joyce's elaborately girlish bedroom, I wasn't prepared for this room's austerity: one bed, one dresser, one nightstand; white-washed walls, no pictures. It was as severe as a monk's cell. A darkly stained Parson's table served as a nightstand. The twin bed had no headboard and was covered with a crisp white spread. The bed was pushed against the far wall under a small and high window decked with white curtains and a white shade. I opened the curtains and lifted the shade to take advantage of the setting sun.

A mirrored dresser sat across from the bed. This ponderous piece of furniture seemed to give the room its only weight. Simple and dark, it stood like a sentinel watching over the room, reflecting the bed and the window. The room had probably been used as a guest room. I shuddered, imagining rising each morning surrounded by the purity of all this white and seeing myself in that overpowering mirror, revealed at my most vulnerable before I could prepare my face and my body for the day.

I sat on the bed and looked through the items on the nightstand. There were two books and a prescription bottle. The books were from the Egg Harbor library. One was a sci-fi novel and the other a collection of essays. Bookmarkers protruded from each book. I picked up the prescription bottle. The label bore Joyce's name and read "Take one tab by mouth at p.m. bedtime as needed for insomnia."

I scrutinized the room again. It suddenly occurred to me to question this being a guest room, and the girlish bedroom down the hall where Joyce slept. If I'd reversed the functions of these rooms, then why such austerity for her room and the peculiar décor of the guest room?

The light was starting to go. I took a deep breath, questioned my willingness to invade a dead woman's privacy, and without further introspection, quickly went through the dresser drawers. The top drawers were empty. But the other drawers were filled with sweaters, underwear, shirts, some slacks. I quickly became convinced that this was indeed Joyce's own bedroom. I opened the closet. A cedar smell filled the room. Inside were wool skirts, jumpers, a few sensible dresses, some hatboxes circa 1950.

Neatly placed on a shoe rack were several pairs of those "industrial strength" shoes. I might as well have been looking at Ida Reeves' closet. I closed the door and was about to leave when something under the bed caught my eye. I knelt down and lifted the spread's edge. A metal box, the kind people use to store their important documents, was partly hidden under the bed. Not a very astute hiding place, I thought, since it drew my attention. I pulled the box out and tried the lid. It wouldn't budge.

Okay, where do people hide keys to home safes? I stood up and searched through all the dresser drawers again. Nothing. I went back to the closet and felt in all the pockets of the clothes hung there. Still nothing. As I reached up for one of the hatboxes, it tumbled down, hitting me on the head. Out of the box rolled a black cloche hat and a key.

I snatched the key and tried it in the box lock. It turned easily. Inside, I found the usual documents: Joyce's birth and baptism certificates, her parents' birth and death certificates, her high school graduation diploma. There was a separate rather bulky envelope addressed to Joyce from the Adoptees' Liberty Movement Association. I pulled out one letter and read it:

Dear Ms. Oleander:

We have listed you on our registry using the information you provided. As our brochure explains, ALMA is voluntary; the organization can make a match only if both parties are registered.

We suggest that birth parents searching for their adoptive children use all methods available. Enclosed you will find a list of other resources that will help you in your search.

Sincerely,
Marsha Ann Hodges

Besides the ALMA letter, brochure and list of resources, the envelope held four other letters. Joyce had followed ALMA's advice and contacted several of the other resources.

I read through the other letters. One was from a national adoption clearing house called Soundex. Apparently, Joyce had registered with them as well. The next two letters were actually billing statements from the *Chicago Tribune* and the *Milwaukee Journal*. Last Mother's Day, Joyce had taken out ads in both papers. Other than the number of words in the ads and the amounts due, there was no indication of the content of the ads.

I quickly read the last letter. It was from a private detective named Barry Snyder. He did not find any record of adoptions twenty years ago in Door County, or with agencies that had accepted a female infant from Door County. With so little to go on, he concluded, he was unable to narrow his search enough for it to be useful.

Before putting the letters back in the envelope, I reread them and checked all the dates. The letters spanned the last six months. And the only specifics about the child I could find were in Snyder's letter.

The sun had set, so I used my flashlight to make my way down the stairs. On my way out, I took the mushroom field guide and slipped it into my jacket pocket. "Forgive me, Father, for what I do in the name of justice," I muttered. Or in the name of obsession, I could hear Lydia and Jake Stevens hissing.

A jumble of suppositions ran through my head as I drove toward home. First off, let's suppose Joyce Oleander had a child about twenty years ago—a girl. She gave the child up for adoption and most recently wanted to find her. But all her efforts were unsuccessful. I thought about the bones I'd found, whose age had yet to be determined. But Joyce was looking for her child, so she assumed her child wasn't dead.

Up ahead I could see the old gas pump that marked the gravel road leading to my cottage. I put on my signal light and slowed the truck. As I began to make the turn, I jerked the truck back onto Highway 42. I seemed to remember that the library stayed opened until six. I had about fifteen minutes.

The library's front door was already locked, but I could see a rectangle of light coming from the back office. I banged on the door as hard as I could. Ida Reeves peered out from her office. I banged on the door again. She came out and walked toward me. Even in the dim light, I could see the pursed annoyance on her face.

"We're closed," she said through the locked door.

"I know. But I just need to ask you something. It won't take but a minute. It's very important."

"Come back tomorrow. We open at ten." She pushed her glasses up on her nose and retracted those large lips.

"Please, let me talk with you. It's about Joyce's baby."

There was no hiding the look of shock on her face. Her hand actually went to her throat like the requisite damsel of classic melodrama. She unlocked the door and walked quickly back to her office.

We were both too agitated to sit. In the full light of the office, I noticed changes in Ida's appearance. The top button of her blouse was unbuttoned and part of her collar was caught under her sweater. Errant hairs stood out all over her head, as if she'd just come in from outside. And that crisp posture was gone. Her shoulders stooped inward, almost as if expecting a blow.

I had rehearsed what I was going to say, what ploys I'd use to get Ida Reeves to open up. I was sure that she knew more than she had originally told me about Joyce. Her altered appearance almost changed my mind. I reached into my pocket and handed her the letters.

She looked at them a long time, then looked away. "Where did you get these?"

"Ms. Reeves, Joyce is dead. There's no need to protect her anymore."

She put her hand up to stop me. "You came to Joyce's funeral and that shows character. I respect that. But I want it understood that I don't owe you anything."

I shook my head in agreement.

"I also want a promise from you that what I tell you is off the record. Nothing goes in the *Gazette*. You may not think so, but the dead do need protection. And Joyce was like a daughter to me." She struggled to control her voice. "Do I have your word?"

"Yes, you do."

She pulled back a chair, sat down and put her hands together as if in prayer. "I'm not going to sugar-coat this or beat around the bush. Joyce told me that when she was in high school, she had a child out of wedlock. Before you ask, I don't know who the father was. She didn't even tell me about this until a few months ago. 'I was young and stupid and naive' was the way she explained it."

Ida took a deep breath. "She wanted to find her child, and she asked for my help. I told her that it wasn't a good idea to dredge up the past. The child was probably being well taken care of. Locating her might bring grief to everyone." Ida shook her head as if she was trying to clear it. "Joyce said that she was worried. She had read some story about an adoptive mother who had killed her adoptive child. I told her that was nonsense. But nothing could dissuade her. I really think it had more to do with the hysterectomy, and her never being able to have any more children. She was frantic. She even hired a detective." She glanced at the letters. "Well, you already know that."

"Yes. Go on, please." I didn't want Ida to close down on me before she completed her revelations.

"I told her that her child probably didn't want to be found, or she herself would have registered with that organization, the AL-something. Let me think." She rubbed her forehead, then glanced at the letters before I could prompt her. "Oh yes, ALMA, I see here, the Adoptee's Liberty Movement Association. Alma, did you know it means 'soul' in Spanish? Anyway, most adopted children don't want to be found. It's too disruptive to their lives. Those happy reunions you see on television are rare, and just so much media hype. At least that's what the literature I've read indicates."

She stopped. I had started drumming my fingers on the table in frustration.

"I'm sorry," Ida said. "I know I get carried away sometimes. It's how I deal with things."

"Someone must know something, Ms. Reeves. How could a high school girl hide something like this, especially in a small town?"

"When I asked her that, she said she wore baggy clothes and that her grandmother didn't pay much attention to her most of the time."

"She was living with her grandmother?"

"Yes, after her parents died. Nice old lady, but too infirm to care for a teenager."

"But where did she give birth? What hospital? Who adopted the child?" I ran my fingers through my hair and rubbed the back of my neck.

"I don't know. She told me a friend helped her out. That the friend had handled everything."

"A friend? She didn't give you a name?"

"No, she wouldn't tell me. She said she couldn't tell me. She had made a promise. Whenever I tried to get a name out of her, she'd shut down. Joyce had a way of with-drawing into herself. When she got like that, there was no reaching her."

"Do you think the father could have been Elliott Stillwater? But if that were the case, then why break off the engagement?" I answered my own question.

Ida sat very still, looking at her hands. "I don't think it was Elliott's child."

"Are you sure there's nothing else?"

"I should have helped her. I could have, but I didn't."

She brought her folded hands up to her mouth. "I turned my back on her. Just before the surgery, she said to me, 'There's not a day goes by that I don't think about my child. All I want is a picture, a letter, something to tell me she's happy and safe.' You know what I said? 'You gave up that right when you gave up that child. It's better this way.' I should have thought about what that surgery meant and how much Joyce loved children. Then maybe things would have been different. Maybe she'd still be alive."

So that's why she'd been so cold when we first talked. To feel anything would open the door to feeling everything. "You don't know that."

She put her hands down and looked into my eyes. "Yes, I do."

We sat in silence for a moment. I could hear the wall clock ticking in the next room. I realized that any reassurance I could offer Ida Reeves would be useless. Her neatly constructed world had collapsed with her admission of guilt.

"Take these." She handed me the letters. "Maybe you can find Joyce's child."

I took the letters and put them in my pocket. "Ms. Reeves, a lot of things could have pushed Joyce over the edge."

She walked over toward the office door. "You have what you came for. So if you don't mind . . ."

As I walked past her, she switched off the lights in a place where Joyce Oleander had found solace.

"In such a night," I said aloud, slamming my truck door and looking up at the sky. The orange harvest moon ran close to the fields and cast an umber light. "In such a night," I said again, not remembering the rest of the line from Shakespeare's *The Merchant of Venice.* But I did remember that like me, the characters couldn't bear being indoors on such a night. However, my reasons had nothing to do with romantic love or love of any kind.

I opened the back door of the cottage. Salinger jumped up at me, panting and crying.

"Okay," I said, patting her thick sheen of fur. "I'm with you."

She ran past me and tore through the aster field. I followed her, knowing I'd never catch her. As I crossed the field, for the first time I saw that the whiteness of the blooms was gone, and the field had browned. The small flowers were all closed in upon themselves. Whatever had kept them thriving had departed. I shivered. Winter seemed imminent. I headed toward the bay. I needed the water's hypnotic spell.

The wind along the rocky shore bit into my exposed face with a longing I understood. I could see lights on the far shore, steady and small. The moon had slipped behind a bank of clouds, casting everything into bas-relief. I sat down on a flat rock and let the cold seep up into me. The water was dark and restless. It would be a quick and cold death.

I touched my head to free me from such thoughts. But like the water, my head continued to throb. Who had fathered Joyce's child? It couldn't have been Elliott Stillwater's baby;

according to his brother, Joyce and Stillwater had never been intimate. And the timeline I'd cobbled together suggested she had broken off the engagement after the child's birth. If it was his child, wouldn't she have married him? So if not Stillwater, then who was the father?

I breathed deeply, taking in the briny scent of decaying fish mixed with the smell of crushed pine needles. And who was the friend who had helped Joyce? Where was her child now? I shivered. Hopefully not attached to the identity of those bones sitting in a drawer in the forensic anthropologist's office.

A wave rushed up the shore and wet my shoes. I inched back on the rock and hugged myself for warmth. Joyce had a child twenty years ago, so she would have been sixteen when she conceived. If only I knew the age of those bones. But that child had most likely been murdered. Surely Joyce's child had been adopted.

Salinger startled me out of my thoughts. She stood beside me, shaking her wet fur and crying. She smelled like mold. "Where have you been, my one and only guard dog?"

She cried again. "All right, I guess I'm hungry too."

As we neared the cottage door, Salinger began to howl. "Quiet," I cautioned her, my whole body tensing. I approached the back door slowly. No lights were on inside, and the door was slightly ajar. I hadn't locked it.

I realized I had two choices: circle around to the front of the house, jump into my truck and go for help. The problem with that idea was that the keys were in my purse, and my purse was on the kitchen floor where I had thrown it in my haste to be outside. That left the other option: confront whoever had sneaked into my house. Maybe I had left the door open myself? I had been so preoccupied that I couldn't remember. Still, I decided to go around the front and see if there was another vehicle parked in the drive besides mine. I pulled on Salinger's collar and shushed her vehemently.

There was no other vehicle in the drive. I reached into the back of my truck and grabbed the bow and arrows, feeling foolish as I did it. I moved slowly back around the side of the house to the back door. Ready or not, I said to myself, drew the arrow, then swung open the door and walked inside.

Quickly I switched on the lights. Salinger jumped in front of me and started to growl. "I've got a weapon!" I shouted. "Show yourself and you won't get hurt."

Silence. Salinger growled again. I went into the living room, flipped on those lights. No one. I was definitely feeling foolish. I threw the bow and arrow on the floor, walked into the bedroom and turned on the bedside lamp.

There on the dresser mirror written with lipstick were the words: *freek bitch*.

I ran to check the bathroom. Then I opened every closet door in the house. But whoever had left the message was gone. He must have sneaked into my house while I had been sitting by the water. I immediately ran to the back door and locked it. This coward had apparently watched me leave the house, and then slipped in to scrawl the message.

I looked around the room again. One of the dresser drawers was open slightly and askew. Had I left it that way? I opened the drawer. Everything looked in place. I pushed aside my silk panties and slips. There, still neatly hidden at the bottom of the drawer, were my breast prostheses. I re-adjusted the drawer and closed it.

I stared at the scrawled words again: *freek bitch*.

"Illiterate loser," I said aloud. "It will take more than words to scare me."

In the kitchen, I mixed up a cleaning solution strong enough to melt road tar. It consisted of ammonia and pine-scented floor cleaner. I scrubbed back and forth on the mirror over and over until the letters smeared, faded and finally disappeared into my pail of pinkish water. I kept scrubbing, even after the mirror was clean. There was a taint in the room that had to be obliterated. Finally, when the ache in my arm became insistent, I threw the sponge in the pail, and dumped the water.

My scouring completed, I burrowed into the green velvet chair and enjoyed the crisp, cool taste of a glass of chardonnay. One went down easy, and I had a refill, thank you. I hate cowards, and this had been a cowardly thing. If Sarah Peck hadn't been so recently in the hospital and Rob Martin for the most part sitting at her side, I might have figured this for her post-suicide-attempt acting out. So I could think of only one other person who would do this: Renn Woulff.

For a brief moment, I considered calling the cops. Then rejected the idea, since I wasn't sure that they'd believe me— and especially since I'd destroyed the evidence. He could always claim he hadn't really broken in, because my back door was unlocked.

I poured my third glass of wine and took a generous gulp, feeling the wine's warmth spread through my body, relaxing me, making me feel less scared and vulnerable. What would I say when the cops asked? What would I say when they wanted to know if anything was out of place? And then there was that word. The word that I couldn't make go away: freek. No matter how he spelled it, I knew what he meant.

I stayed in the velvet chair all night and didn't fall asleep until early morning light forced its way under the door.

24

Friday, November 17, Present day

The rest of the week had been long, tedious and un-eventful. Whoever had written that message on my mirror had backed off. I made myself sleep in the bedroom—if you could call it sleep. I kept dreaming about the cancer surgery: the pain and the waking realization that they had cut off my left breast, that I would never be whole again.

Stevens had successfully avoided me by communicating through notes and Marge. The one time I had walked by his office, his door was closed. It was going to be a long winter.

He had assigned me a story on two fish poachers that kept me tied up in court until late Thursday afternoon, when they were sentenced to eighteen months in prison. They had sold about 120,000 pounds of illegally caught perch and made about $350,000. So much for protecting the environment. But at least I was finally off obits.

During several court recesses, I sacrificed lunch to sit in the Sturgeon Bay Library's microfiche room looking for the ads Joyce Oleander had placed in the *Chicago Tribune* and *Milwaukee Journal*. The ads were small and hard to read, and scanning microfiche on an empty stomach made me nauseous. But I persisted. What kept me going was the belief that if Joyce's daughter was somewhere out there alive, I would find her. I needed a happy ending to match that fairy tale bed-

218

room in her town house. I now believed Joyce had prepared that room for a daughter who never came home.

After all the searching, the ads turned out to be another dead end. Except for the adoption search site, they were identical. "Birth mother desperately seeking daughter given up for adoption twenty years ago in Chicago area. Birth name Oleander."

I also left several voice messages for Barry Snyder, the private detective Joyce had hired to find her daughter. But so far he hadn't returned my calls.

By Thursday night, I was having extended conversations with Salinger. The dinner party was starting to look like a better alternative than another night alone. Besides, it would give me an opportunity to observe Sarah and Rob in a social situation. I left a message on Lydia's machine that I'd be coming to her soiree, and that I'd bring wine. By Friday, I was actually looking forward to it.

I chose my dress carefully, selecting a combination of velvet and silk. After a long soak in a bubble bath made with freesia, honey, and sweet almond, I slipped into a purple, high-necked silk blouse, long black velvet skirt, and a midnight blue velvet cape lined in blue silk. My spiked heels were black suede. Before the mastectomy, I had taken great pride in my body. I always thought of myself as being built like a Vegas showgirl: five-foot-seven, 130 lbs., with long slender legs, a flat stomach, and full breasts. I had studied dance when I was younger, and had briefly been a member of the Ruth Page Dance Company in Chicago. Until I was thirty-four, until the cancer, I was still taking ballet and jazz classes. I could have kept at it, even with the damage done by the mastectomy, but I lost my motivation.

I had left the house early so that I could stop by the Egg Harbor Market and buy some decent wine. I headed toward the wine section at the back of the store and chose a gold medal winning California merlot called French Hill that only set me back twenty-eight dollars. I was coming back down the aisle, when I saw Eva Peck. She had her back to me, but there was no mistaking that hairdo. She was in rapt conversation with a black man who was dressed entirely in white, including a white baseball cap turned backwards on his head. As I neared them, it occurred to me that he was the only black man I had ever seen on the entire peninsula.

Eva was pointing to a plastic wrapped package. "Do these muffins have real butter in them?" she asked the man.

"No butter. Margarine. I baked them this morning." He grinned at her, and I could see that he had a large gap between his two front teeth.

"You're sure, there's no butter. I can't have butter."

He grinned again at Eva. "Mrs. Peck, I didn't use any butter."

She looked again at the package in her hand. The man must have thought that the conversation was over, because he walked past me toward the front of the store. When he was out of sight, she put the muffins back on the shelf. As she turned, she saw me.

"I usually bake. But with just me now, it's too much," she said, glancing vaguely back toward the muffins.

"I can't remember the last time I baked," I responded.

"Oh, that's right, you live alone too." She looked at the bottle of wine I was carrying.

I wasn't going to tell Eva Peck that the wine was for a dinner party. If she thought that I was going home to drink alone, all the better. Maybe I could use it to my advantage.

"Are you in a hurry to get home?" I glanced stealthily into her basket. There were two cans of salt-free soup, a quart of low-fat milk, and bran cereal.

"Well, not in a big hurry."

"Would you like to go to the Olde Stagecoach and have a drink?"

Eva's expression registered something between judgment and surprise. "I don't drink. But I suppose I could have a cup of tea."

The Olde Stagecoach was a few doors down from the Market. We stowed our respective purchases in our vehicles and met inside. I secured a table in the back of the bar. It was around 6:45 p.m. A few men dressed in Lions Club jackets were bellied up to the bar. It wouldn't be long before the rest of the group showed up, and then it would be impossible to hear each other talk in there.

"Is this okay?" I asked Eva, as she gracefully positioned her bulky body on the tall, narrow barstool.

She smiled without showing her teeth. "I suppose if we're only having a drink."

The waitress, who looked about fifteen, took our drink orders. I ordered a glass of pinot grigio and Eva, to my surprise, ordered a grasshopper.

"When in Rome," she shrugged.

There was a sudden looseness to Eva that made her seem almost as girlish as the waitress. We made the usual small talk about the weather until the drinks arrived. Eva sipped delicately from her foamy drink, and for some reason, I thought of Lana Turner.

"I haven't had a grasshopper since . . ." She crinkled her forehead. "Since when Carl and I had Saturday night card parties at our house. In the winter, we'd take turns at each others' houses. Sometimes we'd have a theme, like German night." She had that faraway look people get when they go down memory lane. I always figure they're making up half of what they remember.

"Sounds like a lot of fun. Do you still get together with the same people?"

"Oh, you know how it is. People drift apart for one reason or another. But I do try and stay active in my church."

A man who smelled like he had already made a dent in a gin bottle stumbled to the rear of the bar. "Hi, Eva," he said, as he sat down near the Lions Club boys.

Eva merely nodded her prim head in his direction. "That's Floyd," she sniffed. "He's always had a crush on me. Now that I'm a widow, I don't want to encourage him."

"I can understand that." Not really, especially since the only interest Floyd seemed to have was getting another drink. The waitress made her rounds to our table. I ordered another drink, hoping Eva would too. The atmosphere of the bar and the alcohol were beginning to melt away her reserve. I had some difficult questions I wanted to ask her. To my relief, she did indeed order another grasshopper.

"Did you hear that Sarah's out of the hospital?" she asked.

"As a matter of fact, I went out to her place on Monday to see how she was doing."

"I hate the way she lives." Eva siphoned the foam from the bottom of her glass with her straw. "Smoking, drinking, those crazy paintings. You know, she never sells any. Who would buy them?"

Eva didn't sound much like a mother grateful that her only daughter had escaped a suicide attempt.

"Has she talked to you about why she tried to kill herself?"

"No, and I have no idea. Doc Porter said she has amnesia about it, like it happened in a blackout. He says she's probably upset about her father's death."

That's putting it mildly, I thought. The waitress returned

with our second round of drinks. "I'm sure that you're very upset yourself."

"You're right, I am, but you don't see me trying to kill myself."

"You're a stronger person. You can face things. I mean, right from the beginning, you were suspicious about your husband's death. And you insisted on an autopsy." I was shamelessly appealing to her vanity, but I suspected it was her Achilles' heel.

"I was suspicious. And I still am." She removed the straw from her drink and drank from the glass. "Carl knew his mushrooms. I don't think he'd make a mistake, even if he had been drinking. But that's what everybody else believes happened."

"Do you remember him eating any mushrooms before he became sick?"

She thought for a moment. "Yes, I remembered that later when the results came from Indianapolis. But nobody even asked me about it. About five days before he became sick, he brought home a bag full of white mushrooms. He liked to fry them in garlic and butter. Always looked like fried slime to me." She shook her shoulders and took another drink. She'd given up sipping by now.

I recalled that the mushrooms didn't react in the body immediately. But I was certain that the latency period was more like six to twenty-four hours. "Do you remember what he ate the day before he became sick?"

"What would that matter? It was the mushrooms that he picked that poisoned him."

"Not necessarily, Mrs. Peck. Usually the toxins react in the body about twenty-four hours after."

"That can't be right. Everybody's system is different." She shifted her bulk on the stool.

"That's true. Still, I'm curious, what did he eat the day before?"

She rubbed her forehead. "I think that was the night we had stew."

"We?"

"I mean, he had the stew. I didn't eat it. It was rabbit stew. I can't even stand the smell of it."

"But you cooked it for him?"

"No, I didn't make it. Sarah made it. She said they had some left over from the restaurant."

"Were there mushrooms in the stew?"

"Why, yes. Sarah always uses mushrooms in her stew."

I twirled my wine glass. Eva frowned, and I could see the suggestion about the stew mushrooms beginning to form in her thinking.

"I need to ask you something else, Mrs. Peck. Something about your husband and your daughter."

In the smoky light of the bar, I could see her eyes widen. Then she blinked them quickly, as if there was something in them.

"Sarah seems to harbor a great deal of hatred toward her father. In fact, she told me she's glad he's dead. And that his death put a lot of people out of their misery. Do you know what she meant by that?"

Mrs. Peck looked around quickly to see if anyone had overheard me. "I don't know what you're talking about. How dare you say that to me? Sarah loved her father. Carl was a, was a wonderful man."

"I'm only telling you what Sarah told me. And Rob Martin says Carl called her a slut and a failure. He says they were always at each other."

"Sarah's making that up."

"Rob said he was there when it happened."

"That's not right." Eva took another substantial drink, followed by dabbing nervously at her mouth with the cocktail napkin.

"Why is that?"

"Because I wouldn't allow such a thing. You think I'd allow anyone to talk to my daughter like that?"

"Then why is Rob Martin contending this?"

"I don't know. Maybe he thinks he'll get on Sarah's good side. You know, he still wants her back. Anyone can see it, the way he looks at her."

I couldn't argue with Martin's obsessive devotion, but Eva still hadn't answered my question. "But why would Sarah say these things about her father in the first place?"

"Sarah likes to blame her problems on other people. She doesn't take disappointments very well. She thinks life owes her something. Ever since she went to Chicago, she changed. That place changed her. Don't you believe what she says about my husband."

I didn't buy Eva's explanation. From experience, I'd learned that the truth was usually somewhere in the middle. I took a sip of my wine and considered my next question. "Mrs. Peck," I began. "I might do a follow-up story on Joyce Oleander because of her volunteer work at the hospital. Did you know Joyce very well?"

"Everyone knew Joyce. She worked at the library for years. But are you sure you should be doing another story on her?" She lowered her voice. "Considering what happened."

"So you didn't know Joyce very well?" I asked, trying to clarify her vague answer.

"No, not well. She kept to herself a lot."

I placed the photo of Joyce and Sarah down on the round table. "Do you know who this girl is with Joyce?"

Eva bent forward for a closer look at the photo.

"That's Sarah. Sarah and Joyce used to play together as girls." She pushed the photo back toward me.

"So they were friends in high school?"

"Why are you asking me this? What does it have to do with your story and her volunteer work?"

"Joyce had a baby when she was in high school. I thought maybe Sarah knew something about it."

"Who told you that?" Eva gulped the rest of her drink.

"I can't say." I was protecting myself as much as Ida Reeves.

"Well, I never heard such a vicious rumor. Sarah never said anything to me." She took a deep breath and let it out slowly.

I caught the strong smell of mint from her drinks.

"You know, young woman, it's not a good idea to spread gossip. Especially about the dead."

"It's not gossip, Mrs. Peck. I happen to know that Joyce was searching for her child before she died. She'd given the baby girl up for adoption."

Eva's mouth pinched with disgust. "I don't know where you got that from, but it can't be right. And even if it was, people in a small town don't like other people, especially outsiders, sticking their noses where they don't belong. Or making up things just to write about them."

I wasn't sure if that was a warning or merely small town paranoia. Either way, I wasn't going to drop it. "So you don't know anything about Joyce having a baby."

"No, of course not. Isn't that what I just said?" She clutched her purse to her like a life jacket. "I thought you were different. I thought you were a nice girl who understood about etiquette and good manners like Sarah used to understand."

Before I could respond, our waitress returned. "Another round?" She picked up Eva's empty glass. My glass was half full.

"Not for me. I'll just finish this," I answered.

Eva just shook her head no and smiled her pained smile.

I stood up. "I'll be right back. Ladies room." I wanted to give her a few moments to digest what I had told her before I asked her any more questions about Joyce.

When I returned, Eva was gone. She had stuck me with the bill. I finished my drink and left twenty-two dollars. As I turned to leave, I saw Renn Woulff's face reflected in the bar mirror. His back was to me. I was so engrossed in conversation with Eva Peck that I hadn't noticed him come in.

I could easily have left without him seeing me, but that grinning face made me shake with fury. I walked up behind him, my high heels clicking loudly on the wooden floorboards.

"Next time you have something to say, say it to my face," I whispered to the back of his greasy head.

He turned sideways to look at me. "What?" he slurred.

"You're not just a drunk, you're a coward too," I said in a low and menacing tone.

"Hey, everybody. It's the lady reporter. The one looking into everyone's business. She's a real dick, she is." A few snickers punctuated the room.

"Just stay away from me, or you'll be sorry." It was an idle threat, and I knew it. But I was pulsing with anger, blurting out whatever movie cliché popped into my head. If I'd had a revolver, I'd have had it drawn. I had to get out of there before I told him that this town wasn't big enough for the both of us.

"What you talking about, you freakin' bitch?" he shouted.

I turned and walked toward the door. I could feel every pair of eyes in the bar follow me.

"Hey, where're you goin'?" Woulff called after me. "Let me buy you a drink. No hard feelings."

25

Of course I was an hour late for Lydia's dinner party. An assortment of trucks and cars were parked haphazardly in front of her shop. I recognized the black Dodge Ram and Stevens's MG convertible. He had finally given in to winter and put the top up.

As I trudged up the wood chip walkway, I saw the flickering light of candles in the upstairs windows. I knocked at the back door. Riffs of classical music drifted outside. It sounded like Mozart. So that was the kind of evening it was going to be.

"Well, it's about time!" Lydia opened the door. She was holding a glass of champagne. Her hair cascaded around her shoulders in loose curls. She was wearing a black body suit that adhered to her like another skin. Her waist was cinched with a silver belt. All she needed was a whip, and she could have become Cat Woman.

"Didn't want to come empty handed." I raised the merlot.

She read the label. "You're forgiven. We're just about ready to eat, so go on up. I have to fetch some more candles from the shop. I think you know everybody." She smiled.

The main room upstairs swam in candlelight. There were candles on end tables, on the fireplace mantle, on the window ledges, and on the dining room table. Lydia had created a shadowy ambiance where subtleties of expression could easily go unnoticed or even be misinterpreted. Despite the subdued light, there was no way to enter unobserved. I took a deep breath and strode into the room, trying not to brush against any candles and set myself ablaze.

The only two people in the room were Jake Stevens and Deputy Chet Jorgensen. Although they were both about the same height, they were a study in opposites. Jorgensen, whose physique could make Arnold Schwarzenegger self-conscious, was decked out in a navy sport coat, dress trousers, white shirt and tie. The lean and lanky Stevens wore his usual attire: jeans and a work shirt. This one was dark blue. His only concession to the occasion was a tie: a skinny black one that any of the Beatles might have worn in the early Sixties.

Stevens and Jorgensen were leaning against the stone fireplace, drinks in hands, deep in conversation. The Deputy was gesticulating with his free hand. Stevens was shaking his head. Neither one acknowledged my arrival.

I untied my cape and threw it on the sofa. I looked around the room and spotted a makeshift bar set up on a glass cart between two windows. Under each window was a pile of floor cushions. They were the ones we had sat on at the women's meeting. Maybe after the liquor had done its job, we'd all sit around and spill our souls.

Ignoring the "never mix, never worry" rule I'd developed in college, I poured myself a glass of champagne and joined the men.

"Is this a private conversation or can anyone join?" A lame opener, but I've never been good at party chitchat.

"Didn't see ya come in, there," said Deputy Chet. "How's the bow huntin' comin'?"

For once, Stevens looked taken aback.

"Haven't really had much time to hunt." I avoided looking at Stevens, but he recovered in record time.

"You'll have to take me hunting sometime, Leigh," he said, with a sardonic expression.

"Hey. I been asking you to come huntin' for years." Jorgensen looked from Stevens to me, then grinned. "Ya puttin' me on again, okay then."

Stevens patted Jorgensen on the back. "I think Leigh's putting us both on."

"Now would I do that?" I asked, widening my eyes.

"I think you might." Stevens jiggled the ice around in his glass.

"Listen, then, no kiddin', she's a pretty good shot." Chet wasn't going to let this drop. Too bad such doggedness didn't extend to criminal investigations.

"I'm sure she is," Stevens concluded. He stared at me past politeness.

For an uncomfortable moment, I studied my drink.

Chet shifted his weight from foot to foot. "Didn't ya say somethin' then about huntin' before?" he asked.

"Not hunting, shooting," I answered.

Stevens was about to ask something when Lydia walked into the room.

"Dinner's ready. Everybody, please sit." She moved toward the stereo in what could only be described as a bona fide, movie star slink. "Any musical requests?"

"How about some low down dirty blues?" Sarah Peck emerged from the kitchen, carrying a gold-filigreed soup tureen. And right behind her came Rob Martin, with a steaming platter exuding a lemony fish scent.

"Do you have Muddy Waters?" Rob asked.

I was shocked by Sarah's appearance. Her hair was cut so close to her head that patches of scalp showed in places. It looked like she had taken a knife to her hair and hacked away in a frenzy. She was wearing another leather mini skirt whose black surface looked hard as a lead shield. Her gold lamé blouse shimmered in the candlelight, showing off her braless breasts.

Lydia fumbled through her stack of CDs. "How about Vivaldi's 'Four Seasons' or Bach?" Without waiting for an answer, she made a selection.

"Lydia, why'd you bother asking?" Martin grumbled.

She pressed the start button. "Just teasing. Will Charlie Parker do?" She stood up and ran her fingers through her lush hair.

I was getting the feeling that everything everybody was saying had an undertone to it. That they were all speaking in another language that I had yet to tune into.

"Boy girl, boy girl," Lydia said, pointing round the table. Her voice had a tenseness to it, as if she were on the verge of hysterics.

As if playing some bizarre game of musical chairs and the music had suddenly stopped, Sarah quickly plopped down next to Chet. Trying not to appear piqued, Rob casually slid back the chair on Sarah's other side at one end of the table. I sat down on Rob's other side across from Sarah. In our haste to be seated, we'd all crowded around one end of the table.

"Well, I guess I'll sit here," Stevens said, rather ungraciously pulling back the chair next to me.

Lydia sat at the opposite end of the table from Rob. She didn't look too happy about it. She bit the side of her lip. "Sarah, would you do the honors?" Lydia pointed to the covered soup tureen. "Hope everybody's in the mood for fish."

Sarah stood up and took the lid off the tureen. A strong odor of spices and fish drifted out. "Just pass your bowls down." As she ladled the chowder, her hands trembled. Rob perched on the edge of his chair, as if he were about to catch Sarah if she keeled over.

"Food looks mighty good. Which lovely lady do I give my condolences to?" Chet asked, after the food and wine had been passed around.

I wasn't sure if he was trying to be amusing or had misused the word.

"I made the stuffed sole," said Lydia. "Sarah made the chowder."

I automatically stared down into my soup bowl. There were dark brown mushroom slices floating in the broth. I realized I was holding my spoon aloft. I quickly took a sip of the broth.

"Suppose everybody heard about the council approvin' that Chicago developer's plan for the Egg Harbor subdivision, then." Chet popped half a buttered roll into his mouth.

"So you're happy about it?" Stevens queried.

"Not unhappy," Chet responded.

"What's that supposed to mean?" Rob scowled. "You know damn well that the council sold us out. That land was supposed to be set aside for preservation."

"Hold on. Don't ya read that paper of yours, Rob? Part of it's goin' to be." Chet took a long pull of his wine. "That developer there's preserving five acres of wetlands near the south quadrant."

"If the council had any sense, they'd put a stop to all development," Martin said.

"Is that realistic, Rob?" Lydia asked.

"What does it have to do with being realistic? Do you want this place to look like every place else in this god-forsaken country—strip malls, subdivisions, and more strip malls?" Martin stopped eating. A thin sheen of sweat shone on his forehead.

"Rob, you've seen them plans there. That place ain't goin' look that way. We're goin' about our development very conservatively." Jorgensen sounded annoyed.

"It's going to happen regardless," Stevens said, "whether we like it or not."

"That's a hell of an attitude, Jake," Martin snapped. "But of course, I figured you'd take that tack."

"What tack's that?" Stevens asked. His voice had gone flat.

"Rob, do you always have to be so . . ." Lydia ran her tongue over her top lip as if the word she was looking for was there. "So passionate?"

I got the distinct impression that she was enjoying the exchange, despite her protest.

"What do you think?" Martin asked.

It took me a few seconds to realize that he was addressing me.

"Well, I don't know all the particulars of this new subdivision. But having watched my town in Illinois go from a few scattered subdivisions and cornfields to endless strip malls and countless subdivisions, I'd probably be against development. In fact, the lack of development was one of the reasons I came here."

"You outsiders always feel that way," Chet harrumphed. "Us natives understand the economics. We don't come here with no money. We gotta scratch out a livin' from this place."

"I would think you of all people would be against development, with your concern for the natural order," I countered.

"It's like what I told ya there about nature. There's gotta be that balance. If we control development, we can have that balance."

"You're not accounting for human nature," I answered

sharply. For some reason I was irked with his naiveté. "How do you control greed?"

Chet began to say something about the council, but Martin wouldn't let him finish. "Then you believe humans are basically evil?" Martin asked. "If we don't have rules and punishments, we'll sin indiscriminately?"

"Leigh likes to see the worst in people. It keeps her mind off her own problems," Lydia grinned.

I didn't find her funny. But whatever game she was playing, I wasn't going to participate. "That's one way to look at it," I said, forcing a grin in return.

"Lydia, that's not what I'm asking," Rob said, dismissively. "I want to know if she thinks we're all natural born sinners kept in check by rules and punishment."

I felt I should put him out of his misery. "Yes, I think people will sin when they get the chance. Some of us commit little sins, others of us . . . and then there are some people who sin indiscriminately even with rules and punishment."

Sarah stared across the table at me as if daring me to say something. I was starting to feel outnumbered. I felt my face flush.

"It's human nature," Lydia commented as she passed around my expensive bottle of merlot. "People always want to see what they can get away with." It was obvious she wanted to change the subject, but Rob Martin wasn't going for that.

"So you do think humans are basically evil?" He held my eyes with his own.

"Some, not all. What do you think?"

He didn't answer my question, and his eyes had begun to shine like his forehead. "So according to you, some of us are more evolved morally than others."

He was trying to corner me. I could feel my heart beating harder inside my chest. "I don't know about that. I think it's dangerous to talk in absolutes because people don't fit neatly into categories. But I do believe that some people are evil and irredeemable. Whether they're born that way or they're a product of extreme abuse, I can't say. Nor does it matter really. But you're evading my question, Rob. What do you think?"

He took a deep breath and let it out. "I think people are basically evil. All of them without exception, and that includes myself. I also think it's dangerous not to talk in absolutes. Because that's when you get fooled. John Wayne Gacy, Ted Bundy, Jeffrey Dahmer. Think about how they were able to win their victims' confidence. By appearing 'normal' and cultivating a clever con. But knowing that their victims most likely believed in the basic goodness of people was the other part. No one with any sense of self-preservation these days can afford that belief."

"Sometimes experience is the best teacher," I said, aware that Martin was taking my comments very personally.

Chet chuckled to himself. "Okay then, that's why ya spend so much time with them plants and animals, eh, Rob?"

"Well, here's to human nature." Lydia lifted her glass in a toast. "And if Rob is right, our first McDonald's north of Sturgeon Bay."

Sarah was the only one who drank to Lydia's toast.

"Sarah," Lydia said, "you'll have to give me your chowder recipe. You know how I'm always looking to try new things." She peered over the rim of her glass at Rob.

"I'd like a copy too," I chimed in, seeing a perfect opportunity. "Is this one of your specialties from the restaurant?" Adrenaline was charging through my system and seemed to have surged into my mouth.

"Yeah, I've got lots of specialties," Sarah answered, smiling at Chet.

"Such as?"

"Beef Wellington, poached salmon, the usual."

"What about rabbit stew?"

"What about it?" There was a hard edge to her blackened lips.

"Nothing, just that your mother happened to mention rabbit stew was one of your dishes." Reason told me I should keep my mouth shut, but it was like being in a car wreck, right at the moment of collision.

"She did, huh?" Sarah laughed. "Did she also tell you that rabbit stew was one of old Carl's favorites?"

"Sarah, don't." Rob gave her a panicked look.

"Where's your sense of humor, Rob? Oh I forgot, you never find anything funny anymore."

Martin tried not to look hurt. I almost felt sorry for him.

"But you already know that. About the rabbit stew being his favorite, and probably his last meal. My rabbit stew, left-overs from the restaurant." Sarah glared at me. "I'd be happy to make you some sometime."

"I don't think that's funny," Rob said under his breath.

"See what I mean?" Sarah leaned toward Chet and whispered something into his ear. He laughed uncomfortably.

"Now that there would depend on you," he said, looking up at Rob. Sarah said something else that I couldn't hear. Rob stabbed a piece of cold asparagus viciously.

In the background Charley Parker was squeezing notes out of his sax to "Sweet Georgia Brown" that seemed beyond human ability.

"Speaking of interesting recipes, Rob, did you pick the mushrooms for the soup?" Lydia asked.

"What? Oh, yeah," he said, glancing at me with a smirk.

"You didn't happen to find them at Lynd Point?" I asked, and saw his eyes widen. "I understand that's an excellent spot for mushrooms." I decided to play along with Rob and Lydia's little joke.

Martin had a perplexed look on his damp face. I could feel Stevens shift in his seat.

"Lynd Point? That's not a good site for mushrooms," he scoffed.

Now I was perplexed. Either he was lying or Sarah's painting was a figment of her artistic imagination. "Really? Well, where did you get the mushrooms for this chowder, then?"

"I bought them today," Sarah piped up, "from the market. So if anyone drops dead, you know who to blame."

"No one's accusing you of anything, Sarah," Stevens said in a matter-of-fact tone.

"Jake is right, Sarah. Rob and I were just having a little fun." Lydia smiled broadly at me.

Sarah pulled at her sliced hair. "You and Rob have as much fun as you want. You have my permission."

"Anybody for dessert?" Lydia quickly parried.

After dessert, everyone drifted away from the table in twos. Chet and Sarah huddled in a dark corner on several floor pillows. Lydia would only allow Rob to help her clean up. So Stevens and I were left to each other.

"You never give up," he said, sitting beside me on the sofa and handing me what had to be my twelfth drink. My head felt disconnected from my body. Although he had been drinking throughout dinner, he seemed completely sober. That ability put my teeth on edge.

I was conscious of having lost control over all words containing the letter S. "I had a drink earlier with Eva. Shhhh.

Um, I found out Carl'z final meal wuz rabbit sz-tew. With muss-rooms, no lez."

"So?"

"You heard her at dinner, admitting bringing it from the reztaurant. Eva didn't make it or eat it. Sz-arah made it."

"That doesn't prove she put the fatal mushrooms in the stew. Or even that the fatal mushrooms were in the stew."

"Maybe not. But therez more." I was about to tell him about Joyce and the letters.

He quickly put his finger across my lips. "Can we not talk about Sarah or Carl Peck, for one night? You look pretty wasted. I think you'd better let me drive you home."

So that was how it was going to be.

26

The fire crackled and shot sparks against the sooty screen. Stevens and I were lying in front of it. He was on his side, facing me. I was on my back, trying not to be sick. Like an expectant lover, he had let Salinger out, built a fire, and made me some tea.

After the second cup, the room stopped spinning in its wild orbit.

"You're not going to get sick on me, are you?" Stevens asked, as he reached over and pushed a strand of hair off my forehead.

"Sick? Me, no. I never get sick." The alcoholic fog had lifted somewhat. I remembered that I had said those same words to Tom. Right before the diagnosis of cancer was confirmed.

I turned over on my side and moved closer to Stevens. I reached up and pulled him toward me. I told myself that I could always blame it on the alcohol in the morning.

He was slow, he was methodical and the feel of his tongue traveling down my neck had my body and brain in overdrive.

This will work, I told myself. There's no need for words. I'll guide his hands. I won't let him near the breast area. He'll chalk it up to some eccentricity. You can make love without involving the breasts. I deserve this.

He started to unbutton my blouse.

"No." I pushed his hand away and sat up, tugging at my open blouse like a high school virgin.

"What's going on?" He sat up and faced me.

"Look, Jake. I can't do this. I thought I could, but I can't."

"Okay. Whatever." His tone was sharp.

I had initiated the sex. I owed him some explanation. "It's just . . . it's not about you."

"What's it about?"

"It's just not a good idea."

"Why, because we work together? Because I'm your boss? What?"

"Those are good reasons."

"But they're not 'the' reason, are they?"

"I don't have to give you any reason." My nerves were fraying.

He stared a moment into the fire. "What are you hiding?"

The question stunned me into silence.

"I'm right, aren't I?"

"Can you wait here for just a moment?"

He looked at me perplexed, but remained sitting. "Sure."

I hoped that he didn't think I was slipping into something more comfortable.

I wasn't sure where I had stored the poster of the one-breasted woman. But I was pretty sure it was somewhere in my bedroom closet. Sure enough, I had shoved it in the back under a pile of clothes.

I grabbed it and headed toward the living room. I'd show Stevens the poster and then he'd leave me alone. There'd be no need for tortured discussions and reassurances. I had used the poster with Tom as a preamble to showing him the mastectomy. He had glanced at the poster and said, "Now, can I look at you?"

He had taken one look at the "new" me and said, "You look fine." I hadn't believed him.

I strode into the living room. Stevens was still sitting on the floor in front of the fireplace. I knelt down beside him and unrolled the poster. He looked at the woman in the poster for what seemed like a very long time. Then he looked up into my eyes. It was only when I broke the gaze that his eyes moved to my chest and then away.

"Personally, I've always been a leg man."

In spite of myself, I laughed.

"But that can wait for another night," he said, standing up.

27

Saturday, November 18, Present day

There was a buzzing inside my head like a thousand angry bees that wouldn't stop. Automatically, I reached over toward the alarm clock and pushed down on the button several times before I realized that it was the front door bell.

I sat up, and a wave of nausea rolled through me. I ran to the bathroom with Salinger at my heels. After retching several times, I was able to stand up, but my throat was raw and my side hurt. Clutching my side, I staggered to the front door. Whoever was there was insistently pressing the doorbell. I had to stop that noise.

I peered through the etched glass. It was Lydia. She was holding a covered bowl. I inched the door open.

"God, you look awful. Your face is flushed. Hung over? I brought you some leftover chowder."

At the mention of the chowder, my stomach heaved. Without a word, I ran to the bathroom but didn't quite make it. I fell on my knees and vomited on the bathroom floor. I was sweating and shaking with dizziness. This was like no morning-after hangover I'd ever had.

"Leigh?" Lydia had come into the bathroom.

I watched Lydia's face as it faded in and out of darkness. Then everything went dark.

★ ★ ★ ★ ★

The tubes were back as if they knew their way and had proprietary rights. One was in my right hand and was attached to an overhead drip. There was another inserted in my side. The familiar antiseptic smell stung my nose. I started to reach toward my left breast and stopped. The pain was in my stomach, not my breast. From habit, I looked over at the next bed. It was empty.

I pushed the call button. Almost immediately, a nurse appeared.

"You're awake, excellent." She had overpermed, hay-colored hair and a blue ink stain on the pocket of her uniform.

I started to talk, but my throat felt like it had been sandpapered.

"Don't try and talk. I'll get Doctor Waters. He's the admitting doctor. Lucky you, he's still on the floor making rounds."

I floated somewhere above the hospital bed, remembering the fire and Jake Stevens slow, methodical fingers and then everything disappeared into a fog. Suddenly at my bedside, the nurse reappeared with a thirty-something doctor with a crew cut that was as clipped as his bedside manner.

"The long and short of it is that you ingested a toxic substance. Until we run some tests on what we flushed out of your stomach, we won't know for sure what it was. Unless of course, you know what it was?"

I struggled to speak above a whisper. "I don't know. No way did I do this to myself."

"All right, then." He jotted something on my chart. His professional face didn't give much away, but his manner suggested he didn't believe me. I didn't take it personally. Emergency room doctors were a skeptical lot.

"As soon as we have the results, we'll let you know."

★ ★ ★ ★ ★

Sunday, November 19, Present day

The next morning, Doctor Waters delivered the test results to me in person. I suppose I should have considered it an honor. He stood at the foot of my bed as if he were giving a lecture to first year interns.

"You ingested a drug called Antabuse. It's not harmful unless the suggested dosage is exceeded, or it's combined with alcohol. The severity of the reaction is tied to the amount of the drug and alcohol taken. From your symptoms, I'd estimate that you ingested about 250 grams of the drug in combination with a great deal of alcohol."

"But there's no permanent damage?" I asked. First things first. I'd worry about who gave me the drug after I knew I was okay.

"No. But you were quite fortunate that someone got you to the hospital so quickly. If not, you would have gone into convulsions and possibly cardiac infarction."

"I didn't take that drug," I said, adamantly.

"I'd like to see you in a week for a follow-up. And you won't be able to drink for several weeks."

The very mention of alcohol was contracting my stomach muscles. "Why is that?"

"We have to be sure that your system is free of the drug. We did a gastric lavage." I looked at him like he had three heads. "We washed out your stomach and lower bowel. But the drug is still in your system."

"I'm missing something here."

"Antabuse is used to treat alcoholics. It usually takes about twenty-four hours on the drug before drinking alcohol will set off a reaction. On the other side, a reaction can still occur several days to several weeks after the last dose, depending on the amount of the drug taken. That's how it works."

244

He rechecked his notes and finally made eye contact. "This doesn't have anything to do with the cancer?"

"The cancer?" My brain was still trying to digest what he had told me. "No, I'm okay with the cancer. I mean, this has nothing to do with my mastectomy."

"All right, then. Well, there's a deputy from the sheriff's office outside. He needs to ask you some questions. I'll see you in a week, Ms. Girard." Doctor Waters shook my hand and left.

Chet Jorgensen stood next to my bed, trying not to look at the various tubes sticking out of me. "Can't stand hospitals," he stated tersely, taking off his hat and placing it gingerly on a chair. He was in full uniform today, complete with sidearm.

"Why don't you sit down?" I whispered.

"No thanks. This'll only take a few minutes, then." He flipped open a notepad. "Doc tells me ya overdosed on some drug called Antabuse, used to treat alcoholics." He studied the ceiling for a few seconds. "Now don't get upset, but I've gotta ask this. Did ya take an intentional overdose while you was drinkin'?"

"No. Nor did I take it accidentally. I never heard of this drug until two minutes ago. Chet, somebody poisoned me."

"Okay then, I know you're upset. But ya don't want to jump to conclusions."

I nodded my head emphatically yes. "Think about it. Why would I take a drug and then drink, if I knew that it would make me sick?"

"Okay, that's what I'm here to find out." He cleared his throat. "Um, are ya or have ya ever been treated for alcoholism, then?"

I rolled my eyes. "No. Someone slipped me the drug, knowing that I would be drinking. He or she tried to kill me."

"Okay, let's assume for now you're right. Since the Doc tells me the drug takes about twenty-four hours to get goin' in the body before ya get sick from drinkin', let's go over what ya did during your last twenty-four hours."

"Starting with the obvious, there was the dinner party. Anybody could have put something in my drink or drinks at the party."

"Thought about that already. What about before or after the party?"

"Before the party, I spent the majority of the day alone. I had a few drinks with Eva Peck at the Olde Stagecoach." His left eyebrow went up. Probably not because he suspected Eva, but because Eva and I were socializing. "And after the party, Jake made me some tea, at my house." I was trying not to dwell on that part of the evening.

"That there's a lot of potential suspects. Can ya think of any reason somebody would want to poison ya?"

"Chet, you know the reason as well as I do. Now are you going to look further into Carl Peck's death or not?"

"Ya think there's a connection between ya bein' poisoned and Carl Peck's death?"

"Isn't it obvious? Why else would someone want to poison me? Either they think I know something or they're afraid I'm too close."

He seemed to consider what I said and jotted something down in his notepad. "I need ya to make a formal statement when you're up to it. And I'll tell the Chief what ya said about the connection." He put his hat back on. "But I think you're wrong. Dead wrong."

"Why Chet, you just made a pun."

"You just stay away from the sauce for awhile. Okay, then?"

The overpermed nurse came in the room as Chet left. "Aren't we the popular one," she said, checking my tubes.

If I had attempted suicide, her cheery demeanor would be sending me over the edge about now. "Could you do me a favor?" I asked.

"Depends on what it is."

"Could you see if Doctor Porter is in the hospital? I'd like to talk to him."

"Is he your regular doctor?"

"Yes." The white lie was in a good cause. I had a hunch about the drug used to poison me.

"I'll check."

"And one other thing, could you hand me the phone?"

If it was possible, Doctor Porter looked older than the last time I saw him. He sat in the chair beside my bed, reading my chart and nodding his head. "Everything looks in order. How are you feeling, young lady?" He patted my leg paternally.

"Except for the tubes, the pain in my stomach and the sore throat, hunky-dory."

"Don't worry, you're in good hands. Doctor Waters is first rate."

"That isn't exactly why I asked you here. I didn't take the Antabuse. Somebody slipped it to me."

"If you're sure that's what happened, then you should tell the police, young lady."

"I did. But you might be able to help."

"How can I help?"

"Did you ever prescribe Antabuse for Carl Peck?" I asked, playing out my hunch.

He moved his jaw from side to side as if he were re-aligning his dentures. "You know I can't tell you that. That's confidential information between a doctor and his patient."

"I realize that Doctor Porter, and I wouldn't ask except that someone tried to kill me with that drug."

"What does that have to do with Carl Peck?"

"I'm not sure. All I know is that within the last twenty-four hours, someone poisoned me with Antabuse, and several people close to Carl Peck had the opportunity to get their hands on that drug if he had a prescription for it."

He started to get out of his chair. "I think you need your rest."

"Wait, Doctor Porter, please. Think about it. Carl Peck is dead. What difference does it make now?"

He sat back down and looked again at my chart. "The only reason I'm going to say anything at all is to prove that you're barking up the wrong tree."

"So, did you prescribe the drug for Carl Peck?"

"Carl came to see me last March. He looked pretty bad. He was retaining fluid, and his whole body was swollen. His skin was yellowing as a result of jaundice. I told him if he didn't stop drinking, he'd be dead by Christmas. He said he wanted to stop and had tried but couldn't.

"And that was why he'd come to see me. Finally scared, I guess. He wanted me to give him a prescription for Antabuse. He'd read something about it somewhere. Carl was a great reader. I told him his liver cirrhosis was too far advanced, and to take that drug would outright kill him. He lost his temper and told me he didn't need my help, that he'd find a way him-self. The next time I saw him was in the hospital, right before he died."

"So you didn't prescribe him the drug?"

"That's what I'm saying."

"But that doesn't mean he didn't get it from another physician."

"Any physician who would prescribe Antabuse to Carl Peck would be writing his death warrant."

It was dark outside. I must have slept for hours.

"You're looking better. Green just isn't your color." Lydia stood in the shaft of light from the hallway.

"What time is it?"

"About five. Sorry I couldn't stick around yesterday, but there was no one to cover at the shop. I didn't leave though, until Hank, er Doctor Waters, assured me you were out of danger. Here, I brought you something. A get well present."

She handed me a small box wrapped in deep blue paper studded with silver stars. "Go on, open it. Considering what's happened, I think it'll come in handy."

It was a greenish-black stone attached by a silver-filigreed cap to a long silver-linked chain. The necklace was similar to the one I'd seen Lydia wear.

"The stone's malachite. It heals and balances the whole system. It's especially good for healing from poisoning."

"So you believe that I was poisoned."

"Of course, what else? I told Hank that. But you know how doctors are. He kept asking me if you were depressed, you know, about the cancer."

"What did you say?"

"I told him that any demons you might have lurking about because of the cancer, you exorcised through your work. I was right to say that, wasn't I?"

So she wasn't sure I hadn't tried to kill myself. I wondered why she had defended me to Doctor Waters.

"You were right."

"Good, now you can let the police handle this thing. Your day nurse told me Chet was here earlier. What did he say?"

"He's going to look into it. But he doesn't believe that I was poisoned. He thinks I have a drinking problem."

Lydia laughed. "Chet can be so literal sometimes. He has a real problem seeing beyond the obvious." She checked the tube attached to my side. "Did Doctor Waters say when they were taking this out?"

Something was on Lydia's mind, and it wasn't the tube removal. "I thought this evening. Any guesses who slipped me the drug?"

She turned toward me, her eyes bright with interest. "I've been trying not to think about that. And I suggest you do the same."

"Lydia, that's a little difficult considering that someone wanted me dead and might have succeeded, if you hadn't shown up."

"Then that eliminates me as a suspect." She was trying to make light of the situation, which infuriated me.

"If it was you lying here, I'm sure you'd be thinking about it night and day."

She shrugged her shoulders. "I suppose I would. Not to sound insensitive, but it isn't me. And quite frankly, I think you're partly to blame for what happened." Her contrite manner had disappeared. "I warned you about pursuing this Carl Peck thing. You were downright rude to Sarah at the dinner party. I wanted to kill you myself."

Realizing what she had said, she flushed. "I'm sorry, that came out wrong. It's just that I can't understand you. Whether Carl Peck died accidentally or was poisoned has nothing to do with you. From what I know of him, he was a nasty man, and the world is probably a better place without him."

"Those are pretty harsh words from someone who's dedicated her life to healing people."

"Some people are beyond redemption. Didn't you say that at the dinner party?"

I was starting to feel nauseous again. "That doesn't mean we have the right to kill them. And in case you haven't noticed, this Carl Peck thing now has a lot to do with me."

"Look, I can see we're getting nowhere with this. You need to rest. I'm going to take off."

She picked up the necklace and turned it in her hand. "You really are going to need this."

I looked at her skeptically.

"Besides helping flush your system of the poison, malachite has spiritual properties. It can reveal one's deepest fears about change and growth. It's sort of like a mirror of your soul. Of course, you have to wear it in order to receive its benefits."

She placed the necklace in my hand. As she turned to go, I called out to her. "Lydia, thank you for saving my life."

"No problem. It's what I dedicated my life to, remember."

"So you see, it had to be one of four people," I explained to Stevens, who had his size eleven cross-trainers propped up on my bed and was leaning back on his chair. "Eva, Sarah, Rob, or Renn Woulff."

He had shown up around 7:30 with a book of poetry by someone named Jean Valentine. I knew it was to keep me quiet. When I asked him who Jean Valentine was, he replied, "Just read it and find out." Neither one of us brought up our last exchange at my cottage.

"So according to your reasoning, whoever poisoned you also poisoned Carl Peck. That leaves Woulff out," he decreed.

"Not necessarily. He was at the Olde Stagecoach when I

was there with Eva. He could easily have slipped something into my drink when I went to the washroom."

"Most of the time, Renn Woulff can't remember where he parked his truck. I don't see him doing something like this. He's a pathetic drunk who blames everyone else for his own screw ups."

"Maybe," I said, debating whether to tell Stevens my suspicions about Woulff leaving me that freek-y message on my mirror.

He leveled his infamous blue stare at me. "What?"

"Nothing. Let's forget about Woulff for a moment. So you do believe someone poisoned Carl Peck?"

"It's possible."

"It's more than possible and you know why." My throat hurt from talking.

"Because someone poisoned you."

"Are you making fun of me?"

"I'm only following your deductions."

"There's something else," I said, pinching the stiff sheet between my fingers.

"Out with it, Girard. You've got that look."

I told him what I knew about Joyce Oleander and her illegitimate child, skipping the part about breaking and entering and stealing important papers. "I don't see how any of this ties in with Peck's murder, but I've got a gut feeling that it does," I concluded.

"Who told you this information about Joyce Oleander?" His face went blank except for that almost imperceptible nerve twitching along his jaw. I was beginning to read this faux blankness as an indicator of some strong emotion he had to keep in check. The stronger the emotion, the blanker his expression. And not for the first time, I wondered what his story was.

"Ida Reeves," I revealed softly. Suddenly driving home my point became secondary to Stevens maintaining that blank look.

He stared out the window, lost in his own musings. Finally he said, "That explains a lot."

I waited for him to elaborate, but he just kept staring out the window.

"Joyce had exhausted every avenue to find her child." I reached for my notepad from the bedside table. "She even called a detective named Barry Snyder." Earlier I had checked my answering machine for messages. Wonder of wonders, Snyder had finally called. He said if I wanted to talk to him, I should call today before 7:30. After that, I'd have to wait until he got back from New Mexico.

"You're lying here with tubes sticking out of you, and you're conducting research?" He shook his head. "What did you find out?"

"Not much. The guy didn't have anything to go on. Joyce couldn't even say for sure if the child had been adopted in this state. She did tell him about the friend who took the baby. But when he asked for the friend's name, she clammed up. He said, 'It was pretty much like finding a needle in a hay-stack.' "

I laid back on the pillow. "Do you know the last time she contacted this guy?"

"The day she died?"

"Right," I rasped, more than a little disappointed. "She wanted him to widen his search to other states. He told her she'd be wasting her money. But if he could talk to her friend, then maybe he could gather something more to go on in the search. She said that she'd think about it."

"And you think this ties in with Peck, how?"

"That's just it, I don't know."

We sat quietly for a moment. A disembodied voice kept paging a Dr. Andrews to surgery.

"Has it occurred to you that Sarah's shooting her mouth off about how much she detested her old man was pretty stupid if she did kill him?"

Maybe he did believe Peck was murdered. But he still couldn't see Sarah as a murderer.

"Or maybe it goes along with her whole victim mentality. She feels guilty and wants to be punished."

"That's stretching it." He crossed arms and pushed back against his chair.

"I've been doing some reading on this abuse thing. The way Sarah acts, it fits the symptoms."

He held up his hand. "You mean her extreme anger, self-destructive behavior—drinking, smoking, sex, her problems with relationships?"

I frowned at him.

"If you make it through a few winters up here, you'll see that long about January, after we've been snowed in for weeks, about an eighth of the population decides to beat up another eighth of the population. Usually the population they're related to. Alcohol, the Door County antidote for all those long lonely nights, is usually the culprit. We periodically run a few articles on warning signs and where to get help."

"Can't wait," I said. "But those symptoms could also apply to sexual abuse."

He leaned toward the bed and put his hand on my forehead as if feeling for a fever.

"It's not that much of a leap." I pushed his hand away.

"Doesn't fit. Sarah would be shouting from the rooftops if her father had touched her. Besides, abuse victims—and victim is the crucial word here—don't often turn to murder.

They usually take their anger out on themselves, not others. Suicide or self mutilation is usually the route they take."

"But sometimes they don't."

His mouth turned downward with skepticism.

"If Sarah did kill her father, and she's so guilt-ridden, then why not come out and admit to killing him?"

"I don't know. That part has me stumped. Unless Rob killed him, and she's protecting him out of some weird sense of loyalty." My head was starting to hurt again.

"You're forgetting Eva Peck."

I knew he was playing devil's advocate. "I haven't forgotten her. The problem is, what motive would she have to kill her husband? She surely already knew he was dying of alcoholism. But of course, that would also apply to Sarah and Rob, and old Woulff-ie as well. According to Doctor Porter, if Carl Peck didn't stop drinking, he would have been dead by December. Why hurry the process?"

"An act of premeditated passion."

"Are you making fun of me again?"

"I just wanted to see how that mind of yours works." Stevens sat up in his chair. "Look, Chet called me this afternoon. He's following through on what you told him. So right now, the best thing you can do is let him handle it and get out of this hospital. We have some unfinished business."

I squirmed under the sheet.

"That is, if you want to finish it."

I fiddled with the malachite necklace. In a sudden fit of superstition, I had slipped it around my neck.

"What's that?" He touched the necklace.

"Get well present from Lydia. Supposed to help heal me from poisoning."

He laughed. "Is it good for anything else?"

"You mean besides conversation? I think she said it's a

mirror of the soul." I looked down at the shiny, greenish-black stone. It reflected my face in miniature. "Sometimes Lydia's a little too clever for her own good."

"What do you mean?"

"Look."

He leaned over and looked at the stone.

"If only it were that easy."

"Maybe that's the point."

28

Tuesday, November 21, Present day

A spatter of blues and grays littered the indeterminate sky as I drove north on Highway 57. A sharp wind whipped across the truck, sending gusts of cold air inside the cab. A few snowflakes melted on the windshield. My dull headache was gone, but I still felt as if a horse had kicked me in the side.

I was supposed to be at home, getting a week's bed rest, but Rob Martin had called me around eight. Said he had to see me, something that couldn't be discussed on the phone. I didn't want him coming to the cottage. Since the attempt on my life, I needed to feel that my home was sacrosanct. So I agreed to meet him at the Ridges Sanctuary, a protected boreal forest bordering Lake Michigan. I knew that the grounds would be strewn with volunteers. The third Tuesday of every month, volunteers work on various projects—from repairing the boardwalks to gathering seeds. So I felt I'd be safe. I was used to Door County people viewing the vast outdoors, even trails close to the water's edge or deep in the woods, as normal haunts to meet for a chat. After all, this much nature was one reason I'd come here myself. In the short time I'd been here, it seemed obvious that the natives grew up on this peninsula so tied to the natural world through their art, their recreation, and their livelihood, that "off the beaten path" never occurred to them.

As I walked the circular path toward the Nature Center, I saw Rob Martin bent over what looked like a bunch of scraggly weeds. His red hair stood out against the surrounding pines like a cardinal's wing. He was so intent on what he was doing that he didn't hear me approach.

"Picking weeds?" I asked, coming up behind him.

He turned his head in my direction but didn't get up. "Hardly. Blue fringed gentian." He pointed to a small blue flower. "Very rare, especially this late in the fall."

"I thought it was winter already. Okay, I give, what makes a fringed gentian so special?" I figured he was going to tell me anyway.

"First of all, it's a native wildflower and quite beautiful. If you look real close, you can see where its common name came from."

I squatted gingerly down beside him to get a closer look at the fragile plant. Sure enough, the deep blue flower's petals were delicately fringed as if fashioned by a seamstress.

"It's lovely," I whispered, as if we were in a church.

"What makes this plant so fascinating is its habit of turning up in the most surprising places. That happens because its seeds get blown great distances from the parent plant." He gave me a sidelong glance to see if I was listening. He must have been satisfied because he continued. "There's a Hungarian folk tale that credits this plant as named after a King Ladislas. According to the legend, during a terrible plague, the King shot an arrow into the air, asking God to let it fall on a plant he could use to cure his people. The arrow landed on a gentian, which as the legend goes, the King then used to stop the plague in his country."

It was obvious why Martin was such a good naturalist. Chet wasn't half wrong, plants and animals probably provided him a world he could decipher and count on. "That's a big claim for such a fragile flower."

"Sometimes a plant's appearance can be deceiving. But in the natural world, it all makes sense."

"You didn't ask me here to talk about botany." I was starting to get cold.

"Still in a big hurry, huh? Okay, let's walk the trail to the beach. That way I can check out some plants along the way. And you can keep warm."

"Fine by me. Where are the volunteers?" I asked, as casually as I could. I hadn't seen any around.

"Upper Range Lighthouse. They're painting the interior walls."

I shoved my right hand in my pocket and felt for the thick cylinder of pepper spray I put there just in case.

As we crossed the wooden bridge that led into the forest, the bark chip path quickly narrowed and became jagged with stones. The preservationists had done a convincing job: except for the numbered signs, I felt as if I had entered the forest primeval: a green tangle of ferns, cedars, pines, spruces, so many deciduous trees that I couldn't name, and here and there where light had found a way in, clumps of asters persistent as an errant wish. I followed Martin's blue checkered back at a distance. Occasionally he stopped and jotted something down in his notebook. Ideas for his column, I figured.

As the trail became increasingly overgrown and dark, mushrooms began to appear. They sprang from fallen trees, between rocks, along the forest floor, wherever something needed to be consumed. Martin bent over and examined a group of mushrooms the color of Halloween pumpkins.

I stepped off the trail to get a closer look at the abundant variety of mushrooms. Some were smooth and white, some a smoky yellow, some had convex caps, and some concave. Others looked soft and shiny. "Deliquescence," I whispered to myself, squatting down to look closely. Too lovely a word to describe decomposition, that stage when a mushroom's flesh softened and then turned to liquid. I remembered the term from the book I'd borrowed from Joyce Oleander's condo.

"Deliquescence." Martin came up behind me.

I stood up to face him, slipping my hand in my right pocket. "I know," I said. But he had already moved away down the trail.

It wasn't until we reached the wooden bridge that we were able to walk side by side, and he shoved his notebook into his rucksack. "This walkway leads to the beach." Without waiting for a response, he crossed the one lane road and headed down the beach. I was beginning to wonder why he had suggested meeting at the Ridges, and why we were on this secluded stretch of Lake Michigan beach. All my senses clicked into high gear. What if this was more than just "the Door ways"? One attempt on my life was enough for a week, thank you. I looked back over my shoulder toward the upper range lighthouse, but no one was looking out. I can still turn back, I told myself.

Instead, I increased my pace and caught up with Martin. The sky had gone slate gray, and snow was falling. The wind was fierce off the lake, and I had to shout to be heard.

"Where are we going?"

He strode ahead of me without answering. I had no choice but to keep up with him. Finally, he slowed his pace and headed inland. About ten feet ahead was a snug shelter of pine trees. By the time we reached the pine shelter, I was shivering.

I plopped down on the hard white sand next to him. "Now

that we've had our morning constitutional, will you please tell me what's going on?"

He reached into the inner pocket of his jacket, pulled out a crumpled piece of paper and handed it to me. Two sentences were scribbled in pencil on the paper. "I killed him. God help me." It was signed, "Sarah."

"Where did you get this?"

"It was next to Sarah on the bed, the night I found her when she took the Valium." His hands were shoved under his arms as if he were holding himself together.

"Did you show the police?"

"Sarah said she didn't write it. She looked confused when I showed it to her." He gnawed at the corner of his mouth, not making eye contact.

"Is it her handwriting?"

"It looks like hers. I can't be sure."

The handwriting was erratic. But considering what Sarah's condition would have been when she wrote it, erratic fit. "Why are you showing this to me?"

I was watching him intently. His green eyes narrowed with a fierce determination. I realized that he had been debating that question for himself the entire way here. He probably hadn't resolved it until just now.

"Because of what happened to you. Don't get me wrong, this isn't out of any concern over your welfare."

"As long as we have that straight."

He ignored my remark. "Chet called this morning and told me about the Antabuse. He asked me a lot of questions about the dinner party." He stopped. "I'm afraid for Sarah."

"You think she poisoned me?"

"I can't protect her anymore."

"You've got to give Jorgensen this suicide note."

"I don't have to do anything," he spat in my face.

"Let the police decide if Sarah wrote it. It's out of your hands now."

"I won't do it. I can't do that to her. She would see it as the final act of betrayal in a long line of betrayals by people who were supposed to love and protect her."

So that was it, he wanted me to turn the note over to the police. "I can give the police the note, but I'd have to say where I got it. It would all come down to the same thing."

"Here's the way I figured it. I let you see the note, because I thought you deserved to know. Now it's in your hands. Do what you want with it. But if you give it back to me, I'm going to tear it up."

"She's still going to know you gave me the note."

"Maybe, but at least I'm not the one giving it to the police."

His reasoning was convoluted, but Martin always seemed to be ruled by passion when it came to Sarah.

"What are you going to tell her?"

"I haven't decided. What's important is that Sarah gets help."

"This would all be a lot easier if you gave the note to Jorgensen," I reiterated, reading the note again.

"This is way past easy," he snarled.

"Besides me, have you shown the note to anyone else?"

Martin hesitated for a second. "Just Eva. I thought she should know."

It wouldn't have been my call. "You thought she'd give the note to the police?"

"No, I wouldn't ask her to do that," he snapped. "I wanted to prepare her. She's been through so much."

"What did she say?"

"That Sarah's sick, that she needs help. That I'm the only one who can help her now."

"So it was your idea to show me the note first?"

"What difference does that make?"

"I don't like the idea of being a go-between. I feel like I'm being set up."

"I told Eva, just like I told you, that I wouldn't take the note to the police. She said to show it to you. You'd know what to do."

That sentiment didn't seem to jibe with Eva's last words to me. But then, she had been angry at the time.

"So you'll do it?"

"Okay," I answered reluctantly, shoving the note in my pocket. Suddenly the sun slid from under some clouds and turned the water silver. I felt my face warm with the light. We both looked up.

"Well, that's pretty spectacular," I said, shielding my eyes from the glare.

"What?" he asked.

"The sky, that sudden burst of light, the water turning silver."

"It's because we're surrounded by water," he answered in an even tone. "The two bodies of water play off each other and that creates the sudden changes in the light." He waited a moment to see if I understood.

"You know how to get back," he said.

I drove straight to the police station in Sturgeon Bay, another aging stone edifice in the older section. Lucky me, Deputy Jorgensen was in his office. The receptionist directed me to his desk. Behind the partition and against the wall. I expected to find a deer head sprouting from the knotty pine. Instead, his work area was the picture of police décor, right down to the miniature American flag on his desk.

"Aren't ya supposed to be in bed?" He blushed to his blonde roots.

"Something too important came up." Now I was blushing. I took out the note and handed it to Jorgensen.

He stared at it so long, I thought he'd dozed off.

"Rob Martin gave it to me this afternoon. He found it next to Sarah Peck the night of her suicide attempt. He's pretty sure it's her handwriting."

"Why'd he wait so long to turn it in, then?"

"You'll have to ask him that." I had agreed to deliver the note, not to be the lawyer for the defense.

"We'll have a handwriting expert take a look at it. Ya know I gotta check out your story with Rob and Sarah."

"I wouldn't expect any less from the county's finest deputy."

He smiled. "Okay then, if this is legit, he's an accessory."

"In his mind, some things supersede the law, God, and country."

"Anyways, I questioned everyone who coulda slipped you that drug. Nothing much came of that. 'Cept Eva Peck remembers Carl bein' prescribed some drug to stop him drinkin'. Last time she remembered seein' it was in the medicine cabinet. I told her, check it out."

"That's odd," I said.

"What's odd?"

"How did Carl Peck get the drug? Dr. Porter told me that he refused to prescribe it to him. He said the drug would kill him, because his cirrhosis was so far advanced. So how did he manage to get a physician to write him a prescription for it? And why would he want it, if he knew it would kill him? This isn't making sense."

Chet's phone rang. "Hold on."

While he took the call, I studied the photo on his desk. In

it, Chet posed next to a ten point buck with an arrow sticking out of its chest. The buck's eyes were open.

Chet hung up the phone. "That there was Eva Peck. Medicine ain't there."

Summer, 48 years earlier

Her mother had poured that smell into the bath water again. Lavender. She wanted to tell her the smell made her sick. But the words for it hurt her stomach. Only the shiny razor took the pain away.

Like a string of kisses across her wrists, she made one X after another. Not too deep, just break the skin. Bring a slight rise of blood. No veins or arteries severed, nothing severe.

29

"We think Sarah Peck's left the peninsula." Even over the phone, I could tell Deputy Chet was rattled.

I was on my bed watching a woman on one of those talk shows tell her husband that she's in love with his sister. I muted the sound.

"What happened to the drawbridge? Couldn't get it up in time?" I was going stir crazy just lying around the house. Stevens had banned me from the office until Monday. When I told him about Sarah's note, he had grumbled something about my not leaving the house, and his coming over later with dinner.

"Have ya seen her or heard from her?" Chet asked. His cheerfulness sounded forced.

"Nope. But then, I'm probably the last person she'd contact. What did you find out about the note?"

"Okay, I guess I owe ya one. That handwritin' expert said that note's a pretty close match to Sarah's writin'. And we found Carl's prescription bottle." I waited, already sure of what he was going to say. "It was in the back of Sarah's medicine cabinet. Two tablets were missin'."

"Are you charging her with murder?" The evidence certainly pointed at Sarah, but instinct told me that it was too clean and neat. Too much like a script.

266

"Right now, all we want ta do is get her in here for questionin'.""

"Then Rob confirmed my story?"

"Haven't found Rob neither."

"Nothing like leaving the best part out."

"Look, ya hear from either of 'em, call me. Let us deal with it."

"Of course."

Summer, 51 years earlier: Chicago

It was hot, and the bathroom smelled of urine and lavender. He knelt beside the bathtub. The water was slick with bath oil. He had come in to wash her back. But now his hands were on her belly, then between her legs. The light from the shaded window yellowed his skin, her skin, the cracked floor, the peeling walls.

"You're so beautiful, you're so beautiful," he whispered over and over as his fingers moved back and forth.

Then he lifted her from the slick, cold water, dried her and took her to another room. The damp bed held her body, but she floated to the ceiling. The smell of onions filled the room as her body was peeled back by his mouth.

When it was over, when she returned to her body, she put on her cotton panties, undershirt, white anklets, red sandals, blue starched sundress. He came into the room holding something in his hand. He was smiling.

"This is for you," he said, putting the gift in her small hand.

It was a pin studded with green stones. They were the same color as his eyes. Her tiny fist closed around it. She felt the prick of the pin through her palm. She kept her hand shut.

As he drove her home through the long shadowed streets, her head fell forward and hit the dashboard. Then someone was slapping her face gently, saying "Wake up, wake up." She opened her eyes. They were two blocks from her house.

267

"You must never tell anyone what we did. Or I'll have to hurt every member of your family. Understand?"

She shook her head yes.

Once inside her bedroom, she opened her hand, removed the pin and hid it in the bottom of her jewelry box. In the middle of her palm was the indentation of a heart and a small red dot of blood. She watched as the heart slowly faded, leaving only the small wound in the center of her hand. For two weeks, she kept her hand closed around it, afraid someone would see. Then it too disappeared.

Every time he saw her, he gave her a dime. She bought candy with the dimes: chocolate bars, peppermint sticks, lollipops.

He never touched her again.

30

"Meet me at the cave. You know the one, South Heaven." Her voice was tight with fear. "I've got a gun. If you bring anybody, I'll kill myself."

"Sarah, don't do anything rash. Let me help you."

"You've got forty-five minutes." Her voice faded in and out. I could hear the crackling of a cell phone connection. "Come alone. I mean it."

"I will, Sarah, I promise. But wait . . ." The line went dead.

I threw on jeans, a sweatshirt and my down-filled parka. As I was closing the front door, I remembered Stevens and his promise of dinner. I tried him at the office, but he'd left for the day. Marge told me to try his cell phone. When he didn't pick up, I left him a voice message. "It's Leigh. Sarah Peck contacted me. I'm meeting her at Peninsula State Park, Eagle Trail. By the South Heaven cave. She's got a gun and is threatening to kill herself if I don't come alone." In case he didn't pick up his voice messages, I also wrote a hurried note with the same information and taped it to the door.

As I drove up Highway 42, I called Chet Jorgensen at the station on my cell phone. The dispatcher told me he was already out combing the peninsula for Sarah, so I left him the same message I'd left for Jake, except that I added he should get there fast, because Sarah was armed and threatening sui-

cide. Even using extreme caution, it was impossible to approach the caves unseen. Besides, Sarah was sure to be on the
lookout. I didn't want her to do anything foolish. If a bunch
of cops showed up, she might panic.

Though I sped through the fading light, it occurred to me
more than once that I should turn around, go back home, and
let Chet handle this. Sarah's insistence that I come alone had
my hackles up. She could use me as a hostage to get off the
peninsula. Or maybe she wanted to kill me for giving the police her note, or for pursuing her father's death, or just on
principle, before she took her own life. And then there was
Rob Martin, who also was missing. Was he a player in Sarah's
plan?

By the time I reached Eagle Tower, a quarter moon was
cresting the trees, even though the sun had yet to set. The
black Dodge Ram was parked near the trail head. I looked at
my watch. Thirty minutes had passed since Sarah's phone
call. It would take me at least fifteen minutes, if not more, to
reach the caves. Where the hell was Chet? I sat in the truck
nervously tapping the steering wheel and staring out into the
woods. I looked at my watch again. Five more minutes had
passed. Sarah had said forty-five minutes. Her voice had
sounded desperate and scared. She had attempted suicide
once, and I had felt some responsibility for pushing her too
hard. If she used the gun on herself this time, there'd be no
saving her.

I jumped out of the truck, slammed the door, and started
for the trail head. Before I reached the caves, I'd have to find
something to use for a weapon—maybe a thick tree branch.
Then I remembered the extra set of bow and arrows that I'd
stuffed behind the truck's cab when Chet loaned them to me.
After my encounter with Woulff at Newport State Park, I had
decided to keep them in the truck. Now I hurried back,

grabbed the bow and slung the sheaf of arrows over my shoulder. The bow beat a tree branch, but a gun would beat both. Nonetheless, I would play what I was dealt.

I took one more look toward the road for Chet's police car, but the asphalt road shone empty. I decided not to wait any longer. I felt in my jacket pocket for my flashlight and pepper spray.

Just as I began the difficult descent, the sun slid into the bay, turning the air sharp and the woods dark. A burst of panic surged through me. I stood still on the sharp incline for a few moments, taking deep breaths, letting my eyes adjust to the moonlight. The landscape was leached of color and definition. Then slowly, as if a door was opening, the trees, rocks, and cliffs emerged into black and white shapes: the colors of night, the colors of dreams. I blinked several times.

When I could distinguish the birches from the other trees, I moved cautiously down the trail. A thick crust of snow and ice covered the path and my every step sent a slippery, crunching sound echoing through the woods. Animals I couldn't see scurried through the snow, startling me. I kept hearing Chet's words: "There's some bears in the forests," he had said, "so bear huntin's limited." I dug in my pocket and retrieved my flashlight, switching it on.

I shook my head as if that would free me of the fear that was now seeping into every fiber of my body. For a moment I stopped and listened, hoping to hear Chet making his way down the trail. But all I heard was an owl somewhere in the distance who seemed to be repeating the phrase, "Me too." I took another deep breath and looked up. A cloud had momentarily smothered the frail moonlight with its vast white body. I slowed my pace, directing the flashlight beam on the trail that wound downward like a white river. By the time I reached the pine forest, the moon had freed itself from the cloud and once again the night sky was filled with icy light.

Along the shore path, the snow was deeper, and I was glad I had worn my hiking boots. I could hear the restless crash of the icy water hitting that stony beach. I didn't like it. The night seemed too quiet, too expectant.

I was beginning to question the wisdom of not waiting for Chet, of coming here armed only with a bow and some arrows. What made me think I could talk Sarah into giving herself up? There had never been anything veiled about her hostility toward me. A moment of hubris had set me on this course. I could still turn around; I could still head back. Let Chet deal with Sarah. A more looming question arose: how was I going to prevent Sarah from using her gun on me or herself? Then I realized that my charging out of the trees armed with bow and arrows might trigger her to drastic action sooner, so I decided that I'd find a spot to leave them, near the cave where Sarah couldn't see them.

The trail opened up to a clearing. As I walked along the shoreline path, I stared out at the water. Even in this light, I could see one of the nearby islands—a dark mass surrounded by water. For some reason, I was reminded of Rob Martin's explanation for the sudden changes in light on the peninsula. How had he explained it? "The two bodies of water play off each other and that creates the sudden changes in the light."

Two bodies playing off each other? That could describe Sarah and Rob and their volatile relationship. But it could also describe Sarah and her father's relationship. Whether Sarah killed her father alone or Rob helped her, I still didn't know. But I felt I was definitely about to find out. Maybe that was my real reason for coming to this isolated place alone?

I shook my head again. That wasn't why I'd come. I was here because right now with the cold biting into my skin and a mad woman waiting for me in a cave, I felt alive. For the first time since my cancer, I felt alive.

The cancer had robbed me of that feeling. In relinquishing myself to the doctors, I had relinquished myself to fate and with it, all sense of control. I had lost that woman who used to move through life with a dancer's balance.

My memory flashed on the blue recliner at the hospital where I sat weekly, monthly, trying to distract myself by reading or watching television as the chemo's slow drip entered my body. Hoping the chemo would save me. One day toward the end of the treatments, I felt my body slip away like a dress I was tired of wearing. That day I crossed over a great divide—finally knowing death was always just a matter of when, and that I had no control over it. I was no longer afraid to die. It was a heady realization.

Now against all common sense, my gut was telling me that if there was a chance I could stop Sarah from ruining her life, I had to try. I would make her see that she still had a choice about living or dying, that she could reclaim her life. That as long as she was breathing, there was hope. And for once, it would be my choice, not fate's, to stare death in the face.

Another gust of wind hit my face, savagely stinging my skin. But it felt good. I turned from the shore and trudged on down the snowy path. I ascended toward the South Heaven cave and increased my pace. As I came toward the first set of caves, I saw the flickering of a small fire. Sarah was nowhere in sight. Before I reached the South Heaven cave, I slipped off the sheaf of arrows and placed them with the bow just inside the adjacent cave. With the fire drawing all the light within its circle, I felt sure Sarah could not see where I'd hidden them.

Before approaching the fire, I switched off my flashlight, slipped it into my pocket and called out. "Sarah, it's Leigh Girard."

I heard a stirring from inside the cave. A flashlight bounced its beam from wall to wall. For a second, the words South Heaven were illuminated. Then the flashlight blinded me. My hand went across my eyes, trying to deflect the light. "It's Leigh. Like I promised, I'm alone."

"You shouldn't have come," Sarah said.

"Sarah, come on. Give me the gun, and let's get out of here."

"You don't understand."

"Sarah, I can get you help. There's no need for you to do anything more drastic. To yourself, or anyone else."

"No. Listen, it wasn't me. She did it. All those years, it was dead. Buried, right here. Poor Joyce." Sarah's voice sounded tight and thready, as if it might break.

When she mentioned Joyce, a cold fear crept up my spine. "What are you talking about?"

"Those bones you found . . ." She held the flashlight beam steady on my face, as if she needed to contain me as she studied my reaction. "They were the bones of Joyce's baby. Her little girl. And now she's going to kill me and you."

I moved back away from the cave, but it was too late. As I turned around, Eva Peck stood in front of the fire. She held a rifle in her hand that was pointed at me.

"I knew you'd come," she said.

"What's going on?" I asked, looking from Eva to Sarah. Eva's eyes looked clouded, as if she was blind.

"She said if I called you, she'd tell me where Joyce's child was. I knew Joyce had been looking for her right before she . . ." Sarah let out a deep breath. "I thought the child was adopted. I thought . . ." She choked on the words. "I didn't know she killed it."

"It wasn't killed." Eva's face glowed and glistened in the light. "It was suffocated." The way she emphasized the word suffocated seemed as if she thought that made the outcome different.

"You made a promise, Mother. To Joyce. You promised you'd take care of her child," Sarah whispered.

"There was no other way, Sarah." Eva talked slowly, as if she was speaking to a child. "She would have ruined everything. I thought you'd understand that. You know the family has to come first. Haven't I always told you that? If you don't have a family, what do you have?"

"Mother, I believed you. Joyce and I both believed you. How could you have done that? Not just to Joyce, but to that innocent baby?"

"Be quiet and sit down. Both of you." Eva motioned with the rifle toward the fire. Her voice was low and menacing. "Put out that flashlight."

Sarah switched off the flashlight, slipped it into her pocket, and sat down. My mind was racing as I sat down on the hard, snowy ground.

So the killer had never been Renn Woulff or Rob Martin or Sarah Peck. But Eva Peck? Why on earth would she kill her husband or Joyce's baby? In some degree of shock, I asked, "Why did you do all this, Eva?"

With some effort, she squatted on her haunches in front of the fire, cradling the gun in her arms. "I don't know what you're talking about. I didn't do anything." She twitched the gun in my direction.

"Then why are we here? And why are you holding a gun on us?"

"No one can know."

"Know what?"

"Who the father was," she answered. "That silly, stupid girl. What did she think, he was going to leave me? He didn't love Joyce. He always came home to me." Her eyes were so wide I could see the dark, muddy pupils. They looked like brown glass. "The only thing she did right was to keep her mouth shut. But I knew. He could never hide anything from me. I followed him once. He took her right there in the woods, on the ground like animals. Disgusting." Eva closed her eyes for a moment.

She shifted the gun slightly. "But things have a way of working out. No prayer goes unanswered. One night Sarah comes to me, says her friend needs help. She's outside in the car. So I go. And there she is, lying down in the back seat and clutching her big ugly stomach. Crying in pain for me to help her. It was perfect. I took her out back to his workshop. I could see she was close to birthing the baby. She begged me to take her to the hospital. I told her they'd ask too many questions. She'd have to say who the father was. 'You want to bring that shame on your grandmother?' I asked her. She didn't say anything, just kept moaning. I told her I'd help her if she'd let me take the child. I'd see it got adopted. Nobody would ever have to know. But she could never, ever try to find the child or talk about it to anyone. I made her promise."

In the firelight, Eva's eyes had a dangerous glint. She gripped the rifle stock. "But Joyce broke her promise."

"What about him?" Sarah gasped. "It wasn't just Joyce, Mother. Can't you see that? He was always after some woman or other."

"He was like all men, Sarah." Eva sounded endlessly patient. "He'd have his good days and his bad. But the worst thing would be to lose him and break up the family. I couldn't let that happen."

Sarah's laugh came out choked, as if it had been trapped inside her. "When were the good days, Mother? When he let you go to church? Let you cook and slave for him? How about when he wouldn't let you work? When he twisted your arm in front of his friends until you cried out? How about the late night beatings?"

Eva's eyes flared, and she covered her mouth, shaking her head.

"Did you think you could hide that from me?"

"Sarah, your father was a flawed man, but you know he wasn't horrible twenty-four hours a day."

"Spoken like a true victim." Sarah's words were tumbling out as if they had a will of their own. "I was glad when I thought you might have killed him. I didn't care. I wanted to celebrate. I was on your side. Finally, I thought you'd mustered the guts to stand up for yourself. But now, after what you did to Joyce's baby. Then not to tell me it was my own father. Did it occur to you, Mother, that baby was my half sister? You killed my baby sister."

"I told you, I didn't kill anyone. Carl picked those mushrooms himself. Came home with two kinds. Asked me if I could tell the difference between the angel of death and a harmless mushroom. He said it would be easy to make a mistake if you didn't know what you were doing." Eva was becoming so agitated, she was jerking the rifle from side to side. "He made the mistake. Him, not me. You think I would kill my own husband?"

"Of course it was someone else's fault, Mother, that's the whole story of your life, isn't it?" Sarah's tone was bitter and biting.

I had to somehow get her to stop inciting her mother. "Eva, of course, it wasn't your fault. Whatever happened . . ." I tried to cajole her. I had to keep this crazy woman talking until I could think of some way out.

"It wasn't my fault. I was just a girl, a child," Eva began. "He was a friend of my father's. He said he was going to visit the grave of his dead wife. I waited in the car while he did. It was hot that day. There was sweat on the back of my legs. They stuck to the leather seat." She gripped the rifle, but stared past me, past Sarah, past the fire and this place.

"But I could have run away. The car wasn't locked. But I was used to doing what adults told me. I was a good girl. I was brought up strict. Then we drove to a run down house he owned. Then . . ."

Her eyes went dead with the memory. Sarah and I looked at each other, unsure what Eva was referring to, but only able to wait in the firelight; I could feel the air grow more dense, like something besides weather or time had thickened it.

Eva was suddenly in a place that we could not see or know. "After that, he'd give me money. A dime. I'd buy candy. I loved the taste of sugar." She sighed, and spoke now more to herself than to us. "He gave me a pin shaped like a heart. A green rhinestone heart."

Certainly I hadn't been prepared for Eva's revelation. I suddenly realized she had been wearing that pin when I had first interviewed her after her husband's death. She had sat in that tidy living room feigning grief, wearing the pin of her abuser. My stomach roiled with disgust, but I managed to ask, "And you never told anyone about what that man did to you?"

"He said he'd hurt my family. So I bore it, I kept quiet. But I never forgot what he did. Where he touched me. How he looked, how he smelled of onions. Just thinking of that smell makes me sick. I hated him for what he did to me."

I heard Sarah gasp, still she and I waited here under Eva's control, the twigs snapping in the fire, the icy air closing in around us. Eva remained far away, her face strangely calm. Finally Sarah said in desperation, "Mother, you could have told me. We could have gotten you help."

Eva seemed not to hear her daughter. "Then that night

when Carl came home after being with Joyce again after all these years, he told me he was leaving me. 'You fat, stupid cow,' is what he said. 'You make me sick.' After all the humiliations, after everything I did to make a home for him. I made him sick. That was the worst thing, the thought of him leaving and taking away our family name. I simply couldn't allow that. After all of those years of keeping quiet, of keeping our secret for the sake of the family. Hadn't I done my part? And now he was leaving me."

Somehow in Eva's damaged mind, the man who abused her and Carl Peck had merged. She aimed the rifle at Sarah. "That friend of yours. It was all Joyce's fault. She did it, she told him about that child. After she promised not to tell. 'You bitch,' he called me, 'You lying bitch!' He was ranting and raving that I had betrayed him. Me. After all the women. I had betrayed him."

"And that's why you killed him?" Sarah asked. "Why didn't you just let him leave?"

"Poisoned, not killed. He was poisoned." She spat at Sarah. "After he was dead, I thought he was playing a joke on me, pretending to be dead. I sat there with him, waiting for him to say something. Then I thought, now I can hold my head up in town. People feel sorry for widows. Now I don't have to be ashamed."

All the horrible pieces of this family tragedy were falling into place for me. "You slipped the Antabuse in my drink when I went to the bathroom."

"It was only a warning. For your own good."

"I almost died!" In spite of Eva's waning grip on reality, I felt indignant.

"But you didn't. I knew what I was doing. Only you didn't leave well enough alone, did you?"

"And Sarah, you overdosed Sarah and wrote the suicide

note. You wanted her to be blamed for Carl's death. In fact, you had this planned from the beginning. That's why you insisted on an autopsy."

"You're not as smart as you think you are." Eva got to her feet with surprising agility, and now leveled the rifle at me.

I knew I had to keep her talking. "And Joyce. How did you get her to take the pills?"

She let the rifle drop a few inches. "She took those pills herself. I didn't do anything. By the time I got there, she was already dead. I turned her over and made sure the whore was dead."

With my eyes glued to the rifle, I shifted my legs to the right and leaned forward, ready to make a move of my own. "If you didn't have anything to do with Joyce's death, what were you doing there?"

"You're trying to confuse me!" she shouted, bringing the rifle up level with my heart. She stepped toward me and pressed the barrel hard against me. I caught my breath. With one twitch, my life could be over.

I racked my mind, trying to think of anything that would calm Eva and buy us some time. Enough time for Chet to get here. By now he should have received my message. At any moment, I expected him to burst onto the scene. I only had to hold Eva off a little longer.

"Eva, I can see you had no choice. Carl pushed you to it. But you still have the choice to tell the truth and make this right. You'll be the one who saves your family name."

She slowly backed away from me several steps. "I am going to let you go." She smiled broadly.

I didn't like her tone. It was otherworldly and ice cold. "You'll go first. Then Sarah. Sarah, stand up."

Sarah didn't move.

"I said, stand up!" Eva's face contorted with rage.

Sarah got up slowly, as if in a trance, and I could see the child who had grown up following the orders of an often enraged, drunken father.

My heart was pounding loudly, and I felt hot at the temples. "This is cold-blooded murder, Eva. This isn't you. This isn't a good mother taking care of her daughter."

"More like murder, suicide," she said, circling behind Sarah with the rifle, her eyes focused in that other place where Eva was all alone.

"I know that you were justified in killing Carl. I see that now," I continued. "After what that other man did to you as a child, and then to endure those years of torture from your husband. I can see how you had every right. You had to do it to survive. But if you kill us, everyone will say you're a killer. Your family name will be ruined for good. No one will understand."

"If I shut you up, no one will know! I don't want to think about those things anymore. They disgust me. But soon my problems will be gone and so will you. Sarah, take the rifle."

"How can you possibly hurt Sarah, Eva? She's your only child. You're her mother. You're supposed to take care of her."

"That's what I am doing."

I could tell by her eyes, nothing I was saying was getting through to her. Where was Chet? Or for that matter, Jake? Why weren't they here by now? Surely someone would come. And where was Rob Martin? Had Eva already taken care of him, like she was going to take care of us? Why hadn't I at least brought Salinger with me?

"Don't worry, Sarah, I'm going to help you." Eva positioned Sarah's hands on the rifle and put her hands firmly over her daughter's.

"Mother, please don't, don't make me do this!" Sarah pleaded.

"It'll be all right, honey. You'll see. It'll be over quickly. You won't suffer, not like that old bastard suffered. Then no one can hurt you ever again."

"Eva, wait, there's more of a chance here than you might think!" I was talking fast, trying to stall her, desperately hoping for one last attempt to reach her through her delusion. "Did you poison Carl?"

She seemed not to hear me. She was looking at Sarah with her strange, dead eyes. "We're going to pull back on the trigger and kill her."

"I have a right to know. Answer me! Did you poison your husband?" Now I was hoping for a second of inattention. Just enough time to dash out of her line of fire.

For a moment, her expression seemed to clear. But she kept the rifle steadily focused on me. "I don't know. I don't remember anything. If I don't remember, it can't be my fault. He blamed everything on me for years. You can't know what I'm talking about. You can't know what it was like. Covering up the bruises. Smothering my cries so Sarah wouldn't hear. Now move away from the fire, Leigh."

I stepped back a few steps.

"Mother, I won't do it." Sarah began to squirm against her mother's hands.

"You don't have any choice, Sarah. I can't trust you to keep quiet, like I did when you were little. Like I did when I was little."

"You can trust us, Eva," I pleaded. "We've come out here alone to this deserted place, we don't blame you for what's happened. Not like when you were a child. What's happened isn't your fault."

"Step back!" She raised the rifle slightly, engulfing her

daughter with her bulk, amazingly strong in her ability to keep Sarah's hands on the gun.

I stepped back further.

"Since Carl's death, I haven't had one nightmare, not one. And the flashbacks are gone too. They were the worst. When they'd come, it was like I was back there, and it was happening to me again and again. What could you know? If they found out about the baby, they'd put me away. Then I'd have to talk about it. It would be like that man touching me. I'd never be clean, never."

"Eva, you're right. I can't know what it was like. But I can help you. Give you some peace and justice, if you let me. Just put down the rifle."

Sarah was crying and slumping toward the ground. "Mother, please, I can't . . ."

I watched in horror as Eva's eyes glazed over again. Then as if emerging from a deep trance, she spoke softly, looking up into that icy sky. "Thy will be done."

I said a prayer of my own.

The bullet hit me like a mule kick grazing my left arm and propelling me backwards.

At the last moment, Sarah had jerked the rifle up.

"Bitch! Evil bitch!" Eva swore, and swung the butt of the rifle at Sarah's head.

I hoped Sarah ducked but didn't wait to find out. I ran into the darkness, toward the only weapon I had to defend us. My feet knew the path with some Divine guidance, because I couldn't see anything. My hands found the prize, and I grabbed the bow and arrows and crashed heavily into the evergreens.

Another bullet sang past me as I ran deeper into the woods. The moon had disappeared behind a tuft of clouds, and the darkness was absolute. I didn't dare switch on my flashlight and give myself away. I could hear myself panting. I could hear Eva panting behind me. Should I burrow in and wait until I could hear her closer, possibly make out her shadow?

I chose to keep moving. While staying a distance ahead of her, I made enough noise to keep her trailing me. I knew it would be impossible to make it back to the truck without Eva getting off several clear shots at me. I didn't want to take the chance. My best bet was to trick her out into the open.

When I reached the beach, I hid in a copse of trees and undergrowth that faced the trail. There was enough moonlight for me to see shapes about ten feet out. I readied one of the arrows in the bow.

Within minutes, Eva strode onto the beach with rifle at the ready. The moon edged out further from the clouds and shown on the white sand. She scanned around, turning slowly, then back again. Then she stopped, pointed the rifle where I crouched, and started walking forward.

I jumped out from the trees and released the arrow with all my strength. The force of the bow string vibrated against my fingers hot as fire.

Eva crumpled backwards on the sand. I sank to my knees, shaking. She had gotten a shot off, and my ears rang.

In the moonlight, the water was black and silvery as it flowed around Eva's head like tendrils of seaweed, and glistened in her hair. I stood over her. Her right hand was clutched around the arrow shaft where it pierced her chest. She stared up at me in disbelief, gasping for air.

31

Sunday, November 26, Present day

"That's some shot ya made. Got her right in the lung."
Chet took the last swig of his beer. "Sure I can't change your
mind about huntin'?"

It was my third day home from the hospital.

"I've had enough hunting for one season," I replied. My
left arm ached as I ran my fingers through Salinger's abundant coat.

"Why don't ya get Jake there to go with ya?" Chet suggested, raising his eyebrows.

I smiled, but I didn't want to talk about the shooting anymore. I was still having nightmares. Always ending the same
way: with Eva's eyes gazing up at me, her mouth stretched
open as she struggled for air.

"Chet, how many times do I have to tell you my opinion
about hunting?" Jake grinned at me. "Best left to the ex-
perts."

Lydia put down her wine glass. "Speaking of which, has
Eva admitted to killing her husband and Joyce's baby?"

"She's not talking," said Chet. "Maybe those docs at the
psychiatric hospital can get somethin' out of her."

"But there's no question Eva committed those murders?"
Lydia looked at Chet, then me.

"She's where she should be," Chet answered.

Lydia was staring at me expectantly.

I took in a deep breath and let it out slowly, trying to quell my sudden trembling. "I'm sure she killed them both," I said, taking no pleasure in my certainty.

"I'm betting they find her incompetent to stand trial and lock her up for life in a county mental hospital." Jake's eyes met mine with reassurance.

Chet squeezed his empty beer can flat. "Makes me sick, thinkin' what she did to that poor little baby. Do you think Joyce knew?"

It was a question I'd been wrestling with since that awful night at the South Heaven cave. "Joyce must have suspected something. After all, her attempts to find the child had turned up nothing. I imagine she went to Eva as a last resort." I rubbed my forehead, trying to clear my thoughts. "She probably called Eva and made one last appeal, then when Eva refused, she . . ." The memory of Joyce's blood on the carpet rose up before me.

Chet piped in. "We're already tracking Eva's phone logs. We'll know if Joyce called Eva that night."

"She . . . I mean Eva," I struggled to make sense of the images flooding my head. "She insisted Joyce was already dead when she got there. And I believe her. I'm not saying she didn't go there intending to dispose of Joyce once and for all. But by a twist of fate, Joyce had saved her the trouble." Why was I feeling like the story had suddenly become mine? I hugged Salinger to me. It had become mine the minute I sat down in Eva's carefully ordered living room.

"Joyce must have been in deep despair over knowing she'd never find her daughter. And that the one person she hoped might help her, wouldn't," Lydia said.

That's what I had told Joe Stillwater this morning when I called him. He had been right; Joyce had had her reasons for

286

taking her own life. But I wondered if knowing those reasons now gave him any comfort. I thought back to what Joyce had said to Lorraine Birch about feeling relief when it was over. I now knew she hadn't been speaking of her hysterectomy or of Carl Peck's death. She'd been speaking of the unburdening of her secret to the man who had fathered her child. Maybe seeing him dying brought that truth home.

A sudden picture of Eva's face flashed across my brain—right before I had let the arrow go. She had no expression, her eyes glazed with madness. "Eva was completely insane."

"Is completely insane," said Lydia. "Though she was pretty methodical in her madness, right down to drugging you with the Antabuse. I mean she had the presence of mind to steal one of Porter's scrip sheets and write a prescription in Carl's name for a non-narcotic drug. Then drive all the way to Green Bay and have it filled there. That's one smart, crazy cookie. Maybe you should have aimed for her heart and put her out of her misery."

I stirred uncomfortably in my chair. There was sweat on the backs of my legs. "I had no intention of killing her." I had been aiming at her shoulder, but I had missed. I shuddered thinking about how close I had come to actually hitting her heart.

Lydia's face flushed. "Of course not."

"Does anyone know where Rob was that day?" Jake asked, maybe wanting to change the subject.

"He was in Chicago meeting with a lawyer to represent Sarah if she was charged with murder," Chet answered.

"Always the dutiful lover," I said. The words were out of my mouth before I realized what I had said. I glanced over at Lydia, who was turning one her many rings nervously around on her index finger.

"Well, I've got the late shift at the hospital." Lydia stood up to go. "I'd tell you to take it easy and rest, but I know I'd be wasting my breath." She bent down and kissed me lightly on the cheek. "Sorry about that killing crack. I can't even imagine what you've been through."

As she pulled away she looked at the malachite necklace around my neck. "I wasn't sure you liked it."

"I do, very much," I said, smiling up at her.

Lydia grabbed her coat and headed toward the door. Salinger followed her, sniffing at her heels.

"Hold up," Chet called after her. "I'll walk out with ya. Just let me say goodbye."

Chet leaned toward me. He reeked of lime-scented after-shave. "As I told ya, there will be a court hearing before a judge, then. But don't ya worry about it. What happened out at the caves is pretty open and shut. And with Sarah's testimony, it's clear as hair on a pig that it was self-defense. Now take care of yourself." Chet patted my head as if I was his favorite tomboy.

"Thanks. I'm not worried. I'm just glad you got there when you did. You don't know what the sight of you coming down that trail meant to me."

"Too bad I couldn't have gotten there sooner. But let this be a lesson for ya. From now on, ya let the police do their job. And that's an order."

"You'd better ask her," Jake said, standing inside the open door. No sooner had Chet left than the doorbell rang.

Before I could respond, Jake led Sarah into the room.

She stood before me looking as ashen and depleted as the November fields. The zipper on her black leather jacket had separated at the bottom. A large safety pin held the two ends in check. Her hair was ragged looking. The bruise on the side of her forehead from the rifle butt was starting to yellow.

"I've got to go by the paper," Jake said, throwing on his coat. "I'll be back in an hour." I wasn't sure if his gesture was one of consideration or cowardice. Regardless, I forgave him. It was just so damn good to see him.

After the door slammed, Sarah sat down. Salinger jumped up beside her and nudged her hand. I was glad to see Sarah get Salinger's special attention. "Salinger, you're shameless. Get down and leave my guest alone."

"It's okay." Sarah petted Salinger while she scanned the dusky room. She was avoiding eye contact. "Pretty gloomy."

"It was cheap," I conceded.

"How's your arm? I would have come by the hospital, but you know. Do you mind if I smoke?" She reached into her duffel bag and pulled out a pack of cigarettes.

"My arm's fine. The bullet only grazed me. And yeah, I do mind. You know, the cancer. Sorry."

She stared at me a second too long, then shrugged and shoved the pack back into her bag. Her foot was nervously moving side to side. Then she took a deep breath, as if she were inhaling a cigarette. "I thought this was going to be easy." She started to cry. "Damn, I can't seem to get a grip."

She ran her thumb over and over her right palm, as if there was something there she couldn't remove. "She used to take me there, you know, when things got bad at home. To that cave, South Heaven. It was our safe place. Sometimes he'd be so drunk, we had to get away. But then for her to kill Joyce's baby and bury it there . . ." She shook her head. "She used to be a teacher, you know, my mother. First grade. Do you believe that? But after they got married, he wouldn't let her do it anymore."

Sarah stared at the dusty light filtering through the windows. "And all that time, I thought she was weak, because she wouldn't leave him."

"Sarah, you can't blame yourself. Your father pushed your mother over the edge. Not you," I reasoned, wanting to mitigate her guilt and with it some of her pain.

Sarah pulled her gaze from the window and finally looked directly at me. "Yeah, but maybe, I could have done something, then this thing with Joyce wouldn't have happened. She wouldn't have. . . ." She took a deep breath, trying not to cry. "Killed anyone."

"Sarah, your mother is insane. If anyone's to blame it's your father for his relentless years of physical and emotional abuse. And then before him, that man who sexually abused her."

I sensed my words were having little impact. We sat for a moment listening to the wind whipping the trees against the windows.

Finally Sarah broke our silence. "I brought you something. I left it outside the door. Sort of a peace offering, for running you off the road." She said it quickly, with a trace of defiance.

"So it was you." I almost wished it had been Rob.

She ran her hand through her ragged hair. "Not my smartest move. I only meant to scare you, but I got carried away. I'm really sorry."

I had two choices: send her packing or let her give me her gift. I felt we both needed to turn a corner. "Let's see it."

Sarah went to the door and opened it, dragging in a large canvas. As soon as she turned it over, I recognized the painting: the dark colors of the deep woods and the halo of light at the foot of an oak that was no halo, but a circle of white mushrooms. *Destroying Angels* by S. Peck.

"Can't stand having it around. Thought you might want it. If it wasn't for you showing up that night, well, I know what she would have done to me." Sarah paused. "You know, she had me convinced I wrote that suicide note in a blackout. I thought I was losing my mind." Sarah rested the painting against the couch and sat down.

"It's almost funny, when you think about it. I mean, in a way, she was the destroying angel. My mother actually believed God was guiding her. That's why I can't have this painting in my house. If you don't want it, just chuck it out."

I studied the painting's eerie loveliness. I didn't know if I wanted it either. It would be a reminder of how close I had come to death, how close I had come to killing Eva Peck. But I understood the courage it took for Sarah to bring it to me, and that was the real gift. We had both shared a horror and survived. "You care where I put it?"

"Long as I don't have to see it when I come over."

"That mean you're staying?"

"I was going to take off. Maybe go back to Chicago. Lose myself in the big city, and forget it all happened. But I think this is where it ends. Yeah, I'm staying. At least for a while."

Her hair stood out thin and wiry from her head. For no logical reason, I sensed she was going to be all right.

"Well, you know where I live," I said.

She stood up and swung her bag over her shoulder. "Likewise."

"Sarah, thanks." I glanced down at my left arm.

When I looked up, a shy smile played across her lips.

32

"So what happens now?" I asked. Jake and I had been discussing Rob and Sarah over shrimp stir-fry. I had supervised while he chopped, diced and cooked. We were camped out in front of my fireplace, eating off recycled paper plates: the good kind, double reinforced with individual compartments.

"I don't think they have a chance." Jake wiped soy sauce off his chin.

"Too bad. I think she needs him." I popped the last shrimp into my mouth.

"Too much history." Jake piled my empty plate on top of his. He stretched out his long legs in front of the fire and leaned back on his elbows.

I nudged closer to the fire and stirred the embers. "I think she's afraid. That Rob may not accept her as she is, in her mind, damaged." I kept staring into the fire. Oddly, Sarah and her mother felt the same way about themselves, because of how men they trusted had treated them.

"I don't think that's it," Jake replied.

"Really. Then what is it?"

"I think she's afraid he will accept her. As she is, damaged and all."

I knew we were no longer talking about Rob and Sarah.

We watched in silence as sparks flew up the chimney. There were so many ways I could begin what I wanted to say

292

to Jake now, ways to ease into it. Ways all well thought out and logical. But with the moment here, none of them seemed right. I stared hard into the fire. "I don't look like a normal woman."

"I got the idea. Do you take that poster on every date?"

"Jake, I want you to understand what you're getting into." I turned and faced him. "I mean, the scar, it cuts across my left side from underarm to sternum." I indicated the scar's direction with my right hand. "It's long, deep and red."

"Leigh, I've seen scars before."

"Not like this. And it's not just the scar. It's the shock of the emptiness, it redefines me. . . ." I stopped.

"What are we talking about here?" He sat up and crossed his long lean legs under him.

"I'm trying to explain why this isn't going to work."

"You mean why you don't want it to work." He leaned forward and touched my arm. "Look, I wouldn't be here if I didn't want to take this risk with you."

I wanted to explain how the cancer could come back. At any time, with no warning. Instead, I said, "Are you sure?"

"Yes, but it's your call."

Every light in the house was off. Salinger kept a silent vigil beside the bed. The waning moon slit the window's edge with a light as delicate and determined as a first snow.

I pulled away from Jake slowly. "I want to show you something." I pointed to my left side between two ribs. "See it? It's my heart."

He looked closely, then put his hand in that place which no longer seemed so transparent, so thin and fragile.

"How are you going to write it?" he asked, kissing the flat place where my heart beat. He looked up at me.

I took a deep breath. I wanted to see the whole story on the page, but I didn't see it yet. Instead I saw a flash of words, "South Heaven." Then myself going in the front door of the *Gazette*, and Jake's socked feet propped on his desk—a hole in one heel. I thought of the safety pin holding Sarah's jacket together. And that yellowing photo of Sarah and Joyce in matching swimsuits—Joyce's strap slipping down, her small hand held in a fist. I saw the green rhinestone pin, shaped like a heart, rise and fall on Eva's chest.

About the Author

Gail Lukasik was born in Cleveland, Ohio, and was a dancer with the Cleveland Civic Ballet Company. She has worked as a choreographer and a freelance writer. Lisel Mueller described her book of poems, *Landscape Toward a Proper Silence*, as a "splendid collection." She also has been published in over fifty literary journals, including *The Georgia Review*, *Carolina Quarterly*, and *Mississippi Valley Review*. In 2002 she was awarded an Illinois Arts Council award for her work. She received her M.A. and Ph.D. from the University of Illinois at Chicago, where she taught writing and literature. She lives in Libertyville, Illinois, with her husband and their Shetland sheepdog.